Here at the Gate

by

Christine Campbell

To Maureen,
Thank you for coming today.
It was nice to meet you,
  Christine Campbell.

Published in 2014 by FeedARead Publishing

Copyright © Christine Campbell

First Edition

All characters and events in this publication, other than those clearly in the public domain, are fictitious and any resemblance to real persons, living or dead, is purely co-incidental

The author asserts the moral right under the Copyright, Designs and Patents Act 1988 to be identified as the author of this work.

All Rights reserved. No part of this publication may be reproduced, stored in a retrieval system, or transmitted, in any form or by any means without the prior written consent of the publisher, nor be otherwise circulated in any form of binding or cover other than that in which it is published and without a similar condition being imposed on the subsequent purchaser.

A CIP catalogue record for this title is available from the British Library.

My grateful thanks to all the friends and writing buddies who have beta read, proofread, critiqued, advised and generally encouraged me in my writing, especially Sharon Scordecchia, Jane Blewitt, Launie Lapp, Amanda Staley and my son, Andrew Campbell, who listened patiently while I tested my story out on him as it took shape.

The cover of this novel has been a family affair, and my grateful thanks go to my daughter-in-law, Michelle Campbell, and my son-in-law, Tim Pow, who transformed the image I had in my mind into the book cover I have on this novel, Michelle for the painting, Tim for converting the painting into a book cover.

Most of all, love and thanks must go to my dear husband who has always been a tremendous source of help and encouragement.

Without him, I doubt I could write a word.

contents

Here at the Gate   9

The Author   291

The Books   292

Here at the Gate

by

Christine Campbell

A chill wind blew through Mhairi's life.

With no warning — no flash of lightening, no rolling thunder — she was caught in a storm of her daughter's making: the echo of a storm that had swept her away before, submerging her for thirteen years.

'This too shall pass,' she thought. But she didn't believe it. She believed it was only the beginning and she couldn't see the end.

Had she but recognised it, there was a calm before the storm.

She had spent it baking.

Packing boxes of supplies.

Shopping for her granddaughter, Katie, who was leaving home to flat-share with a friend.

Standing at her daughter, Rhona's, garden gate, waving Katie off in her tiny car.

Calm. No hint of a storm brewing.

Katie's car was loaded to the gunnels and was closely followed by her father's larger model, also fully loaded. The addition of Mhairi's boxes had almost tipped them over to needing three cars, but Steve had wedged the gift in somehow and off they went.

She and Rhona moved along the neatly-clipped front hedge, waving until the cars were out of sight and they stood at the end of the driveway, unable to turn away: a joyous new adventure for Katie but a poignant moment for them.

Perhaps Mhairi should have heard the distant rumble of trouble in the resigned sigh from Rhona's throat.

"It's the end of that whole part of my life," Rhona said, picking off the few leaves that dared to break the line of the hedge. "The bringing up kids part, I mean." She nodded in the direction the car had taken.

"Mmm, I suppose so," Mhairi said with a sigh of her own. "But you'll still be 'Mum.' You're not out of a job yet."

"I suppose."

Or seen the lightening in the tearless flash of Rhona's eyes.

"It's a job for life. Not like one of those bags you get in the supermarket."

Rhona turned to look at her. "What bags?"

"You know. The ones they call 'a bag for life'?"

"Y-e-s." Rhona frowned.

"But it's not really, because the deal is, if it wears out they'll replace it."

"Y-e-s." The frown deepened.

"Well, when you have kids, it really is a job for life." Mhairi gave her a moment for that to sink in. "You know what I mean. If you get worn out, you've just got to get on with it."

Now Rhona laughed. "You calling me an old bag? You're taking a risk, mood I'm in."

"Wouldn't dare. Anyway, just a thought — and a vain attempt to lighten the moment." Mhairi sighed as she watched her daughter's attention turn back to the empty street. "I know you're going to miss her, sweetheart." Mhairi pulled her close.

"She was such good company."

"Ah-ah! She *is* such good company. She's only gone to flat share, she hasn't died!"

Rhona nodded and leant her head against Mhairi's shoulder, allowing herself to be cuddled for a while.

The air settled around them.

Mhairi inhaled the scent of her daughter's hair — rose and lemon, clean and fragrant, a smell Mhairi had grown to love and associate with her daughter — it had been Rhona's signature for years and Mhairi never smelled it anywhere without getting a rush of tenderness for her girl.

Being a few inches taller than Rhona, she was able to kiss the top of her head. "Oh, sweetheart, I know, but she's not gone far. Twenty miles is nothing in the car. Besides, she'll be back all the time, you wait and see."

"I know."

"Whenever they run out of food in that tiny wee flat, or space to dry their washing, you'll see, she'll appear in your kitchen right when you and Steve are in the middle of a nice, cosy evening. You know, after-dinner cup of tea, film on the box?" She snuggled in as though it was they who were sitting on the sofa. "'What you having for dinner, Mum?' she'll ask as she pushes the door open. 'Mind if I put a wash in while we're eating?' she'll say, parking her backside on a chair, chatting all the while, as she watches you load the washing machine and make her some food."

With a laugh, Rhona acknowledged, "Like I did to you, you mean."

"Exactly!" Mhairi gave her waist a squeeze before releasing her and turning to go back in the house. "And you'll love it, just as I did."

As they walked up the path, arm in arm, flanked on both sides by the last of the roses, Rhona dead-headed a few of the bushes as she passed, causing Mhairi to smile.

No matter the crisis, Rhona would always want things to be tidy. She couldn't help herself, bless her.

Mhairi, on the other hand, had to restrain the urge to scatter rose petals over the path, just to break up the perfection of it all.

While Rhona put the kettle on to make them a welcome cuppa, Mhairi stacked away the few boxes and bags that hadn't been needed after all, despite Katie's frantic phone calls, 'Gran, Gran, please can you find some boxes on your way over. I'm never going to have enough.' "What shall I do with these," she asked Rhona. "I can't imagine the supermarket will want them back."

"Oh, pop them out by the back door. I'll get Steve to flatten them and put them in the recycling bin."

"I can do that, love."

"Well, if you don't mind. Keeps the kitchen tidy." Rhona stood watching the kettle for a while. "Anyway, she's only nineteen," she said as Mhairi finished her task and came in the back door. "She might be back if things don't work out with Anna and the flat."

"Mmm, wouldn't bank on it, sweetheart. Besides, you'll be surprised how quickly you'll get use to the quieter house." Mhairi negotiated the climb onto the high stool at the central island, bumping her knee on the unit underneath. "Ouch! I keep forgetting there's not a lot of leg-room under there."

"'There's plenty if you pull the stool out a bit."

"Sorry." Mhairi always felt a bit clumsy and out of place in such modern surroundings.

"Huh!" Rhona gave her a scathing look. "I hope I get used to the peace and quiet quicker than you get used to these bar stools."

"Sorry." Always felt a bit like a schoolgirl, too, in her daughter's house. "Not a great percher."

"Yeah, well, the kids like them." Rhona sniffed at what she clearly felt was an implied criticism of her ultra-trendy kitchen. "Breakfast won't be the same without Katie hopping on and off that stool, picking at her toast."

"Eating like a bird."

"Driving me crazy leaving a trail of crumbs across the kitchen."

"See? There's a plus already," Mhairi said, helping herself to a biscuit. "You'll get your kitchen back just as you like it. And, your remote control." She slid the biscuit tin across the tiled island top to Rhona.

"My remote control?"

"For the TV."

"Oh!" Rhona laughed. "Yeah! It'll be quite nice for Steve and I to get choosing the television programs." She put a mug of tea in front of Mhairi and rummaged through the biscuits. "Did you take the last caramel wafer?"

"Oops! Sorry!"

"You're not sorry at all," Rhona remonstrated with a grin. "You know they're my favourites?"

"Mine too." Mhairi grinned as she flicked the wrapper across the surface.

Laughing, Rhona snatched it up, and put it in the bucket. "Clearly! I'll have to double up on them next time. As long as caramel wafers don't go up in price, we should be all right."

"Don't worry. I'll sub you for them if needs be."

They 'high-fived' on the deal.

These were precious times, Mhairi thought: time spent with her daughter, sharing life's ups and downs. She knew she was thinking in cliches, but she didn't care. Rhona would call it her 'Little House on the Prairie' thinking, but she still didn't care. Happy families were what it was all about.

Wasn't it?

the project

Sitting with Rhona in her daughter's immaculate kitchen, she watched sadness flicker on Rhona's face as she drank her tea.

"You do know you're going to be okay without Katie, don't you?" Mhairi said, placing her hand over her daughter's, imparting a promise of love and support in her touch.

"I do know." Rhona nodded and shrugged. "Nothing else for it. Anyway, what I thought I'd like to do …" She sat up straighter, her eyes widening, her smile returning. "And you might find this interesting …"

"Ooo! I'm all ears." Mhairi leaned forward.

"You know how I was always good at English Composition when I was at school?"

Mhairi nodded.

"And I loved History?"

"Yes."

"Well, I fancy combining the two and writing a history book."

"Oh, what a lovely idea! You'd be good at that." Mhairi smiled. "You're great at putting words together. You always were. Remember those wee plays you used to write? You used to get Dad and I to sit in the 'front stalls' while you and Ewan performed them." She laughed. "Poor old Ewan. He used to have such trouble remembering his lines. Do you remember?"

Rhona put her mug down on its coaster. "Oh, it wasn't remembering the lines that was his problem," she said, donning her big sister mantle. "It was bothering to read them at all. He was such a pain."

"But at least he let you bully him into doing it."

"No, actually, I didn't bully him into doing it, I had to bribe him into it. Cost me half my pocket money to get him to play a part. Then he loved it. Loved being the star of the show."

"He was rather good once he got into it."

"I much preferred writing plays, than playing in them. Which brings me back to what I was saying."

"You fancy writing a book."

"Yes. What d'you think?"

Mhairi looked at her daughter with a mixture of pride and love. "I think it's a great idea. I know you could do it. You're great at sticking with things once you decide that's what you want to do. Me? Now, I struggle to write a letter. But, you? A book? No problem. I think it's a super idea."

"Aw, thanks, Mum."

"What an exciting thing to do. You know how I love reading. I'd be so proud. I'd show it off to everybody. 'My daughter's an author,' I'd say."

"Always assuming I'd get it published."

"Oh, you would. I know you would."

"Your faith in me is touching, Mother. But perhaps we ought to see if I can actually write before we book the venue for the launch."

"Oh, I know you can do it. And do it well." Mhairi laughed. "You wouldn't do it if you thought it wouldn't be good enough to publish. I know you, my precious."

Rhona smiled. "Well, I've set up the computer and I'm all set to start."

"Clever girl. I wouldn't know where or how to start on the computer."

"Yes, well, we all know you're a bit of a technophobe."

"From another era." Mhairi sighed and drank her tea.

"Never too late to learn."

She shook her head. "It is for me." Lifting her mug, "I'm a cup of tea in a world of lattes," she said.

"Hah!"

"And I doubt I'll change. I've no desire to go to school — in any shape or form." Wriggling her bottom into a slightly less uncomfortable position on the stool, "Anyway," she said. "We were talking about you." She smiled at Rhona, feeling so happy that her daughter had a project to help her over this transition. Rhona was always at her best when she had a project. "Do you know what you want to write about?"

"Yeah, well, like I said, I love history, so I thought I'd really enjoy to write up our family history."

"Oh!" The kitchen clock ticked off a beat or two of silence. Mhairi pulled her loose, woolly cardigan closer round herself.

When she closed her eyes, she felt the chill presaging a storm. A whirlwind of emotions sprang up with no warning, snatching away her equilibrium, ripping the years of normal living apart in an instance.

She waited for her heart to start again, clawing at some hope, "You mean like Katie and Michael growing up? Things like that?" she asked.

"Not so much. More like tracing our family tree, finding out the family secrets, seeing what dramas there've been in the family and writing about them. What d'you think?"

"Well, I really don't know what to think." Mhairi shivered. "Shall I put the kettle on? Another cuppa?" Icicle fingers tightened round her throat.

"I'm okay. Still got this one, thanks, but on you go, you have another."

"Thanks." Mhairi busied herself with the kettle, emptying the tea out of her mug, rinsing it, fiddling with the teabags, finding a spoon, all with her back to her daughter. Anything. Anything but turn round to face her. Anything to delay till blood coloured her face again.

The noise of a storm thundered in her ears, and she felt herself transported away from here. This wasn't her daughter's kitchen, it was a time machine and she was eight years old and it was summer and she was playing in the garden and she was at the gate and there were rhododendrons, lots of rhododendrons and roses; she could smell roses and honeysuckle and…

"So what d'you think, then?"

Mhairi jumped.

"Yes." It felt as though hailstones, shards of ice, were piercing her skull, giving her a headache. "Yes. Interesting. I'm sure that'd be very interesting. And, I'm sure you'd be very good at it. Telling stories, I mean," she said, still without turning round. She stirred her tea, then, snatching at another fragment of hope, "Your Dad's side of the family!"

"Yes?"

"I'm sure your dad's side of the family would give you some great stories." Emerging from the storm, she came back to the island unit, climbing on the dreaded stool, a smile set on her face. "I mean, his grandfather was an interesting man. He'd been in India, you know, for years. I think that's where he met Dad's grandmother. Yes, yes. I'm sure you could write a great book about how they met and what they got up to in India and everything."

"That's what I thought."

"Goodness! That would keep you busy, wouldn't it? There'd be lots of things for you to research. Not just the history, what India was like back then and everything, but the geography too. I think they travelled about a lot. And the food, you could write about the food. I'm sure the Indian food we get in restaurants over here isn't real Indian food. You could even include some of your great-gran's recipes. I'm sure Gran still has them somewhere."

Rhona laughed. "You seem even more excited about the idea than I am?"

"Oh, I am. Finding out all about your dad's family would be so interesting. Were you thinking of writing it like it was a story? You know, a sort of docudrama thingy? Isn't that what you call something that's a story but using real facts and real people?"

"I do believe every family has a story," Rhona said. "It's just about finding out the interesting bits and making the most of them. I want to dig a bit deeper, make sure there isn't something else I'd rather write about. Something even more dramatic. Who knows what I'll find in your side of the family, for instance?"

The noise of a storm thundered in her ears, she could smell roses and honeysuckle and... Mhairi slammed the garden gate.

Enough. It wasn't going to be enough. All the colours and smells of India were not going to be enough for Rhona if she thought for a moment there might be more.

"According to all the sites I've looked at, the starting point is just writing down who's who as far as I already know." Rhona drew Katie's now-redundant packing list towards her across the breakfast bar and the pen she'd used to tick things off as they'd been taken to the cars. "Oh, I love making lists," she said, turning this one over to use the other side, her face aglow with the anticipation. "Something I got from you, eh, Mum?"

"Mmm?"

"You okay, Mum? You're beginning to look a bit tired."

"Mmm? Mmm, yes." Mhairi put her cup down and manoeuvred herself off the high stool. "Yes, I am tired. Up early, baking. Think I'll head home, if that's okay with you. Get a bit of a lie down before I have to make the dinner."

"Sounds like a plan. You look done in."

Mhairi came round the island and kissed her daughter on the cheek. "No need to get up, love. I'll see myself out. You get on with your lists. I'm glad you've got a project in mind. Good to keep busy." She gathered her coat and bag from the cupboard Rhona always tidied them into, and almost made it to the back door. She had her hand on the handle, had the door opened, was almost through it when Rhona asked the favour she was dreading being asked.

"D'you think you could jot down your details for me when you get a minute? You know, where and when you were born, your mum and dad's names, dates of birth, dates they died? Those kind of things. Your grandparents' details too, if you know them. Just to get me started. I'll get Dad to do the same." She smiled with satisfaction. "Oh, this is going to be such fun, eh, Mum?"

fearful expectation

'Fun' was not the word that came to Mhairi's mind as she drove the ten or so minutes home. 'Foreboding' more accurately described her feeling.

It reminded her of when Rhona had been about ten or eleven years old and she had pulled out a box of photographs, emptying them onto the rug in front of the fire. 'Why are there none of you, Mum?' she asked, after sorting through them for a while.

'Because it's usually me who takes them,' Mhairi told her, with that horrible feeling in the pit of her stomach, knowing that Rhona would not be satisfied with that as an answer.

'But, I mean, none! Not one!'

'There's my wedding photo.' She pointed to where it sat on the sideboard.

Rhona dismissed that one with a wave of her hand. 'Well, of course there's that, but that doesn't count.'

'And there are the photos Dad takes when we're on holiday.'

A scathing look. 'I'm talking about *old* photos. Like these ones of Dad.' She held up a bundle of photographs tied together with blue ribbon. 'Gran said I could keep these, by the way. As long as I look after them, she said.'

'That was kind of her.' Mhairi started back towards the kitchen, dishtowel in hand, to continue drying the dishes.

'But, why are there no old photos of you?'

'I don't like having my photograph taken.'

Rhona continued to rifle through the box. 'There's not even one of you with anyone else. Don't you think that's strange?'

'Not really.' Mhairi shrugged. 'Like I said, I don't like having my photograph taken.'

'Are there really not any of you as a kid?'

She shook her head.

'Have you got some somewhere else?'

Mhairi sighed, recognising the tenacious streak that Rhona had inherited from Donald. He wasn't one to give up easily either. 'No. There are none.' She tried once more to make her exit.

'Really? Are you sure? You must have some somewhere.' Rhona's face lit up. 'Old school photos. You must have some old school photos. Even in the olden days, when you were at school, I bet they took school photos. Maybe a class photo? What about it, Mum, old school photos?'

'I'm telling you, there are none. In the olden days, as you call them, no, they didn't take school photos.'

"Dad has some.'

'Well, I don't. Now, can you get on with your homework, please?'

'This is my homework.'

'Then you'll have to take one of the snaps Dad took last year.'

'But we were supposed to take the oldest photo we could find.'

'Then one of the wedding photos. And put that box away, please. It's nearly bedtime.'

'But, Mum! It's only eight o'clock. Beth gets staying up till eight-thirty.'

'Well, that's up to Beth's Mum. Anyway, it'll be that and some, by the time you've had your supper. You've to get up for school tomorrow.'

Rhona groaned and rolled over onto the floor beside the pile of photos.

'If you can get into your pyjamas quickly, I'll do some pancakes.'

The sick feeling in her stomach lessened as Rhona was deflected from the photographs and Mhairi was able to put them away.

Now, as she drove home after leaving Rhona making lists of what she knew and what she wanted to know, Mhairi reflected that Rhona may not be so easily distracted this time and she couldn't quite shake off the sense of foreboding.

"Katie get off all right, then," Donald asked later as he hung his keys on the hook and reached across to drop a kiss on her cheek. "Rhona okay?"

Mhairi reached her hand up to his face and smiled. "Yes, both fine." She ignored the flutter of panic that seemed to be resident in her throat and chest, and headed for the kitchen. "Just dishing out," she said.

"Great! I'm famished. Katie okay I wasn't there to see her off?"

"Yeah, she was fine. She knows you had to be in Glasgow. Anyway, knowing you, you'd have been the one to start the tears flowing."

He threw his hands in the air. "Calumny!"

Mhairi laughed and nudged against him as he went past to take his seat at the table. "No, it's true. You're such a sentimental old softie."

"While you're hard as nails, I suppose?"

"Well, I managed not to cry today," she said. "So far."

"Worst is over."

"Yeah."

They chatted on as they ate their meal, Donald updating her on what was happening with his mother. Ruth was in hospital in Glasgow having had yet another serious fall. Since Donald was her only child, it fell to him to meet with consultants and doctors to monitor her care and to visit every day, and she watched the ward door for him every afternoon. At nearly ninety-eight, she felt she had a right to his devotion while she needed him, a feeling with which Donald and Mhairi agreed.

"They're pretty sure it was another stroke."

"Mmm."

Ruth Carlyle, Donald's mother, had never warmed to Mhairi, so it mattered not whether Mhairi visited and Ruth rarely acknowledged her presence when she did. Mhairi had always accepted the unspoken reproof. Her sin being that she had stolen the heart of Ruth's precious boy, and she was unworthy of holding it, according to Ruth. Shivering, Mhairi turned her attention back to Donald's account of today's visiting hours.

He was a good man, her Donald. Retired now, but he had been a hard working man, a good provider. A good father to the children too.

When the children were young, after they were settled, she would pour him a cup of tea and carry it through on a tray for supper, with a plate of scones or cakes, freshly baked earlier. The smell of fresh baking was one of her own favourite smells — there was something reassuring and homely about it — and its association would always be with his pleasure at her efforts. Every evening, she blushed with his compliments as she offered the plate. There was still rarely a day when she hadn't baked bread or a fruit cake, biscuits or scones. Now that there were just the two of them, she often put a selection in a Tupperware for the family, or Donald would take some as a treat for his mother.

It wasn't that she was a particularly good baker, even after all the years of practice, but Donald was an encouraging and appreciative consumer.

As he recounted the afternoon's hospital visit, she watched the wrinkles deepen round his eyes as he laughed, the merriment in his eyes matching the amusing anecdotes he told.

The frown lines on his brow, how they would deepen when he talked about his mother's failing health. "I swear, if Mother asked me once if I'd come straight from work, she asked me a hundred times. It's like she's on a loop. You know, like in the supermarket at Christmas time, when they play the same blooming carols over and over and over, until it's all that's in your head for days."

She had loved this man for such a long time: long before they started going out together. She had watched him back then too: watched those same eyes sparkle when he laughed, watched how they shadowed in sadness but never in anger. He held his temper well, so well that it could almost be frustrating when she was riled up about something herself. She had learned to trust him completely by the time she yielded to his persistence and agreed to go on a date with him. He was the only person who knew her story.

diversion tactics

Three days later, Rhona shouted hello as she came through the back door: three days during which Mhairi had kept herself busy, pulling everything out of the hall cupboard and sorting through the junk that had accumulated since the last clear-out; three days trying not to let her imagination run ahead, trying to disperse that ever-present feeling of foreboding that had haunted her since their last chat, and three days not answering the phone in case it was Rhona.

"You stopped answering your phone or what?" Three days that had clearly not gone unnoticed.

"Oh, sorry! Had my head in the hall cupboard all day. Having a clear-out. You any use for this old toaster? Still works but got the bullet when we redecorated the kitchen."

"No, thanks." Rhona took the toaster from Mhairi's hands and turned it over. "Looks a good one, though. I'll ask Katie if it's better than the one in the flat."

"Oh, that's a good idea."

"Mum, I was wondering if you had..."

"She settled in okay? Texted or phoned or anything?"

Rhona laughed. "Almost constantly. 'How do you work the washing machine?' 'How do you do your scrambled eggs and cheese?' 'How long do you give your broccoli.'"

"Oh, that's good if she's cooking broccoli!"

"I don't think she'd dare not to have vegetables, just in case you ask her next time you see her."

"Well, they are the most important part of any meal."

"So you've been telling us our whole lives.'

Mhairi pulled a rueful face. "Oh dear. Go on a bit, do I?"

"Just a bit. But we love you anyway," Rhona said as she gave her mum a hug. "Anyway, what I was going to ask you..."

"How's Michael? Is he coming over next weekend. I thought I'd buy a bit of beef for Sunday dinner, if that's all right. With broccoli, of course."

Rhona laughed and nodded. "Fine, great, Yes, Michael and Zara are okay for the Sunday. It's not next Sunday, though, but the one after, isn't it?"

"Is it? Oh, well. I've started planning early."

"You've never really had a great sense of time, have you, Mum?" Shaking her head, she went to hang her coat in the hall cupboard. "Will Ewan be coming too?" she asked as she came back. "Shame they didn't make it last time."

"He's planning to, but it rather depends on that old car of his getting through its MOT."

"I don't know why he hangs on to that old thing. He's not short of a bob or two. Why doesn't he get himself a decent car?"

"He loves that old Rover."

"Yeah, well I don't know why Sally puts up with it. It's done and it's unreliable."

Mhairi nodded in agreement. Rhona was right, she knew, but Ewan had always been like that. Even as a wee boy, he hated giving up on a broken toy, would spend hours trying to fix it rather than discard it.

"Something I've never understood, this attachment he makes to old things that need throwing out," Rhona said, shaking her head. "I'd far rather get something new."

"Thankfully, Sally seems to understand and doesn't mind him holding on to the Rover. She phoned last night and said they thought there was quite a bit needing done but hopefully it'll be all right. They'll probably be down about eleven on the Sunday. They usually are."

It had become a family tradition, Sunday lunch at Mhairi's once a month. They were all so busy and scattered here and there, it was a great chance to catch up on all the family gossip and Mhairi loved it. This is what family life should be like. This is what she had read about as a girl: cosy chats round laden tables, love and affection flowing like wine.

"Mum," Rhona said as she sat down at the kitchen table. "You know how I was saying I want to write our family history?"

Mhairi picked up the toaster and went out to the hall cupboard. "Hang on a minute. I'll just put this away till you let me know if Katie wants it." Taking it into the cupboard, she stood a moment, hidden from Rhona by the cupboard door, leaning her head against one of the shelves, her eyes closed, willing herself to stay calm, telling herself she had to stop her heart missing a beat every time the subject of Rhona's project came up.

With a soft whooshing sound, she felt herself transported away from here. This wasn't a cupboard, it was a time machine and she was eight years old and it was summer and she was playing in the garden and there were rhododendrons, lots of rhododendrons and roses; she could smell roses and he was at the gate...

"You okay, Mum? Not got lost in there have you?" Rhona stuck her head round the door.

Mhairi jumped as she crash-landed back in the here and now. "Just coming, love."

"Like I say," Rhona continued as Mhairi followed her back into the kitchen. "I've been working out what I need to find out and how to go about it."

"Hang on a minute and I'll get us a cuppa, pet." Mhairi walked over to the sink and ran the tap full-on prior to filling the kettle. Filling and rinsing the kettle three times before setting it on its stand and clicking its switch on, she then took a couple of mugs from the cupboard and, though they were perfectly clean and dust-free, she rinsed them under the fast-running tap, all of which tasks were accomplished with so much noise talk was impractical.

While she waited for the kettle to boil, she tweaked the pretty multi-pastel-coloured curtains into place, though they were hanging perfectly, she wiped the honey-coloured pine worktop again and she tidied the tidy row of cookery books that sat on the shelf under the cream painted cupboards, all the while chattering, almost without taking a breath, about anything and everything that she could think of. "Probably about time these were painted again," she said as she closed the cupboard door. "Think I'll do them the same colour, though. Just freshen them up."

"Mmm! I wouldn't have thought…"

"I'll give the curtains a wash too, not that it's long since I did them."

"No. Did you not do them just last…"

"Yes. Yes, I did, didn't I? Oh well. Maybe I'll just wash the lampshade."

She could hear herself. Who was this woman falling apart in her kitchen? Where was the calm, collected woman she had trained herself to be? The persona she had chosen?

By the time they were both seated with a cup of tea and some of Mhairi's home-baked lemon drizzle cake, she had managed to introduce the topic of the proposed new shopping centre, a topic she knew Rhona felt passionate about, thereby ensuring at least an hour's safe conversation.

Watching her daughter get impassioned about what the proposals would mean to the neighbourhood — the noise and inconvenience, the dirt and pollution, as set against any benefits they would derive — Mhairi allowed her attention to wander, knowing she wasn't really needed in this conversation.

There was that whoosh again — they were still sitting at the scrubbed-pine kitchen table, where they always seemed to sit when Rhona came round, or any of the family, for that matter — but Rhona and Ewan were schoolchildren.

'Why do you never talk about when you were at school?' Rhona asked, looking up from her homework. 'You never talk about school friends or anything.'

Mhairi froze, her hands in mid-air, poised above the table, the mugs of hot chocolate she had made for them, steaming in her grasp. 'Well … I didn't make many friends,' she said after a beat or two of painful silence. 'I was a bit of a loner.' She took a breath to steady herself and placed the mugs of chocolate in front of the children.

'But you must have …'

'What's the sum of half a pickle of walnuts and a stone of dates?' Ewan asked, putting down his pencil to lift his mug with both hands.

Rhona groaned. 'Please, Mum. You've got to get that joke book off him.'

'Well?' persisted Ewan.

'Hmmm.' Mhairi looked puzzled. 'The sum of a pickle of walnuts and …'

'Half a pickle of walnuts …'

'Let me see …'

"Don't you think so, Mum?" Rhona was saying.

"Oh! Yes," Mhairi nodded, as she made another crash-landing. "Absolutely, dear," she said, unsure what she was being asked to agree with, happy to agree anyway. Anything to keep Rhona off the other, dreaded topic.

'I don't know why you're getting yourself all upset about this,' Donald had said to her last night over supper. 'You know Rho'll get sidetracked with stories about my grandfather if we do my side of the family first.'

'Yeah, but she thinks she knows all those stories. She's probably already added them to her list. Then she'll be expecting something from me.'

'Tell you what. Why don't I take her over to see Mum in the next day or two. I bet she can dredge up enough Indian scandal to keep Rho happy. She'll have enough for several novels once Mum gets talking.'

'Thanks, love.' Mhairi gave him a peck on the cheek as she got up to clear away the supper things.

'Suggest it to her when she pops in tomorrow. Tell her I'll pick her up at twelve, day after tomorrow. That okay?'

Sure enough, when the shopping centre conversation was exhausted, Rhona looked at the clock. "Oh, heck, I'd better get going. It's Steve's badminton night, so early tea." She took her cup to the sink and came to give her mother a kiss. "Oh, and I was wondering..."

"Your Dad wondered if you'd like to go see Gran with him tomorrow. She's been asking to see you." Mhairi went to the cupboard to get Rhona's coat. "Dad says he'll pick you up at twelve if that suits you?" she said as she brought it through.

Rhona checked the day and date on her phone. "Tomorrow. Wednesday." She checked her diary, also on her phone. "Yes," she said as she slipped her coat on and put the phone in her pocket. "That should be fine."

Mhairi handed her her bag and opened the back door. "Twelve o'clock, then. I'll tell him. He'll enjoy having your company."

Mhairi chose not to notice the look of surprise on Rhona's face at her mother's unusual eagerness to show her out and close the door behind her. Though she did notice, with a twinge of guilt, that Rhona stood outside for a moment or two registering her precipitous ejection.

Biting her lip, squashing the impulse to open the door and pull her back inside for an apologetic hug, she held her breath until she saw Rhona continue on down the path, her shape distorted and mosaic-ed by the patterned glass of the back door.

There had to be a better way to deal with this situation, but Mhairi had yet to work out what it was. Until she did, avoidance seemed her only option.

concocting lies

The trouble with lies is the difficulty remembering them.

As she got older, remembering anything was getting harder, but lies, they seemed ethereal, wafting in the air just out of reach.

Like any other children, Rhona and Ewan had asked about Mhairi's childhood, her mother, her father, any brothers or sisters, who she played with, where she'd lived, where she'd gone to school — the usual list, common to any kid, Mhairi imagined. Among all of these questions, there was only one Mhairi answered correctly. 'I lived in a big house near Glasgow,' she said, in answer to the 'where did you live' question.

'With your mum and Dad?'

'Of course.' Though it hadn't been 'of course.'

She had been taken from that house when she was eight years old and had never entered it again. She chose not to add that bit of information.

Every other question, she answered with a fictional story; a lie by another name.

The difficulty was remembering the story. Rhona, in particular, often caught her out and she'd have to dissemble and reorganise, clarifying with more embellishments until they both forgot which particular 'fact' had tripped her up. At one point, Mhairi had written a story to draw on for details, but she was not a gifted writer and the story was lacking in so many details as to be almost useless, and, of course, it was never to hand when she needed it — and there was never a surreptitious way to consult it.

Mhairi knew she told Rhona and Ewan she had no siblings, and that her parents had died, but she couldn't remember if she said anything about how old she was when they died or how they'd died. It hadn't been something they talked about much, Ewan not being terrifically interested, Mhairi being a mistress of evasion and Rhona accepting it might be painful to dwell on, so Mhairi hoped that perhaps her daughter's memory for detail was about as flawed as her own.

On Wednesday, as soon as Donald left to pick up Rhona, she sat at the kitchen table, hunched over a notebook, working out some reasonable dates to jot down, concocting a rudimentary family tree to present to Rhona when she could evade the issue no longer. Her conscience bothered her but she chose to ignore it, though she couldn't ignore the stress headache that was building behind her eyes. Leaning back in the chair, she stretched and sighed, and closed them for a while.

For all she knew they could be dead, since she had no contact with them for sixty years. No direct contact. One brief letter from her father when she turned twenty-one. Not a letter of congratulations, but an intimation that she would not be welcome to return to his home. He had enclosed a bank draft she was to present to his bank when she found suitable accommodation, 'not here in Glasgow, but somewhere like Edinburgh or Dundee,' the letter informed her. He would give her the deposit and the first six months' rent on a small flat, furnish it and open a bank account in a name she chose, not the name she grew up with. He would place 'sufficient funds' in the account to allow her to 'live modestly' for six months until she could get herself 'established in adequate employment.' She must make no effort to contact him, her mother or her brother. The letter made it very clear they no longer existed to her. They were dead.

There had been no visit, no card, no letter from her mother.

In all those sixty years, nothing.

Mhairi bowed to the pain that lodged in the left side of her chest, deep inside her ribcage, each shallow, ragged breath cutting it deeper until she could expunge again the memory of not being loved. She lay her head on the table, her arms hugged across her chest, and waited for remembered pain to make way for resignation.

Her mother didn't love her.

Obedient to the instructions in her father's letter, she made no attempt to contact what, on paper, might be called her family. That didn't mean she didn't think about them. It took a good number of years for the realisation to sink in: she was unwanted, unloved, discarded. Years in which she cried for her mother, her nanny, her baby brother. Years in which she longed for things she'd never had; to be comforted, to be held, to be loved.

Mhairi lifted her head and uncoiled with the slow gentle grace of a daisy seeking the sun after a storm, finished her work of fiction and left it on the worktop, ready to give Rhona if she came by tomorrow.

The trouble with the truth is the difficulty forgetting it.

She could be going about her daily life, thinking of nothing more than the task she was working on, the meal she was planning, when a word, a phrase, a smell, a trick of light. and there, something was triggered in her head and she'd be taken back to that garden or to the life without it.

To the abyss of loneliness: overwhelming despair that had bowed her head and bent her back. To the void of hopelessness: deepening shadow that had darkened her eyes and destroyed her sleep.

It amazed her she had lived through it: shocked her she had been forced to.

Mhairi dragged herself from the brink again, as she had so many times over the years. Whenever she allowed herself, or was unable to stop herself remember those barren years, she came so close to losing her mind that it frightened her. Each time, it took a huge effort of will not to allow the past to drag her down into its morass of hurt and blame. Each time, she had to remind herself she had survived before, she would survive again.

Forcing herself to take a long, deep breath, she gathered her coat and keys and took herself out.

Driving into Edinburgh at this time of day didn't take too long and she reached Holyrood Park in thirty-five minutes. Parking the car, she crossed the road and walked briskly to the bottom of the hill. At a slightly slower pace, sometimes walking the well trodden paths, sometimes scrabbling over rocky parts, she reached the top of Arthur's Seat in not much more than two and a half hours. Breathless and elated, she stood at the top and gloried in her accomplishment. It got her every time. That hard push beyond thinking, beyond pain. No matter how desperate she felt, no matter the weather, climbing this hill imbued her with power. As long as she was able to force her legs and her lungs through the burning pain of this climb, she could believe there was hope that the past would not catch up with her, that she was strong enough to fight against its drag.

The wind was strong up here by the cairn, but Mhairi loved it. Sitting on the grass, she closed her eyes, leant back on her hands and offered her face, feeling the wind chill her skin and whip her hair, taking her breath and throwing it back at her with full force as it swirled. Not until it had whipped the last thoughts of the past from her mind did she open her eyes to look at Edinburgh lain out at her feet.

The city, the castle, the river, the hills: it was all set out before her like an architect's model, with background views all round, full-circle: over the Pentland Hills; the city; the Forth Road Bridges; the Fife coast, and out to Bass Rock and the conical shape of Berwick Law. When she stood up, she had almost a complete three-hundred-and-sixty degrees of ever-changing view — all wrapped in blue sky with heavy white clouds hanging in it, undecided whether to release their load now or wait till later.

Autumn had already rushed in on the scene with a chill wind, ripping half-turned leaves from their branches earlier than they would have chosen to fall. Though there were no trees up here at the top of the climb, she could see them in the vista she surveyed.

Mixed with the peaty smell, there was the sniff of snow in the air and she filled her lungs with the sharp, freshness of it, loving how cleansing it felt.

The city looked very small: cars and buses moved along the grid like tiny ants, insignificant from this vantage point; people were no more than dots, too small to even bear the label 'insignificant.' What arrogance to think mere mortals were the pinnacle of creation. What were they but specks of dust on the surface of the planet: a planet placed in a veritable plethora of celestial bodies all moving in a majestic choreography.

What was her life compared to the vastness of the world around her? What place did she hold in the universe?

Yet there was something in her that clung to life, clung to the value of her own life. She spread her arms to the wind, turning slowly in a circle, embracing the sky, the hills, all of it. "I am here," she told the world. "I am me. This is my place."

No traffic smells, no traffic sounds, but the smell of snow and heather on the wind, the sound of the same wind in her ears, the distant mumble of the earth turning. Up here, she had space in her head to hear the hum of life. It was made up of insect noises and bird calls, human voices and the thrum of her own blood. Up here she could shut out the past and live in the moment, her only thought how to drink it in and hold its healing in her heart. Up here, she knew she was alive. Up here, she felt invincible.

"I am here. This is my time."

There were always walkers on the hill, regardless of wind and weather. She acknowledged with a nod the one or two she passed as she walked round its crest, revelling in the rawness of the day and the bounce of the tough grass beneath her feet, pulling the crisp air deep into her lungs and holding it for as long as she could. Spreading her arms wider and lifting her face back to the sky, eyes closed, she spun slowly round and round, round and round until she felt as though the whole world spun on this axis, this was the centre of the planet, everything spun out from this point.

Other walkers smiled back at her, complicit in her pleasure. It was good to be here. Good to get perspective: to know that just as every blade of grass on that hillside added to the wealth of its beauty, so too, did each one of them have a part to play in the great drama of life. 'I am here. I am me.'

Enough. It was enough. She was restored.

As she made her way to the car, she studied every part of the walk back down the hill as though she would be asked questions about it later. Was there much heather still blooming? Had the wind stripped the gold from the gorse? What about birds? Did she see many? Which ones? She was greedy for it all, anxious to store it for barren days ahead, when this walk might be denied her.

Enough? It would never be enough.

Donald wasn't back by the time she got home from her walk, so she set about making their meal with determination in her heart. She would not be brought down by this thing. With a shrug, she looked at the notebook she'd left for Rhona. If lies were what it took, then that's too bad. She would not be brought down.

The trouble with lies is the difficulty remembering them, so she hastily made a copy of the 'genealogy' in the notebook.

The trouble with the truth is the difficulty forgetting it, but her walk had helped to push the past back into the recesses of her mind and she forbade herself to call it forth again.

desperate impulse

"Thanks, Mum. I'll sort that bit out later." Rhona pocketed the notebook and helped herself to a biscuit. "Mmm, caramel wafers."

"Gran was helpful the other day, was she?"

"Yeah, great! It was fascinating. She didn't know who we were at first, then once we got her on to the stories, her memory was so sharp! Most of them I'd heard before, but it was quite helpful to get the facts straight for the record. D'you know, Mum, she couldn't remember whether the Doctor had been round on Wednesday when Dad asked her, yet she even remembered dates and put the who was who to the stories as I remembered them."

"That's amazing, isn't it?"

"She says she's got some more old photos she'll let me have. Dad's going to go to her house for them tomorrow."

"Good. That should be interesting."

"It'll be great. I think I might have seen some of them before, but they were just old photos of old fogeys, then. Now, they'll have more significance for me."

"Faces to the names."

"Exactly. Plus, Dad said Gran did a bit of research a few years ago into Grampa's family records after he died. I think she'd found his old papers and stuff when she was turning out later. He still had a copy of his own father's birth certificate so she'd dug a bit deeper and managed to find one for his mum, which is great, because that takes me another generation back on that side."

Mhairi nodded. "That's good, isn't it? That should give you enough to be going on with, I should think, eh? Plenty material for your book?"

"Oh, I'd like to find out a bit more."

"Really? How much further do you think you'll go?" Mhairi got up and started tidying the kitchen worktop, wiping the surface, watching how the damp cloth made the pine shine for a moment before it dried to a matt finish, wiping it again, watching how quickly the dampness evaporated away.

"Not sure. Depends how far back the records go."

"Does Dad think he can dig out more at Gran's house, then?" she said, without looking round, her attention focused on the rhythm of her hand as it drew the dishcloth across the wood, back and forth in an almost circular movement.

"Oh, Gran won't have any more. But, when I go online, what she's given me will make it easier to take it a bit further. It's amazing what you can dig up online."

A pause in the wiping, a beat of her heart. "Online?"

"Yeah! I told you, Mum."

Wiping, keeping even strokes, watching the bleached white cloth move across the worktop, forcing herself to resume breathing, slow and steady. "Did you?"

"I told you I've signed up on one of the genealogy sites where you can look up old birth certificates and stuff."

"Oh, I didn't realise you were going to do that."

"I did tell you, Mum."

"Did you? Sorry, dear." She shook her head. "I'm getting so forgetful in my old age."

Rhona got up and gave her a hug. "You're not old, Mumsie."

Mhairi held on to her, leaning her cheek against her hair; that fragrance, rose and lemon, wrapping itself round her heart. "But, I am forgetful."

"Not all the time. Let's face it, you remember the important things." She held up her biscuit.

Mhairi laughed. "Like the caramel wafers."

"Like the caramel wafers." Rhona hugged her harder before moving to sit down. "Anyway, like I say, I've signed up on this site so I can look up everyone's records."

"Wow! That's something, isn't it? Times were you had to go to Register House to do all that."

"I know. Now it's so easy. Type in a few details, click on the button and there it is, 'Hey, Presto!' all neatly spread before your very eyes." She mimicked a magician sweeping aside a curtain to reveal what had been hidden behind it, her arms spread before her, hands stretched out, palms up.

Mhairi laughed as she brought the two mugs of coffee she had made over to the table. "Oh, you looked so like Ewan when you did that. Do you remember the magician phase he went through?"

"Remember it?" Rhona pulled up her sleeve. "I'm sure I've still got the scars from that trick he tried to do with the matches." She studied her arm. "Well, I did have, anyway, for ages."

Trying not to let Rhona see her laughter, Mhairi turned put away the jar of coffee.

"It wasn't funny. It was really sore."

She tried to make her face serious as she turned round. "I know, darling. But it was a long time ago and I think it was your pride he hurt more than your arm."

"Yes, well. He really shouldn't have asked me to be his 'wonderful assistant.'"

"I don't think he ever did again."

"I should think not," Rhona said, gathering her big sister dignity round her like a robe. "So, anyway, Mumsie. I keep trying to tell you about this site I'm on and tracing our family tree and everything."

"Yes, sorry, darling. So, have you started?"

"Yes. I've seen the record of Dad's birth and Gran's and Gramps'."

Picking up the dishcloth, Mhairi squeezed it out in the basin of sudsy water and put it away in the fridge, put the carton of milk in the bread bin, and looked round for the cloth to wipe the worktop.

"It's great," Rhona said. "You'd love it, Mum."

"I don't know what to do," she muttered.

"Sorry? What did you say?"

With a puzzled frown, Mhairi noticed the milk was in the bread bin. "I don't know what to do." She put it in the fridge, found the cloth and started wiping.

"Mum? You okay?" Rhona got up and came over to where Mhairi still stood, leaning against the worktop. "You must've about wiped the surface off that worktop." She took the cloth from her mother's hand and put it beside the sink.

Mhairi looked up at her. "I might need to tell you something."

Rhona waited.

"The dates I gave you. My genealogy. It might not be quite accurate."

"No problem. The site's pretty good at getting results with incomplete data."

"Yes."

"Look. I'll show you." Rhona led Mhairi back to the kitchen table, took Mhairi's notebook from her pocket and pulled her iPad out of her bag. She opened it and went to the website she'd been using. "I've not had a chance to start on your side yet, but we could have a go now." She started typing in Mhairi's details.

It all happened so fast that afterwards Rhona told Donald she had no idea what actually did happen. She just knew that, somehow, Mhairi knocked over one of the mugs of coffee, sending the hot liquid all over the iPad. She then leapt up, grabbed the dishcloth to mop the coffee up and swiped the iPad off the table, sending it crashing against the cooker and skidding across the floor.

"Oh, darling!" she cried. "Your iPad!" Before Rhona could get there, Mhairi had grabbed up the iPad, tried to wipe it and dropped it into the basin of soapy water she had been using. "Oh, no!" she said, her hands up to her face, as water soaked into the cracked screen of the iPad. "I'm SO sorry, love."

"Good grief, Mother!"

Mhairi fished it out of the basin and looked at the mess of it. "Oops!"

"Oops! is right," said Rhona. "What on earth happened there?"

Mhairi shook her head. "I'm such a klutz. And so clumsy. I'm sorry, love." She opened the cupboard door and dropped the iPad in the bucket that sat behind it, then she turned to give Rhona a hug.

Rhona tried to push past to rescue the iPad. "I can't believe you just did that, Mother. That wasn't just clumsy! That was incredible!"

Mhairi didn't move out of the way. "I know. I'm SO sorry. I'll buy you a new one tomorrow.""

"I thought we were going to go duvet shopping for Katie tomorrow," Rhona tried in vain to move Mhairi away from the cupboard.

"Can we not do that too?"

"No, you know we can't, Mum. We'll have to go through to Braehead for an iPad and I don't have time. I've to buy this stupid duvet and get it to Katie tomorrow."

"The day after, then."

"You've got the girls." She succeeded in moving Mhairi aside to open the cupboard door.

"I'm sorry, honey. We'll set a day and we'll go through to Glasgow just as soon as we can."

"Anyway," Rhona said as she rescued the iPad out of the bucket. "I'd better save this in case I can claim on my insurance and they need to see that it really is ruined."

"Oh, I think it's ruined all right."

looking back

Mhairi knew she couldn't go on like this. It was too costly for starters. It was also pointless. Rhona was not going to give up on her project, nor was she going to content herself with tracing half her family tree.

Panic was making a fool of her. Instead of giving into it, she needed to steady herself and face up to the logical outcome of Rhona's search. "But I'm scared," she told Donald. "I can't face her reaction. What if she hates me? Never wants to see me again?"

"Don't be silly," he said. "She's your daughter. She couldn't hate you."

"No? My own mother did."

"You don't know that."

"I was eight years old, Donald. She allowed me to be locked away when I was eight years old and she never saw me again."

Donald had no argument against that.

She was eight years old. A young eight years old. Sheltered and lonely.

There had been plenty of time to think about her early upbringing. Years of solitude and too much time for reflection had allowed her to rerun the first eight years of her life again and again, understanding it better and seeing it clearer with each viewing.

When she thought about that period of her life, Mhairi felt it read like a Victorian novel, and, although she was born in 1945, the twentieth century didn't seem to have 'caught on' in her home. Certainly not as far as her father was concerned. The second world war saw more women working in shops, offices and factories, giving them a taste of freedom, allowing them to be more independent. Even her father had mostly women serving in his shops, though he made it clear it was against his better judgement. 'A woman's place is in the home,' being his opinion and practice. 'No wife of mine will need to work,' he'd say loudly and proudly at the dinner table. Mhairi had heard one of the maids mimic him, saying it when Mhairi was in the kitchen begging scraps to take to the dogs. Most of her understanding of her father originated there.

When Mhairi was a wee girl, the household, and her father, boasted a cook, a housekeeper and two maids as well as Nanny and the tutors. When Mhairi thought back, none of them seemed to have loyalty or affection for their employer, speaking openly in front of her about his failings. It was unlikely he thought any better of them, judging by the way he treated them. In both camps, her presence was dismissed as of no account, as though a child couldn't see, hear or understand, so no-one tempered their criticism or complaint.

Mhairi knew the facts of her upbringing, but it was hard to view them as more than that, just impersonal, cold words. Even when living it, she felt like an outsider looking in through a misty window.

Her father owned a chain of clothing stores in the Glasgow area. He was a man of importance, as he liked to remind his household often. He had earned their respect and appreciation, he told them, and, perhaps he had in many ways, having started as 'nobody,' working his way up from a handcart, or barrow, in The Barras, to a self-made shop owner.

The Glasgow Barrowlands had become a major street and indoor weekend market in the East End and William thrived there when a young man barely out of his teens, having a naturally shrewd, or canny, personality. He seemed to have a sixth sense when to buy, when to sell, what to buy, what to pass on, and he claimed he bargained better than anyone he knew.

Being a shrewd observer of the world around him, he anticipated, not only another war, but also the shortages that would exist during that war and, before the Second World War broke out, he had huge stockpiles of things like underwear, socks and stockings in his warehouse and as the war progressed and these things became more difficult to find, his prices rose cruelly. She imagined him strutting, laughing loudly as his competitors struggled to keep their shops open with low stocks. The war suited William handsomely.

Mhairi knew the story, but, in later years, she wondered if clothes were all he sold. The Barras was a place well known for other, more nefarious business than the goods on display and she didn't remember her father as a man above such clandestine dealings. Try as he might, he didn't quite fit seamlessly into polite society.

However, as his business expanded, and he opened his shops, he lost his working man demeanour and became a gentleman, by his own reckoning at least.

Mhairi remembered him as a gruff authority figure, who wasted no kindness on her.

He was already into his forties when Mhairi was born and had no patience for her. She was rarely allowed in his presence. Most days, her food was eaten in the nursery of the grand house William had acquired in the more rural area just outside the city, though, from time to time, he would order that she be seated at the dining table 'that she might learn manners.' This always puzzled her, since his own manners seemed rough in comparison to those she learned from Nanny.

The rest of her education was undertaken by a series of tutors, each harsher than the last. The only playground she knew was the rambling gardens behind the house and, for the first five or six years of her life, 'play' was limited to supervised daily exercises there, her tutors becoming drill sergeants.

Too young to serve in the Great War, and having developed asthma before the Second, William was never a soldier, though he saw himself as an officer, and always treated his staff as his troops. Mhairi often heard his voice booming out orders as he left for work each morning. According to Cook, 'It seems to count for nothing that he never passed his medical,' she said. 'Still struts like a sergeant major.' How Cook knew this, Mhairi couldn't fathom, but, then, Cook seemed to know a lot about William Anderson and his family.

Mhairi remembered him as a man whose high opinion of himself always did outrank reality.

She reckoned now, with hindsight, her mother, Audrey, must have been a great disappointment to him. His first wife had died in childbirth, his son and heir dying with her, and, second time around, he had chosen a strong young woman he must have hoped would manage the task better. But, when all she produced for him was a puny daughter, he made it exceedingly clear he was disappointed. The sign, 'William Anderson & Son,' remained unpainted.

Then, when Mhairi was six, Audrey did her duty and bore him a son and Mhairi lost the small affection her mother had shown her. Alexander was a demanding baby and took all the attention Audrey could spare from her social rounds, it being important she move in the 'right' company, but equally important that Mhairi did not.

Just as she would hear her father roar and bellow, she would hear her mother simper and whine. The dresses and hats William bought her were paraded for Mhairi and the servants to admire before she flitted off to this one's lunch or that one's dinner. There were occasional glimpses of her mother's friends from the schoolroom window as they arrived or departed for afternoon tea when it was Audrey's turn to entertain.

'Pay attention, Mhairi,' whichever tutor employed at the time would bark at her. 'Stop daydreaming out the window and apply yourself to your work.' The command was usually accompanied by a rap on the knuckles with a ruler. William chose the tutors carefully. The foremost qualification he looked for being a distaste of children, it seemed.

When questioned later, several of them concurred with her father's statement that she was 'a child of low intelligence, prone to periods of dark reflection,' though Mhairi herself knew her daydreams were always of sunshine and freedom.

When her brother was born, there was an upside to the new member of the household. Nanny had more duties and less time for Mhairi. When afternoon lessons were dispensed with, and the tutors went home, Mhairi roamed free and unsupervised in the grounds of the house. Despite their later report that she was 'a stupid child with no aptitude for learning', Mhairi would pull out books about birds and trees, flowers and insects and before she was seven, she could name most of the plants in the garden and the birds and butterflies that shared it with her.

Scraped knees and ripped dresses from climbing trees earned her much censure and Nanny later reported her as being 'an unruly child, lacking discipline.' Her penchant for building hideaways in the bushes, disappearing into them for hours, causing her frequently to miss mealtimes in the nursery, brought Nanny's wrath and the additional report that she was 'a strange child, disobedient and reclusive.'

Her father kept hunting dogs: an affectation she realised now, since he was never invited anywhere to hunt, as far as she remembered. Sometimes, she would spend some time talking to them through the metal netting that enclosed their kennel area, and they seemed to sense her loneliness, muzzling against her fingers as she poked them through the mesh.

Her only ally in the house was Cook and she would save scraps of meat for Mhairi to take to them, earning Mhairi the dogs' trust and affection. She had named each one and they answered to her names more readily than to those her father barked at them, much to his chagrin, the more so because the names were silly, baby names.

She craved company, and, as with any craving, it became all she could think about. In later years, she learned of people who invented imaginary friends to satisfy just such a craving. Nanny and her tutors made the assumption she was no different from any other lonely child and believed she had a legion of make-believe companions. It might have been healthier if they had been right and she had found solace in such company, but unfortunately, Mhairi didn't light on that form of comfort.

a stay of execution, not a pardon

The next day, she and Rhona had an afternoon shopping together and the talk was confined to which duvet was the better quality, which pillows the more comfortable as they shopped for Katie's flat. Apparently, the bedding she had taken with her from home was no longer suitable since she moved into the room with the double bed.

"I'm trying not to read anything into this new arrangement," Rhona said with a sigh. "But, she did say Anna, her flatmate, was between boyfriends and had 'sworn off men' since the last one broke up with her, and that the single bed would suit her in her newly celibate state."

"Mmm! And you think Katie..."

"Exactly."

"Well, let's not jump to conclusions. And let's not fret about it because Katie will do what Katie pleases. She's nineteen and all grown up and living independently of you."

"And maybe this is why," Rhona said with an even larger sigh.

"But you don't know, so let's get on with choosing this duvet cover. Something neutral? Or something really pretty and girlie?" Mhairi held up a frilled, flounced, lacy specimen.

"You have a very mischievous side to you, don't you?"

She picked up another, more outrageously pink and pretty one.

"Perfect!" Rhona said with a grin.

It took all of Mhairi's self control not to remake the display beds in the shops they went to. She hated to see an untidy or improperly made bed. Years of executing 'hospital corners' had made her pernickety, she knew that, so she resisted the temptation and settled for a surreptitious tweak here and and a furtive flatten there as she passed the beds, her hand stroking the surface, ostensibly comparing softness, in reality seeking smoothness at least. After they had moved past a particular bed, she darted back and pulled up a duvet that had been thrown back for someone to examine the undersheet. It was accomplished quickly and efficiently and made her feel a little better.

Sometimes Mhairi wondered if she was obsessive-compulsive, but, on the whole, she thought not. There were only a few things, like untidy beds, that really got to her. In other things, she had a preference for riotous colour and random patterns, plants growing as they would and a home with a lived-in look. But the beds must be made.

When they stopped for coffee, they chose a window seat where they could look out over Princes Street and the Gardens, quieter now that there were not so many tourists. While Rhona queued for their coffee and cakes, Mhairi reserved their table, placing the bags and parcels on the floor beside her. She loved this view of the Castle and the Gardens, especially on a crisp, late-autumn day like this. Mid-October, yet the trees across the road still held on to the last of their multi-hued leaves, and people had started wearing bright hats and gloves, making it a colourful tableau set below her window, but she closed her eyes for a moment and took a deep, contented breath.

Enough.

It was enough to be here, to be free to come and go as she pleased, able to shop with her daughter, meet for coffee with her grandchildren, fill her house one Sunday every month with her loved ones, live a life. It was so much more than she could have dreamed of having.

All she ever wanted was here, in and around this city: her husband, her children, her grandchildren, her friends. As she neared seventy, she had no desire for adventure or excitement. To live out her life in peace and contentment, that's all she prayed for. Nothing else mattered but that they had one another. It was the fear of losing them that drove her almost insane. Drove her to such foolishness as destroying Rhona's iPad to buy herself time, a day or two, a week at most. They were going through to Braehead in a few days time. They would shop for a new iPad while Donald visited his mother. A stay of execution not a pardon.

Often, Mhairi felt like Ronnie Biggs, one of the gang who pulled off the Great Train Robbery of 1963. He'd been captured but escaped in 1965 and gone on the run. They'd watched a film about it, two television films, in fact, that told the story of the audacious robbery and the hunt to bring the robbers to justice. Donald remembered it being in the news all those years ago, and, being a lawyer, it had fascinated him. Watching the films, Mhairi realised their haul of over two million pounds was nothing compared to what she had netted. A husband and children, a house and garden, a life. Yet, daily, she waited to be found, to be caught and everything taken from her again.

Just as the fear of being caught made some of the robbers do stupid things that gave them away, so her fear caused her to do stupid things too. Like the episode with the iPad.

The really stupid thing was, Rhona wasn't even dependent on the contraption. Everything on it had been backed up, and she had a computer at home. So destroying the iPad had been a foolish impulse born of panic, old insecurities making her reckless.

Shaking her head to rid herself of the frustration occasioned by fear, she fiddled with the salt and pepper in the centre of the table, the menu in its stand and the little vase with its imitation flower. Today was not about fear or panic, running away or getting caught. Today was about here and now, being on a shopping spree in this beautiful city with her beautiful daughter.

She watched as Rhona came towards her with the laden tray, and she considered telling her the truth. Right here, right now. Just sitting down and telling her the whole story. But it was a fleeting thought, dismissed as quickly as it came. This was not the place. It was too public for such a private matter. Nor was this the time. They were having a lovely day together, too delicious to ruin. Mhairi doubted there would ever be a right time or a right place, but she knew this was neither.

Her heart filled with love for her daughter. For so long it had seemed an impossible dream. That she could have a husband and children; that she could feel such deep, tender love and affection, for them and from them, had felt unattainable, the barrier to happiness insurmountable. She silently thanked Donald for believing in her, for rescuing her from certain loneliness, for marrying her and giving her children, this life.

"You look pleased with yourself," Rhona said, placing her coffee and cake in front of her.

"With life," she said with a smile. "I'm happy."

betrayal

"Good day, was it?" Donald asked later.

"Lovely! You?"

He pushed back in the chair to stretch his legs. "Traffic was horrendous, as usual. Mother was querulous, as usual. What's not to enjoy?"

"You're a hero!" Mhairi said, giving him a hug as she walked round him to get to the cupboard at his back. "Did she know who you were today, then?"

"Yes, actually." He smiled, leaning back in his chair. "She was quite lucid today."

"That was nice for you." She took down two dinner plates from the cupboard, giving them a polish with the dishtowel before setting them on top of the oven to warm for a moment. "I'm pleased."

"Yes, we were able to have a half decent conversation, for a change."

Mhairi smiled, genuinely pleased for her husband. He faithfully visited each day, coming home exhausted and dispirited most days, his mother having been uncommunicative because she thought he was a stranger. "Lovely."

"I was telling her about how comprehensively you destroyed Rho's iPad. She reckons you did it deliberately," he laughed.

"She would."

"Thought it'd give her a laugh," he said. "But, no, 'we are not amused' was the order of the day."

"I suppose, at her age, she has the right to be 'not amused.'" She walked across to the oven and took out the pie she had warmed, cutting it and serving it onto the plates, spooning potatoes and vegetables beside it, placing his plate on the table.

"She was a bit scathing about your bid to keep Rhona from finding out your past."

"Pardon?" Mhairi dropped her own plate on the table, the food slopping perilously close to the edge.

"Doesn't reckon you'll manage it."

She sat down at the table and stared at him. "I don't understand. How does she know anything about my past?"

"She's always known."

"Pardon?"

"She's always known," Donald said a little louder.

"I heard you." She raised her hand. "Always? What has she always known?"

"I thought you knew she knew," he shrugged and gave a nervous half-laugh. "I though you knew she knew," he repeated in a silly sing-song voice before taking a mouthful of pie.

"But, how? How has she always known?" Mhairi leant forward, her hands gripping the edge of the table.

"Well, I suppose I told her. Mmm! This is good. Marks and Spencer?"

"You told your mother!" She stared at him in disbelief, a belt of pain tightening round her chest.

"Well...yes..."

She threw herself back in the chair, her hands covering her ears, colour draining from her face. "No!" It was a guttural sound, hardly a word at all. "No!" Her head shaking in denial. It wasn't possible.

Donald started to shift in his seat. "Well, it was one of those times..."

Mhairi put her hand up."No! No! No, no, no, no!" She needed a moment. A lifetime of trust was about to be blown to smithereens. She needed a moment before the final certainty of it hit. Before the shock waves of his words smashed into the rock of her trust. She closed her eyes. Pain pulsed in her temples.

She opened her mouth, but words seemed inadequate. She held her head, holding in the explosion. Her voice, when she forced it through the pain, started small. "I can't believe you told your mother."

"Well, not everything, not right away."

"When? When did you tell your mother? **Why** did you tell your mother?"

"Well, she sort of guessed something wasn't right. She knew you'd had to change your name."

"She knew? How did she know?"

"It was when we were getting married."

"When we were getting married!" Mhairi lifted her hand, halting his speech. "Hold on a moment. Are you telling me that your mother has know about me..." She looked to Donald for confirmation.

He nodded.

"She has know all about me since before we were married?"

He nodded again.

She was up out of the chair and stepping back from him. "YOU TOLD YOUR MOTHER! I can't believe you told your mother."

"Calm down, Mhairi. You're going to burst a blood vessel or something."

"Calm down! Calm down! I will not calm down. I feel anything but calm! I trusted you. I trusted you with my life, my heart, my story, and YOU TOLD YOUR MOTHER! No wonder she's hated me all these years." Mhairi was pacing the room, sitting down from time to time, then jumping to her feet again, unable to be still. "No wonder she treats me like a leper."

"Oh, come on, it's not as bad as that."

"No? No?" She snatched up her plate and went to the cupboard under the sink. Throwing it open so hard that it crashed right back on its hinges, smashing into the cupboard next to it and bouncing closed again, she swung it open a second time and scraped the untouched food into the bin inside the cupboard. "It's every bit as bad as that. The woman can't stand me. She can't bear to be in the same room as me." She threw her plate in the sink, where it smashed into the pie plate. She didn't notice or care that one of them broke. "And who can blame her?" She put her hands over her face, shaking her head, closing her eyes against the pain. "I can't believe you told her."

Donald shifted in his chair again.

Mhairi's head snapped up. "Who else have you told? Who else knows?"

He looked straight at her. "No-one! I swear. No-one else."

"That you know of." The words were hurled at him. "That you know of! What about your mother? Who will she have told. Don't try to tell me she's kept that particular nugget of gossip locked away for forty-odd years."

"She hasn't told anyone."

"That you know of."

"She wouldn't."

"You think?"

"I know she wouldn't."

"No?"

"Think about it. Why would she? It isn't exactly something she'd brag about to her friends. It isn't exactly something to be proud of."

Mhairi shivered in the chill that ran between them. It was almost tangible. With all the words that had been thrown across the kitchen, none hurt as much as those unspoken now. "No, I don't suppose it is," she said, her voice quietened at last as she moved towards the kitchen door.

"Aw! Come on, Mhairi!"

A sudden thought made her turn in the doorway. "What if she says something to Rhona?"

"She won't."

"You can't know that. Your mother likes having power. Knowledge is power. She knows Rhona is doing this family tree thing. What if she decides to give her this little tidbit as an I-know-something-you'd-like-to-know sort of thing?"

"She won't, love. You're worrying about nothing."

"Have you met your mother?"

"You're getting yourself all worked up about something that's not going to happen. My mother doesn't even know what she had for lunch, never mind what you did sixty years ago."

"Yeah! Sometimes. Other times, she knows exactly who everyone is and where they are and what they did."

"Nah! Those times are rare."

"Rhona can't see her again."

"Don't be daft!"

"Daft? Yeah! I was daft. Daft to think you were on my side all these years."

"Come on, Mhairi."

"No, I mean it Donald. I don't want you to take Rhona to see her again."

"You're being ridiculous now."

Ice cracked in Mhairi's eyes as she spun from him and stormed upstairs.

When he followed her up a little later, after he'd washed what remained unbroken of the dishes and locked the back door, he found their bed empty and the spare room door shut against him.

a meeting

Wishing she had snatched her pyjamas from under her pillow, Mhairi undressed to her underwear and climbed into the bed in the spare room. Too weary to fold her clothes, she let them fall to the floor and stepped out of them and into bed, shivering until the cool cotton sheets warmed. Had she expected to be sleeping here tonight, she would have put the electric blanket on for an hour or two, but, as it was, she had to wait till its heat reached into her bones with only her anger to keep her warm.

He had told his mother.

In the forty-four years of their marriage, it had never occurred to her that he might have told his mother. She had trusted his discretion implicitly, forgetting how insidious his mother could be, how cleverly she could get what she wanted from her only son. Mhairi should have guessed the woman couldn't leave a secret unrevealed to her. It all made sense: the barbed comments, the snarled remarks, the dismissive gestures, the ignorant snubs. The woman hated her. Hated that her precious son had married 'beneath himself.'

Even worse than the fact that she knew, was the fact that he told her.

Donald, her knight in shining armour had betrayed her. She thought he had saved her, allowed her to start afresh, with a blank, clean page to write a fresh, new chapter to her life. It was all a sham. 'It's not exactly something to be proud of,' he'd said. He had been ashamed of her all these years.

They'd met by a fluke. She was working in a grocer's shop in Edinburgh. Her first job, hard won, not well paid, but hers. The shop was closed and she was tidying in the stockroom — unpaid overtime, but she didn't mind. Her flat was tiny and cold, she was in no rush to go home. Usually, the boss locked the door and he cashed up while she worked, but he'd forgotten to lock up. When a customer walked in, Mr Foster's greed for the sale outweighed his desire to get finished, so he served him.

'Have we any more tinned salmon,' he called through to Mhairi.

When she found a new box, she brought it through to stock the shelf as well as serve the customer.

The customer pulled a face as he took the tin and handed her the money. 'Salmon sandwiches tomorrow. Mother coming for afternoon tea,' he said, though she'd asked no explanation of his purchase. 'I don't suppose you have any decent biscuits I could throw on a plate too?'

'What does your mother like?' she asked, directing him to the couple of shelves of biscuits nearby.

'Honestly? Haven't a clue. I've never bothered to notice.'

'Well, what does she put on the plate when she makes tea for you?'

He pulled a face. 'Not really a biscuit sort of person, so can't say as I've paid attention.'

'What about a mixture? You could either buy a few different packets,' she pointed them out on the shelves. 'Or, you might think about getting a variety box.' She indicated the selection of boxes on the top shelf.

'That might work,' he said, nodding with obvious pleasure at the suggestion. 'Which one would you recommend?'

Mhairi blushed. She had never eaten a biscuit in her entire life. It was not something that had ever been offered in the past and it was not something she could afford at present. 'I really couldn't say.' She turned to her boss. 'Mr Foster?'

He signalled he was counting and was not to be disturbed.

'So, what do you think?' the customer persisted.

Using the steps provided, Mhairi reached down a random box of biscuits.

'Perfect! They'll do nicely.' He paid for his purchases and turned as he got to the door. 'Nice powder,' he said with a grin, pointing to his cheek and nodding in the direction of hers.

She might never have remembered him if it hadn't been for the flour all over her face. When she looked in the mirror in the backroom, she couldn't decide whether to join in his laughter or die of embarrassment.

It was another month before he returned to the shop, though she had noticed him as he walked past each weekday evening and had concluded he must work nearby. An office perhaps? He looked very business-like, always in a suit, carrying a briefcase, sometimes with another, similarly smart, slightly older gentleman.

'Mother coming to tea again?' she asked, blushing at her own boldness. She took the tin of salmon he'd asked for from the shelf.

'Yes actually.' He looked puzzled.

'You were in before,' she stammered out, regretting that boldness now.

'Ah! Yes, I remember. You served me, didn't you? And you had flour on your face.'

'Mmm! I had hoped you'd forgotten that.'

He laughed. A deep, mellow sound that she found she liked very much.

Handing over some money, 'The biscuits were a great success, by the way,' he said. 'Mother enjoyed more than a few. Still plenty left for today. I'm not really a biscuit person myself, so the tin hasn't been opened since.'

Mhairi smiled dumbly as she handed him his change and could only manage a nod in reply to his cheerful goodbye. Unused to social chit-chat, there was a limit to her responses and even that had dried up at the sound of his mellifluous laugh.

About a week later, she almost bumped into him as she left the shop. Mister Foster was closing up early because his wife was having dinner guests and he had been demanded home in plenty of time. Mhairi was buttoning her coat and was not looking where she was going when someone held her elbow and guided her round the baby carriage she was heading straight into. It turned out to be the older gentleman her customer walked with.

She thanked him, not daring to look up, knowing her cheeks would be crimson with embarrassment, and she almost ran down the street and round the corner.

Then something happened that she could not have foreseen. Mister Foster lost the shop. He'd been working on credit for years and it had run out. He'd been unable to pay his debts and he was declared bankrupt. The shop would have to close. Mhairi was out of a job.

The little world she'd been building round herself, her hideaway in the bushes, her place of safety was being demolished. It had taken almost six months to find this job. Six months of walking the streets of Edinburgh, asking in every shop, every office if there was a vacancy. Six months of answering every situation vacant notice she came across. Six months of watching her small amount of money dwindle with every rent payment, every morsel of food she ate, not knowing where and when she'd be able to replenish it. The prospect of doing it all again was crushing.

Mister Foster had needed a lawyer and the lawyer turned out to be Donald Carlyle of Harrison, Tweadale and Bingley, who had offices not far from the shop. The first time Donald came into the shop in that capacity, Mhairi had taken his usual tin of salmon down from the shelf as he approached the counter. He laughed, bought it anyway and then asked for a word with Mister Foster. He was taken into the backroom for the interview.

'You're Mhairi,' he told her when he reemerged.

She nodded, her face reddening yet again. She hated that she blushed so easily, though was not surprised by it. She had so little experience of conversation, she felt certain she would say something foolish as soon as she opened her mouth.

'I'm afraid you are going to be out of a job.'

She nodded again. Mister Foster had said as much earlier that day.

'Can you type?'

Another nod.

'File?'

And another.

'Speak?'

'S-sorry,' she stuttered. 'Yes. I did a course. Not a speaking course, of course, a secretarial course, I mean... of course...' She had secretarial training of sorts, her father having sent her an old typewriter to practice on and arranged a correspondence course for her when she got her little flat. Even when the ribbon ran dry, she tapped away on it, getting faster and more accurate month by month, longing for the chance to use her one and only skill.

Donald Carlyle was laughing at her, not unkindly, but definitely laughing. 'Yet you're working in a shop?'

She nodded. 'Sorry!' Remembered to speak. 'Yes. It was all I could get. I have no experience.'

It was Donald's turn to nod. 'How old are you?'

Wondering if she should be addressing him more politely, she threw in a 'Sir,' when she told him she was twenty-one.

He laughed, that lovely mellow laugh again. The kind of laugh that reached all the way to his eyes — and all the way to her toes. 'Please, call me Donald. You're only a few years younger than I am.' He held out his hand. 'Donald Carlyle.'

Trembling and nodding, she shook his hand.

'This is where you tell me your name,' he said, still holding her hand.

'Mhairi. Mhairi Adams. But I thought you knew that. I thought Mister Foster…'

'Mhairi Adams. Okay, Mhairi Adams, I shall see you tomorrow in your best bib and tucker and I'll take you for an interview with our Mister Bingley. He's interviewing for a typist. Let's see if you're up to speed, shall we?' He winked at her.

She was affronted. No-one had ever winked at her before. She had no idea how to interpret it, no idea how she should respond. So she did and said nothing. Just stood like the mute idiot she felt.

'This is where you say, 'Thank you!' to me for arranging an interview for you,' he prompted in an undertone, leaning in towards her.

'Oh! Oh, yes, of course. Forgive me. Yes. Thank you, Sir… I mean…Don…oh…er…Mr Carlyle. Thank you very much. I'm much obliged to you.' And now she was bobbing and babbling. The colour crept up her neck, burning in her cheeks.

But, he was smiling. 'Much obliged. How very quaint,' he said. 'You are a funny little thing, aren't you, Mhairi Adams? Old fashioned and shy. Refreshing.'

Her whole face was crimson now. She wished he would just go away. She would have run if she could have, but she was rooted to the spot, confused by his kindness and openness, and intimidated by his condescension.

'Tomorrow then.' And, at last, he was gone.

Mhairi closed her eyes and let her breath go. If the man had stayed a moment longer, she would have passed out.

*a sleepless night
and a job*

She must have fallen asleep with the electric blanket still on because she woke up about midnight thinking she might pass out with the heat. Throwing back the duvet, she sat up and took a moment or two to remember she was in her own spare room. Everything looked so different, though the sounds of the house were the same — except Donald was more muted. She could hear him snuffling and snoring as he slept.

Her teeth clenched.

How could he sleep? His conscience should be searing him. He should be writhing in an agony of regret for his duplicity.

Turning off the electric blanket, she sat on the edge of the bed debating with herself whether she should wake him up just for the hell of it. She could go to the bathroom, slamming a door or two as she went, putting the hall light on and making sure his door was wide enough open that the light fell on his face.

Stomping her way across the bedroom, she tripped over the heap of her discarded clothes and remembered last night's crushing weariness.

Of all the people in the world to tell, he had to tell his blooming mother. The person she most needed to impress all these years.

Gathering her clothes in her arms, she threw them over the plush chair by the window, and looked out over the sleeping garden, the half-moon very bright in the clear, cloudless sky, the frost painting the grass and the trees. It gave her no pleasure to see its ethereal beauty.

Oh, dammit, Donald! How could he have done this to her. He had been her hero.

All those years ago, it had been much to her amazement that she got the job in the lawyers office. It was thanks, she was sure, to Donald Carlyle's help, because she knew her typing was not 'up to speed' and, having no interview experience, she didn't feel she exactly shone in this one. However, she got the job and it was a relief. Unemployment was not an option she wished to experience again, it being a miserable, costly affair. The small amount left of her father's bank draft would not have sustained her for long and she dreaded the whole applying, interviewing, rejection cycle she knew would have been her lot. Lack of education and experience did not make a great recommendation to any prospective employer.

The typing pool was not too large and the other typists seem friendly enough, helping her to settle in, explaining her duties, teaching her the rudiments of legal language so that she had a chance of understanding what she was typing up, enough to ensure it made sense. The days passed more quickly than they had in the shop because, where its trade had been slow and minimal, traffic through the lawyers' office was brisk and busy. She loved it and found, much to her own surprise, that she was a quick learner and not 'stupid' as she'd been led to believe.

It was several weeks before she had any dealings with Donald Carlyle, and, when she was sent to his office to deliver some files, she was glad of the opportunity to thank him for his help in getting the job.

'Not a problem,' he assured her. 'Mister Foster spoke highly of you. He felt you had potential and, from what I hear from the ladies of the typing pool, he has been proved right in his assessment.'

Damn! She could feel the blush starting. 'Thank you.'

'Do you think you can be happy working here, then, Mhairi Adams?'

'I am happy, Sir.'

'Good! But, please, not 'Sir.' 'Mister Carlyle' will do in the office and 'Donald' would be more friendly outside it, don't you think?'

She didn't expect there to be an 'outside the office,' and found it hard enough to call him 'Mister Carlyle.' She could not imagine herself ever calling him 'Donald.'

But, she watched him: watched his kindness and good humour with the secretaries and the girls in the typing pool; his courtesy and good manners with the clients; and his respect and deference with the partners of the firm. She loved how his smile reached his eyes, how his laugh lingered in the air after he left the room. She was impressed with the volume of work he managed to get through and the thoroughness with which he completed it. She loved that he didn't flirt with the girls the way some of the young lawyers did: that he wasn't working his way through them, breaking their hearts, as others were. She reckoned he was a man of honour.

carol and letty

Mhairi looked at the little clock on the bedside table. Two o'clock and she was still awake. She had to be up in the morning in time to shower and do her hair before meeting the girls for lunch — 'the girls' being Letty and Carol.

They were her two oldest, most treasured friends: she thought of them as life-long friends because she'd known them since her life began at the age of twenty-one.

They'd worked together in the typing pool at Harrison, Tweadale and Bingley, Lawyers; the first of the girls to introduce themselves when she joined the firm.

Now they were all retired, regular as clockwork, every month, she met them at the West End of Prices Street outside Fraser's. They would do a little shopping together and then have lunch. 'Ladies who Lunch,' Letty said every time as they settled at their favourite table in their favourite restaurant.

They had been the first proper friends she ever had. Friends she could go shopping with. Friends she could go for coffee with. It was they who taught her how to style her shoulder-length, unruly hair: to tame the curls enough that they looked glossy and luxurious instead of frizzy and untidy. The fashion of the sixties was for shorter, bouffant hair, or long, sleek styles, but they convinced her not to have hers cut or to iron it straight because it was glorious as it was, natural and richly coloured.

'A little henna to keep the auburn bright, that's all you need,' Carol said. 'It would be criminal to cut that lot off,' she said. 'I'd love to have hair like that, whatever the fashion.'

'A little brown eyeshadow to bring out the green of your eyes,' suggested Letty. 'Not too much make-up. Nude lipstick. Fab.'

She was thankful for their advice and happy that they liked her natural look because she would have been too self-conscious to wear a lot of make up, and short, sleek hair would probably show her face to be too round and babyish. Besides, having had her hair cropped almost to her scalp for so many years, she loved the feel of longer hair and had not had it cut since the choice had been hers.

It felt like freedom.

She still wore it longish, almost to her shoulders, though the auburn had dulled with the years and there was plenty grey threaded through it.

They would go shopping tomorrow — correction, today — just as they had so many, many times over the years.

Closing her eyes, Mhairi lay on the bed allowing her mind to travel back through the years to the nineteen-sixties when Carol and Letty first took her shopping to help her choose fashionable clothes: a short suede skirt and coloured tights, an angel dress and knee-high boots. The fashion for longer skirts and dresses, inspired by Marianne Faithful and the flower people hadn't caught on yet in Edinburgh, though there were some beginning to appear in the shops and Mhairi found them pretty; lingering, fingering the delicate, flowing materials. It wasn't much longer before she added one to her growing wardrobe, counting the cost in paydays.

Having never had money before, and having been almost flat broke by the time she found work, she bought carefully, one item each week, cutting back on food and heating if necessary until she felt she could blend in with the girls at work. To feel like one of them, to not stand out as the proverbial sore thumb, was worth eating frugally and huddling in blankets rather than switch on the heater, and she often wore damp underwear if it didn't quite manage to dry without benefit of the warmth.

The clothes Mhairi had been wearing were not only old-fashioned, 'If they ever were in fashion,' Letty declared. 'Don't mean to hurt your feelings, kiddo, but, honestly, even my old gran wouldn't be caught dead in dresses like that.' They were also matronly, unflattering, shapeless, tied in the middle with narrow ribbons of the same thin, faded material. They managed to make her look dull and somehow both old yet childish. Worn with equally shapeless, faded cardigans that had seen far too many washes, they did nothing to make her look or feel good.

Grateful for Carol and Letty's guidance and feeling more confident with every item she bought, she would gaze at the few pieces of clothing hanging behind the curtain in her bedroom and smile, her heart bursting with pride that she should possess such wonderful items. It was the first time in her life she had chosen and bought her own clothes, but she didn't tell the girls that, allowing them to believe she just had bad taste.

'You look as if you've joined the sixties now,' Carol said.

'About time,' Letty giggled. 'We're nearly done with them. Can you believe in a few weeks it'll be 1968? What you two doing for New Year? Should we have a party round my place?'

They introduced her to the music of the day, taking her to record shops and listening to the hit parade on the little transistor radio Carol handed on to her when she got a new one. She listened to groups like The Rolling Stones, The Beatles, and The Bee Gees with bemusement at first, then amazement. The Bee Gees became one of her favourite groups, Marianne Faithful and Mary Hopkins her favourite singers.

'How can you have lived without a radio till now?' Letty asked the day Carol brought it in to work to give her. 'I'd die without my tranny.'

Sometimes, Mhairi felt overwhelmed with the amount of information issuing from the small cream and brown box on her kitchen window sill, though she loved to keep up with the news, marvelling that she could hear what happened all over the world on any particular day. Geography and maps had always fascinated her even as a little girl and she loved to imagine herself flying off to exotic locations to taste the food and see the sights. The radio transported her there to at least hear their sounds and she sometimes tuned in to a foreign language station for the sheer pleasure of imagining the enormity of the world she had emerged into.

'You really don't have to keep thanking me for the radio,' Carol said. 'I was only going to throw it out. I'm pleased it's of use to someone.'

'I just love it,' Mhairi assured her, stopping herself from saying, 'Thank you!' yet again.

breakfast at tiffany's

Carol and Letty had been astounded to discover Mhairi had never been to the cinema before. 'Never?' said Letty.

She shook her head.

'Really? Never? Wow!'

'Where have you been?' Carol asked. 'On another planet?'

She said nothing and was relieved when their attention switched to buying the tickets and finding their seats.

They had decided she should see Breakfast At Tiffany's.

'Everyone should see Breakfast At Tiffany's', Letty declared. 'I've seen it already at least eight times.'

'Really?'

'Yup! Once a year since it came out.'

'Why?'

'Why?' Letty turned to Carol. 'The lady asks me why.'

'Oh, you'll understand when you watch it,' Carol explained. 'It's just one of those films that gets to you. Think it's Audrey Hepburn.'

'Nuh-uh! George Peppard.' Letty pretended to swoon.

Carol shook her head. 'Not a patch on Robert Redford.' She turned to Mhairi. 'Next film we'll take you to — Barefoot In The Park.'

'Mmmm!' Letty let herself 'swoon' away again. 'But George Peppard, mmm-hmm.'

The three of them snuggled into their seats and Mhairi prepared herself to watch her first ever movie, unprepared for the enormity of the experience.

The film entranced her. In equal measure, she was shocked and mesmerised by it.

Mesmerised by the huge screen, the colours, the sights and sounds of New York City, sound that filled the auditorium. Music, colour, people larger than life, dresses, hats, taxis, parties, fire escapes, in and out of one another's apartments — it was almost overwhelming.

Shocked at the amount of alcohol consumed by the characters: no matter the day or the hour, someone seemed to be offering or asking for a drink as casually as though they were drinking water. Shocked by the immorality of it: that it was accepted as permissible behaviour to be kissing and cuddling with a string of casual acquaintances, that George Peppard, the hero of the film, should be a gigolo, a kept man, sleeping with someone he clearly didn't love, a married woman at that, and paid for the privilege.

'Welcome to the sixties,' Letty informed her with a shrug when she timidly expressed a little of her outrage.

'You don't drink like that, do you?'

Letty laughed. 'Darling, nobody drinks like that!'

'Except in films,' Carol added.

'Or if they're a lush.'

'And they were never without a cigarette.'

Letty lifted her hand. 'Like me, you mean? Think I'll get one of those long holders.' She held her cigarette at arm's length and pretended to draw on it.

It was Carol's turn to laugh. 'Remind me to keep my distance,' she said as she dodged round the imagined cigarette holder.

'Especially if you're wearing your best hat!' Mhairi joined in the laughter, remembering the scene in the film.

'You should try it.' Letty offered her cigarette.

Shrinking back, 'Never fancied it,' Mhairi said, pulling her sleeves down to cover the round scars on the back of her hand. Any desire to try smoking was always accompanied by painful memories of Peg, one of the orderlies in the Home, who liked to punctuate her reprimands with screams, Mhairi's screams. It had turned out to be great aversion therapy.

'What about those hats, though?' Carol pulled her beret to a rakish angle. 'I loved the one with the long organza ribbons.'

'Oh, it was the pink tiara did it for me,' Letty giggled.

'And the pearls wound through her hair.'

'Think I'd suit a chignon?' Carol swept her hair up, catching it at the back with her beret.

'Gorgeous, daaaling!' Letty drawled, pulling her own felt hat down her forehead, peeping demurely from under it.

Sweeping her moral qualms about the film aside — 'Okay! I've had a sheltered upbringing.' — Mhairi knew she was mesmerised by it.

The 'real phoney' character of Holly Golightly, fired her imagination: that she had reinvented herself, changed her looks, her accent, her aspirations because she chose to chase a life she dreamed of, made perfect sense to Mhairi. Holly did not wear her past, she had discarded it when she moved to New York.

Mhairi determined to do the same and returned the next evening on her own to watch the film again, studying Audrey's mannerisms, her style, her aura. Not that she thought she could, or should become like Hepburn, but she admired her air of vulnerable self-confidence, her mystery.

When the film ended, the theatre emptied as people filed out during the National Anthem. As the last notes hung in the air, the lights came on and the usherettes began to snap the seats up and pick up the sweetie papers and other detritus left between the rows. Mhairi sat, undisturbed by their activity, lost in the world she was building.

She would choose a part to play. The rest of her life would be the film. She would be its author, producer, director. Sitting in the empty cinema, the echoes of Holly Golightly's smile on her face, Mhairi decided to take her life into her own hands, no longer to be buffeted and bullied by circumstance and fortune.

Enough: she'd had enough of the old one. Enough of living a life of quiet desperation, waiting to see what would become of her. She would make her own way.

In studying the character created by Hepburn, perhaps she, Mhairi, could find one she could create for herself, one where she didn't walk with her head down, her eyes lowered, afraid of being found out, but where she stood tall and looked the world in the eye.

Like Holly Golightly, it was time to let the world know Mhairi Adams had arrived.

When the Manager of the cinema put his hand on her shoulder and asked if she was alright, she looked at him with what she hoped was an enchanting, enigmatic smile and said, 'Indeed, Sir, I am. And I thank you for asking.'

Humming the film's theme song, Moon River, she carefully gathered her belongings and walking straight and tall, with a Hepburn swagger, she waltzed out of the cinema.

The song enchanted her and she sang and hummed it almost incessantly for weeks after seeing the film, and, in common with so many of her own and succeeding generations, she fell in love with Audrey Hepburn.

'Wish I could pull off that sophisticated, elfin look,' Carol sighed.

Letty looked at her with a critical eye. 'Bit of make-up, new hairstyle, new clothes...'

'Lose a few stone, grow a few inches...' Carol added, making them all laugh.

Oh, it was so good to laugh. To have something and nothing to laugh about. Not to fear reprimand or censure with every sound she made. Mhairi loved Letty and Carol: loved their easy banter, their teasing, their kindness.

When they asked 'Where you been all your life?' they were satisfied with her answer that she was an orphan and had grown up in a children's home and from then on, they treated her like a young sister, someone they had to educate and protect.

Her childhood and teenage years had been barren, cold winter. Her twenties became suffused with the glow of summer.

Mhairi had discovered life.

Incredible though it sounded, everything was new to Mhairi, she was doing everything for the first time.

It was her first time in Woolworth's, where she marvelled at the cornucopia of delights, costume jewellery, scarves and gloves of every conceivable colour, slippers, sweets, light bulbs and underwear, all vying for their place on the counters and shelves. Such a wonderland of colour and organised confusion.

It was her first time sitting in a cafe. The girls tumbled in through the door of The West End Cafe, laughing at some joke Letty had made, tumbled in to a world of soft lights and juke box music. Carol and Letty surged forward, taking her with them to an empty booth.

Mhairi had never seen or heard anything like it.

The room was divided by rows of colourfully painted wooden partitions that rose to shoulder height. Once they were sitting in their booth, they had a sense of privacy that was short-lived when Sheila from the office popped her head over the blue fence to say, 'Hi there, you lot! Been shopping?' and came round to squeeze along the bench to chat for a while, her blushing young man in tow.

The record that was playing on the juke box, What a Wonderful World, summed it all up for Mhairi and she never again heard the mellow, gravelly voice of Louis Armstrong without remembering that day and that time.

a wonderful life

Mhair must have fallen asleep sometime between three and four o'clock and when she heard Donald's alarm go off at eight, she was not ready to get up, so she lay listening to him stumbling about in his usual early morning clumsiness. Unlike her, he was not a morning person and took a while to wake up properly. She used to love his warm, dishevelled appearance at the breakfast table, his preference being to greet the day with coffee and toast before showering and shaving.

Still befuddled by sleep, she heard him mumble, "Good morning!" forgetting, no doubt, that she hadn't lain beside him. A grunt told her he now remembered. She heard him go into the bathroom, his footsteps pausing outside the spare bedroom. She held her breath.

Once the smell of toast and coffee started filtering through the house, she got up and went into the shower, shampooing her hair and washing in double quick time, wanting to make sure she was finished before Donald reappeared.

As she stepped out of the shower, she heard him wheeling the bucket round for the bin men to empty, so she wrapped a huge bath sheet round herself, a small towel round her hair, and escaped to the spare room, where she waited until he stepped into the shower. Taking the opportunity of his morning routine, she knew she had time to rough dry her hair and choose her clothes for the day while he was not in the bedroom.

Feeling like a sulky teenager, she waited back in the spare room until he was in the bedroom to nip downstairs, grab herself a cup of coffee and a slice of toast and was ready and out the door before he came downstairs.

She'd be early for the girls, but she didn't care. That was better than allowing his duplicitous face to spoil her day.

snatching defeat from victory

Caught in the morning traffic, Mhairi's progress into town was slow, so she turned the car radio on and allowed herself to relax some of the tension that tightened her shoulders, rolling them backwards then stretching her neck from side to side. Her jaw must have been clenched while she slept and she opened her mouth wide, wiggling her lower jaw to release the tension. If she was to fool the girls that everything was fine, she would need to be able to smile and seem at ease with life.

The announcer on the radio informed her the first batch of tickets for the 2014 Eurovision Song Contest were scheduled to go on sale at the end of the month. Mhairi smiled, her mood lightening — not that she would be jetting off to Copenhagen to see it, but the news would be something to share with the girls. Today, she needed something to share with them other than what was on her mind. They would have a good half hour's chat about why they preferred to watch the contest from the comfort of home than join the hysteria it could evince in its followers.

It was with the girls Mhairi had her first taste of The Eurovision Song Contest in 1968, and it became one of her favourite annual programs — more because it was the first programme she ever saw in colour than through any merit it had, though she did love all the hype and fuss that surrounded it. It was so vibrant. Every year, she, Letty and Carol got together for a Eurovision party, 1968 starting the tradition.

When she stepped off the bus in 1968 to join the girls in Carol's mum's house — she being the only person they knew who had a colour television — Mhairi had no idea what to expect. She had been swept along with their excitement, her own building by the day as they talked about the fact that Britain was sure to win this year. 'Even the bookies have Cliff as favourite,' Letty told her, a statement that meant nothing to Mhairi since she hadn't a clue what a 'bookie' was and had long since stopped asking such questions because of the disbelief and consequent threat of exposure they encountered.

'It's such a cop, Cliff agreeing to do Eurovision,' Letty crowed.

'I think you mean a coup,' Carol corrected her.

'A cop, a coup, whatever... it still is. I mean he's so famous. Everyone's heard of Cliff, even in other countries. Everyone loves Cliff. They're gonna vote for him.'

'And the fact that it's in the Albert Hall this year won't do any harm,' Carol said. 'Home crowd, home advantage.'

'It's a lovely song, too,' Mhairi ventured. She'd been hearing it on her radio for weeks and could hardly get it out of her head.

On a Saturday, they would sometimes treat themselves to a 'soup and sandwich lunch' and she would look at Letty and Carol, as the three of them sat round the table, and apply the words to them. It really had felt as though happiness hadn't been invented and the bad old days were fading away since she'd let them walk into her heart, or, more accurately, since she'd been powerless to stop them invading her heart. After her initial reluctance and resistance, she had surrendered with joy.

And the chorus, oh, the chorus...

Mhairi had never known much happiness in her life. Now, it suffused her being. Her every waking moment was filled with the joy of their friendship. Whether she was with them or not, they were embedded in her heart. Their kindness and unconditional affection filled her with such gratitude. She knew she could never repay what they gave her, it was beyond price, she knew very quickly that they would remain life-long friends.

Their Eurovision party was more fun than anything Mhairi had ever experienced or could possibly have imagined. Carol's mother had invited a few of her own friends and everyone had brought something for the table, sausage rolls and sandwiches, cakes and biscuits, juice and crisps: a banquet that took Mhairi's breath away. They cheered and clapped the songs they enjoyed, muttered and booed, with good natured pretence, the ones they didn't. When Cliff took the stage, the excitement rose to a level Mhairi could barely cope with. She thought her heart would burst with it.

When the scoring started, it looked as though Letty and the bookmakers would be proved right. Only four countries gave the United Kingdom no points, their meanness duly noted by Letty, 'Remind me never to go to Spain for a holiday,' she said, sitting back with her arms folded. The others laughed, knowing that foreign holidays were way beyond their reach.

Four points each from France and Switzerland were greeted with cheers and approbation and, when Monaco awarded Cliff five points, they all rose to their feet jumping around like children, certain that victory was theirs. Alas, the five points United Kingdom had generously awarded to Germany, which the girls had nodded and sombrely approved, were cruelly gobbled up and spat out by Germany giving them nothing in return, awarding Spain a massive six points instead. The audience in Carol's mum's living room were stunned into silence for a moment, becoming unrestrainedly vocal and vicious in their condemnation, shocking Mhairi more than a little. The war had meant nothing to her, not being born till 1945, too young to learn about it in the years that followed, and unimpressed by the little she read here and there afterwards. The generosity and the meanness were equally puzzling to her. She sat silent.

Those six points were to mark the turning point for Cliff, and his Congratulations were for second place; Spain, championed by Germany, bouncing into the lead and collecting the winner's trophy.

The mood of the party changed, the girls sitting around discussing the politics of the scores and the countries who awarded them. The sparkling fairy lights Carol had so happily strung round the room earlier that day winked forlornly, trying with every glimmer to lighten the mood again. It was Letty, never one to be miserable for long, who suggested second place was not so bad and they should put Congratulations on the record player and have a victory dance anyway. 'After all,' she said. 'He should have won. We know he was the true winner. It was the best song and he was the best singer.'

The party was saved, the memory secured in Mhairi's heart, and the next year, when Lulu was a joint winner with Boom-Bang-A-Bang, the party rocked from start to finish, Cliff's Congratulations sung again with even greater enthusiasm.

As Mhairi drove to meet the girls, these memories lifted her mood until there was no room in her head for anything but anticipation of the joy she always found in their company.

"How was the traffic from your end?" Letty asked her usual question as she proffered her cheek for a kiss. "If it isn't too rude to ask," she added with a giggle, just as she always did.

"Running well," Mhairi gave the stock reply.

"Aah, that's good."

It was a ritual that Letty seemed to be unaware of. Each month, she made the joke as though it was brand new. Each month, Mhairi laughed as though she was hearing it for the first time and Carol tutted affectionately, happy to supply the supposed mild reproof Letty looked for.

Their friendship was littered with snippets and snatches of rituals and traditions. Letty always sat with her back to the window, Mhairi always faced it and Carol sat between them to Mhairi's right. Letty always scanned the menu then asked for something that wasn't on it, Mhairi chose lemon sole with boiled potatoes and Carol downed the largest steak on offer.

"I was listening to the news on the way in," Mhairi said, handing the menu to the waitress after she'd ordered. "And the tickets for ESCape go on sale at the end of the month."

"Yay! Better start preparing for the party!"

"Plenty time yet, Letty. The contest is months away."

"Still. What was the Boy Scouts' motto?"

They clinked water glasses and said in unison, "Be prepared!"

And they were off...

Reminiscing their way, year by year, through all the ESCape parties they'd enjoyed together since Mhairi joined them in 1968. Having long-since decided 'The Eurovision Song Contest' was too big a mouthful, they adopted the nickname 'ESCape' and felt it fitting since all three saw the contest as an escape from the rush and routine of their working week.

As Mhairi looked at her two friends in animated conversation, she sighed with contentment. Enough. It was enough for her to be here, to be loved, to be cherished by the warm familiarity. They had made so many memories together and she loved days like today, when they took them out and polished them up.

In 1968, all these things had been food and drink to Mhairi, pouring nourishment into the barren soil in which she'd been planted, encouraging growth and strength in her soul.

Whoosh — transported back to that garden, her six-year-old self watching the gardener plant bulbs in late autumn and hide the pots in a dark corner of the potting shed till spring. He'd bring the pots out into the spring sunshine and she would check them every day, watching for the green shoots, then the leaves, the stems, the buds, until, finally, there, in all their glory was a pot of hyacinth or lilies.

In the late 60's, Mhairi felt herself brought out of the potting shed and thrust into the sunshine. She grew and blossomed.

Her blossoming did not go unnoticed and she drew attention from the office romeos. Letty taught her how to flirt back and Carol taught her how to deflect it. She chose to be Carol's pupil, and learned to ignore the double entendres and deflect the requests for a date. There was only one man in the office that she had any interest in, and he wasn't flirting. She liked that.

She watched him go about his work with a singular diligence that she respected, and a kind good humour she found appealing. Whenever he laughed, no matter who he was talking to, no matter that she was not part of the conversation, if she was within hearing distance, she would smile. It just had that magical quality of making her feel good.

Just as she had been watching Donald, he must have been watching her, and he clearly liked what he saw. When he asked her out to lunch, the whole office gasped. He was known to be serious about his career. He was known not to be a womaniser. But, somehow, they were not surprised. It was a good match: this serious young man and this fresh, unspoiled young woman.

Mhairi declined his invitation.

*no lunch then
and no lunch now*

"What am I going to do for lunch?" he asked when she informed him she and Rhona had no intention of lunching in Glasgow with him the next day, as they had originally planned.

"What do you usually do?"

"Well, I don't usually go through till later, do I? So I've usually had lunch before I set out."

"Is there not a canteen in the hospital?"

"I suppose so." Donald looked quite put out. "But I thought we'd lunch together."

Mhairi did not relent. "Oh, don't whine, Donald. It doesn't suit you. Rhona and I want to lunch at Braehead. We've a lot we want to do while we're there, so we thought we could just catch a quick bite on the move."

Donald turned on the television, his body language that of a disappointed child in the huff.

Mhairi ignored him and continued making their evening meal. They didn't often row, but, when they did, it always seemed to be Mhairi who went quiet. She didn't like to think she sulked, but, if she was being honest with herself, there really was no other name for it. She sulked. But not tonight. Tonight she wasn't sulking. She had had a lovely afternoon with the girls, when she'd put other thoughts from her mind to be brought back to the fore once she'd left them. She refused to spoil the day by sulking, although she was undeniably quieter than usual.

She was processing. That's what she was doing. Processing her feelings at his betrayal. This was a new situation, new territory. It would take her a while to gain a perspective on it. In the meantime, she could hardly bear to be in the same room with the man she'd worshipped for nearly fifty years.

Supper was a solemn, silent affair. Although she sat with him at the table, she couldn't look at him, couldn't eat, couldn't make idle conversation. Still shocked at his revelation, still stunned into silence on the subject.

"I'm sorry, love, I hate when we're not on good terms," Donald said as she cleared the table when he was finished eating. "Of course I'll get lunch at the hospital. I was being churlish. I just thought we'd be lunching together."

Mhairi shrugged. "Whatever."

He looked at her, watched her move about the kitchen, her body language cold and distant. "Putting two and two together," he said. "I'm guessing that's not what's bothering you."

She didn't respond.

"You're still cross with me, then?"

'Cross' qualified in Mhairi's mind as euphemism of the day.

"Look, I'm sorry. I've said I'm sorry."

"I know."

"Perhaps I shouldn't have told my mother."

Mhairi stiffened at the word 'perhaps.'

"But we can't undo what's done, love. Let's move on." He tried to put his arms round her but she shrugged off the embrace. "Rhona's going to know something's wrong if we're still not on good terms by tomorrow. She can hardly not notice with an hour and a half in the car with us."

Mhairi sighed. He was right, of course, and she didn't want to explain what was wrong, couldn't explain what was wrong without telling her the whole awful story and she was certainly not going to do that. Nor was she going to pretend nothing was wrong. She wasn't that good an actress. "Well, if she sits in the front, you two can chatter till your hearts' content and she'll not notice that we don't."

"Won't she wonder why you've given up your seat for her?"

"I'll tell her I thought it'd be nice for her to have some time with you, since she and I will be together all afternoon."

Knowing he'd been outplayed, Donald turned his attention back to the dishes with a sigh and a shrug.

In the event, Rhona accepted the front seat without question and, as predicted, chatted to Donald as he drove. Mhairi dozed in the backseat and didn't bother to listen. She had her own chatter going on in her head.

'So, why won't you have lunch with me, Mhairi Adams?' he had asked after her third refusal.

'I don't know you well enough,' she had replied, with no coyness, no teasing.

'Perhaps, if you had lunch with me, we could remedy that?'

'Perhaps.'

'Is that a 'yes,' then?'

'It's a maybe,' she laughed. She couldn't help it. He was giving her his big, brown-eyed, puppy-dog expression, and it was too silly, too funny, and way too persuasive. 'Okay, it's a 'yes,' but only if I pay my share.' This was a fun side of him that she hadn't seen before and she rather liked it.

Lunch turned out to be fun too. Since she had insisted she pay her share, he had taken her to the fish and chip van that circled the nearby streets and paused at the local school gates at lunchtime. At first, she didn't know what to make of his choice, but she soon realised it was perfect. No formal sitting opposite one another wondering what to talk about. Instead, they walked and talked as they ate, and it felt much more relaxed and natural. When they had finished eating, he produced a bar of chocolate from his jacket pocket and shared it with her, joking that tomorrow she could provide the chocolate to keep things fair.

"It isn't fair," Rhona was saying. "Steve hogs the computer all the time with his precious Fantasy Football. I can hardly get near it in the evening to go online."

Mhairi snapped to attention.

"He reckons that I've got all day to do my searching, but I haven't really. I'm hardly in these days, what with one thing and another. Everyone keeps asking how I'm coping with Katie leaving home, expecting me to be pining or something, but, honestly, I've hardly got a minute to myself. Since Steve took on more work, all the business side of things falls to me and there's more than enough to keep me busy. In fact, I think I work more hours now than I did when I worked in Merchiston's."

Mhairi relaxed back in her seat, happy to overhear this snippet.

"You need to tell him to get himself a secretary," Donald said.

"He says he'd rather pay me and keep it in the family, and I suppose it makes sense. Just I thought I'd have more time for the things I want to do."

"He knows he can trust you to do it properly."

"I suppose."

She trusted him. It took a while, but gradually, over cheerful lunches and serious sit-down dinners, she learned that she could trust him. He never pried or pushed her for more than she felt comfortable telling him, yet she slowly told him her story. She expected him to be shocked, to back off their courtship, but he didn't. Instead, he held her close and seemed to listen carefully, seemed to understand that she entrusted to him the truth that no-one else had ever taken the time and trouble to find out.

She thought he'd understood it was classified, a secret, a confidence.

But, he had told his mother.

She couldn't look at him as he got out of the car at the hospital.

"Give my love to Gran," Rhona said.

"Will do."

Mhairi said nothing, just got out the car and walked round the back of it as he walked round the front. She got in the driver's seat. "Braehead, here we come," she said as cheerfully as she could, hoping Rhona wouldn't notice she hadn't sent her love to Gran, hadn't said 'Bye!' to Donald, hadn't said anything at all.

He had betrayed her all those years ago. His mother was welcome to him.

poor opulence

Three days later, the fuse was lit.

Mhairi had come to think of her past as a time bomb waiting to explode, so, when Rhona came round with her new iPad and her questions, Mhairi reckoned the countdown had begun.

"Something can't be right with the information you gave me, Mum," she said, pulling out the notebook Mhairi had given her. "I can't find an entry for you. No record of your birth. Did you give me the right date?"

Mhairi pulled out a chair for Rhona and walked across to put the kettle on.

"I trawled through months of information, but I just couldn't find you. Creepy," she said, with a shudder. "It was as if there was no you."

Mhairi got two china mugs down from the cupboard while Rhona took off her coat and settled at the kitchen table, their usual venue for a cuppa and a chat. It had become a routine. Three or four times a week, Rhona would come over and they would pull out the kitchen chairs, get out the cake tin, and make a cup of tea or coffee. They didn't bother settling in the sitting room because they usually started their catch-up chat while Mhairi made the drinks and set the plates and mugs on the table. Rhona didn't stay too long, so they never seemed to get around to going through the other room.

As Rhona chattered on about what she had tried and where she had searched for notification of Mhairi's existence, Mhairi looked around while she waited for the kettle to boil. She loved her tidy kitchen. Everything had its place, everything was in its place. Her cooking utensils: fish slice, ladle, slotted spoon and serving spoon hung in a shining row against the patchwork of pastel coloured tiles behind the hob. The few pictures that hung on the pale creamy walls were straight and dusted, the clock set to the correct time and ticking softly. Creamy cupboard doors gleamed in the sunshine that flowed through the room at this time of day. She had wiped them with great care and attention this morning.

The curtains were tied back neatly at the long window overlooking the garden, their pretty yellow and blue pattern bright and cheerful, old-fashioned probably, but Mhairi's choice and she stroked them fondly, pretending to straighten them as she looked out at the garden beyond. Not much in bloom at this time of the year, but still a pretty garden, the drying green neatly mown at the end of the growing season, but not too short to help it weather the winter. Still a few autumn flowers proudly showing off their hardiness against the onset of the colder nights.

Taking a jug, she added a little water to each of the flower pots lined up along the windowsill: parsley, basil, coriander, mint — growing well in the weak October sunshine, trimmed into neat mini-bushes as she used the herbs in her cooking. Touching the leaves of the mint, plucking a few to make herself mint tea, she breathed in its freshness on her sigh. She didn't want to leave this kitchen.

"So can you check the dates? I always thought you were born in 1945, but there just doesn't seem to be an entry for you there."

"I was born in 1945," she said as she poured water from the kettle into the mugs.

"What month? Because I just couldn't see you." Rhona had opened her iPad and clicked into the site she used.

"No, you wouldn't."

"How d'you mean? Thanks," Rhona took the fragrant mug of coffee and placed it beside her iPad. "On second thoughts," she muttered, moving the mug well back.

"Not under Mhairi Adams."

"But, that's your maiden name, isn't it? Why would it not be under Mhairi Adams?"

"That's not my maiden name."

"But, I don't understand. That's what you..."

"It's Bellingham."

"Bellingham?"

"If you look for Mhairi Bellingham, I think you'll find me. Fourteenth of October, 1945."

Rhona stared at her, her face contorted in puzzlement.

"Type it in," Mhairi suggested.

Rhona did. "Mhairi Bellingham. 14th of October, 1945." The details sprang onto the screen. "Oh! There you are. Mother: Audrey Anderson, nee Lennox. But, I don't understand."

So Mhairi told her mother's story as far as she understood it.

Audrey Lennox had been very young when she married William Anderson.

"If you type in her name, Audrey Lennox, and her date of birth, February 21st, 1927." Mhairi watched as Rhona did that. "There, you can see the record of her birth."

"Yep."

"And William Anderson, the man I thought was my father, May 19th, I think it was, 1903." She stood behind Rhona, watching her fingers fly over the screen of the iPad, feeling like a wind-up watch in a digital age: so out of date with modern technology. Oh, she and Donald had a computer upstairs; Rhona and Steve had given them their old one when they got a spanking-new, super-duper, fancy, does-everything-with-bells-on fruity one, but she didn't try to do much on it. It didn't interest her. Or, it hadn't, till now. As she watched Rhona conjure up the past with a few swipes and taps on a glass screen, she saw the potential of the machine and shuddered. "Yes, there it is. William Anderson. As you can see, he was much older than she was and he was rather dour and staid, but my guess is that she had been flattered by his attention."

"Huh, he'd have been a hundred and ten years old now if he was alive." Rhona typed in both their details and found the record of their marriage. "March 16th, 1945. So, she was only just over eighteen when they married. You're right, she was young."

"Already a widower and childless, I reckon William was eager to father a son and heir." Mhairi shuddered. "He wasn't the kind of man who would have wasted time on the niceties of courtship. I think he more or less bought Audrey."

"Bought her?"

"Well, in the sense that he showered her with gifts and flowers, which might have seemed romantic, and Audrey probably assumed it was, but I think it's more likely it was the most expedient way to get her to accept his proposal." Mhairi shook her head. "I just can't see him as a romantic or amorous suitor."

"A Mr Darcy, d'you mean?"

"Goodness, no! Nothing so gentile or noble. Much more the cold-blooded, determined-to-get-what-he-wanted-at-any-cost type."

"Right."

"You have to remember, it was the end of the war. There was still rationing. Things were scarce — but not for the likes of William. He had his sources. He showered her with expensive things she and her friends would hardly have dreamt of and no one else could get — even if they could afford them."

"I can see how that might have attracted her to him."

"She had so much jewellery. Oh, and so many clothes," Mhairi said, shaking her head at the memory of it. "Closets of them. I used to hide in one of the closets when she was out socialising. Hell to pay when I was caught, but worth it to handle the beautiful materials and cuddle into the fur coats."

Mhairi closed her eyes and she was there — walking across the deep, soft carpet in her mother's bedroom, lying on the sheepskin rug that stretched across the floor at the foot of the bed, digging her fingers into the deep pile, feeling its springiness, its softness, pretending she was lying in snow: soft, fluffy snow.

Opening the drawers of the dressing table, her hands wriggling in among the silky underwear, letting it slip over her fingers, falling back into the drawer like water.

Opening bottles of perfume, breathing in the essence of Lily of the Valley or Lavender; wise enough, even then, to know better than to spray them on her wrist as she'd seen her mother do, knowing that would give away where she'd been while Nanny was calling her to tea. A whiff or Lavender or Lily of the Valley in a perfume department or a garden she walked past, could transport Mhairi back sixty years in an instance.

Occupying a tiny corner of the closet, breathing in the scent of her mother, buried in the soft folds of satins and silks or the depths of fox fur or sable, she would hide for hours in the winter months when it was too wet or dark to play outside and Mother was out socialising or shopping.

"They were rich, then?"

"I guess so, though I didn't know anything else existed outside the vulgar opulence my parents surrounded themselves with. It was just the way it was. Servants, tutors, houseguests and laden tables."

"Were you spoiled rotten?"

Mhairi looked at her daughter. If anyone was spoiled, it was Rhona, 'the apple of her father's eye', the pride of her mother. She had grown up in a home where she was loved and adored, with a brother to play with and parents who cared, with everything she could need or want and more besides. "No," Mhairi shook her head. "I wasn't spoiled."

"Was your mum beautiful?"

"Very."

"Did she look like you?"

"Hardly! Like I say, she was beautiful."

"You were beautiful. Quite a stunner, actually. I can quite see why Dad fell for you."

Mhairi blushed. "Thank you, sweetheart."

"Well, you were. I was always very proud of my mum when you came to the school for any reason. I loved to show you off." Rhona leant in against her. "You're still beautiful, you know, and I still love to show you off. No-one ever believes your age when I tell them."

This was such sweet music to Mhairi's ears. When the children were young, they often told her she was beautiful, but she supposed all children thought their Mummy the most gorgeous creature to walk the earth. She knew she had when she was young. By comparison, all Audrey's friends seemed dull, drab creatures when they visited.

How lovely to have her daughter tell her she was beautiful now, when Rhona was in her forties and she herself in her late sixties. She touched her hair, still auburn and curly, but a little shorter and streaked with grey now.

She tucked the words away in her treasures.

Rhona had returned to her iPad, still showing the marriage entry for Audrey Lennox and William Anderson. "You would have been a few years older when you married Dad, but still a young woman."

"I was almost twenty-three."

"Did she have your gorgeous auburn hair?"

Mhairi nodded. "She did. She was the most beautiful woman I ever saw, and she was much admired by William's business associates. I think he viewed her as a prize he had won in contest with them, and he bore his trophy home proudly, throwing dinner parties regularly to show her off. They were married within two months of meeting."

Rhona hadn't computed it yet, but Mhairi was born only seven months later.

William was not a stupid man. He had probably realised by the time Audrey declared herself pregnant that he had married an amoral and restless young woman, who had no more affection for him that he had for her. A marriage of inconvenience, if ever there was one. The child was clearly not his and he refused to acknowledge it as his. When Mhairi was born, although he had married to ensure an heir, he was probably pleased she was a girl, not wishing to share his name with Audrey's bastard child, but unwilling to let the world at large know the foolishness of his choice of marriage mate. Had Mhairi been a boy, the whole son and heir thing would have been an issue and his reticence to claim him would have advertised it.

Rhona still sat, mulling over the information she had before her and the details Mhairi had added. She was writing the dates down when she saw the obvious. "Oh, she was pregnant already." She quickly clicked back to the entry announcing Mhairi's birth.

"Yes."

"Ah! Father: Charles Bellingham! That's where he comes into the picture."

"Yes."

"Of course! You weren't William's child." Rhona sat back in the chair. "Wow! This is huge. Do you think he knew?"

"Oh, I think so. He used to call me, excuse my language, 'Your bastard child,' when speaking about me to my mother. I had no idea what it meant at the time, of course." Mhairi smiled. "My mother used to place her hands over my ears as though I was too delicate to hear such things, but she didn't correct him." Mhairi remembered the gesture with a wry smile to herself. A woman who observed the niceties of social behaviour, yet had no natural affection for her child.

"Why didn't he divorce her?"

"You have to remember, in those days, divorce was not a common thing and William was an ambitious man. Being a widower was to be admired. Being a divorcee was to be censured," Mhairi said. "He was the kind of man to whom acceptance in society meant more than personal comfort or happiness."

"Sad, really."

"Very." Mhairi agreed. "I find it hard to imagine what satisfaction he got from life." She shuddered at the memory of the cold loveless household into which she was born.

"So he wouldn't allow your mother to use his name on your birth certificate."

"Exactly."

"Okay, I get that." Rhona held up the notebook. "So, are the rest of these details correct, as far as you know?"

Mhairi turned away. "Can we leave it at that, please, for today? I really have to go into town. There are one or two bits and bobs I need for dinner."

"So, I take it these details are not correct, then?"

Mhairi shrugged, ashamed now of her futile attempt to placate her daughter with a list of lies. She held out her hand and Rhona gave her back the notebook.

finding a father

She hadn't always known the details of her birth. Until she was six years old, she assumed William was her father. A distant, unkind father, but her father.

When her brother, Alexander, was born, she saw that his distance and unkindness was reserved for her.

'Get away from that baby!' her father ordered when she tried to peep in the crib at the newborn infant.

The nurse pulled Mhairi away and hastened from the room with her.

'And, keep that bastard child out of this nursery!' he shouted after them, the first time she remembered hearing him say what then became his customary form of referring to her.

On asking her mother about it, Audrey told her she shouldn't fret about such things. 'He's just sore because you're not his.'

Mhairi puzzled over this, and, getting no further explanation from her mother, asked Nanny.

'He's not yer daddy,' Nanny said. 'That's all.'

Still puzzled about the term, she at least knew now why he hated her so much, so, shrugging her shoulders, she ran outside to play in the garden. Secreted away in her hiding place in the rhododendron bushes, she tried to make sense of it. Having never been encouraged to call him 'daddy' and the term suggesting an intimacy that didn't exist between them, it didn't come as a surprise that he was not her daddy. As for the rest, she gave up worrying about it and got on with her little loveless life.

"So, did you ever find this other man?" Rhona asked as she prepared to take her leave. "Your real father? What was his name? Somebody Bellingham?" She looked again at her screen before snapping her iPad cover into place.

"Charles Bellingham."

"Did you ever find Charles Bellingham?"

"He's dead."

It was one of the first things she did when she started working in Harrison, Tweadale and Bingley, Law Office. When she realised she had access to people who knew how do do searches like that, she asked Carol for help to find someone, an uncle, she claimed. Carol told her about Register House at the East End of Princes Street. 'Set back a bit, you know where I mean,' Carol said. 'Where there's a statue of someone on a horse. The Duke of Wellington, or someone like that. It's in behind that.'

Mhairi nodded. She would find it. She was beginning to find her way about the city, beginning to find her confidence too. At first she had been intimidated by the traffic, the noise, the bustle, having never been in any city until she came to Edinburgh less than a year ago at the age of twenty-one.

One Friday, she asked if she might take a half day from her holiday allowance, and set out to find Register House. The outside of the building was no more imposing than many other buildings in Edinburgh City centre, though imposing enough to cause her heart to beat a little faster, her breath to stutter in her chest.

Mhairi had done her homework and she knew General Register House, designed by Robert and James Adams and completed in 1789, was the first purpose built public records repository in the British Isles and one of the oldest custom built archive buildings still in continuous use in the world. As she stood before it, she had a tremendous sense of its history, of the wealth of information stored within its walls, and felt deeply the importance of this place.

Behind it stood a less imposing, but possibly more pleasing building, New Register House, and that was where she had to go. New Register House was built in 1861 to house the Statutory Records of Births, Marriages and Deaths which began in 1855.

She looked at the leaflet she held in her hand.

'The main feature of this elegant building is the lofty fireproof central repository, the Dome, which consists of five tiers of ironwork shelving and galleries similar to those at the British Museum in London. The Dome is a large and striking circular chamber, over 27m (90 feet) high and of considerable interest as a piece of 19th century functional architecture and structural engineering.'

She was excited to see the central dome, excited and fearful. It sounded so grand, and here she was, a young woman who barely knew how to survive in this city, let alone walk into such an imposing room.

First, she had to get herself across the threshold and speak to the receptionist. She knew how much it was going to cost to spend the afternoon here and she had studied what she was going to have to do in the search rooms. Taking a deep breath and crossing her fingers, she pushed open the door.

The receptionist took her money in exchange for her search pass and another information leaflet, this one informing her,

'The 6.5 km (4 miles) of shelving contain half a million volumes. These included some 400,000 statutory registers of all the births, deaths and marriages in Scotland since 1855; still being added to every year. Red birth volumes are on the first tier, the death volumes in funereal black on the second, and the marriage volumes in green on the third. The original marriage schedules, which are signed by the parties immediately after marriage ceremonies in Scotland, are shelved on the top tier of the Dome as are the open Census records from 1841 to 1901. The old parish registers are perhaps the greatest treasures in New Register House. The oldest volume dates from 1553 and is for the parish of Errol, near Perth.'

The gist of this information was repeated by the search assistant who was summoned to her side as she led Mhairi along a corridor to one of the search rooms, showing her to her allocated seat, where she helped her with the mechanics of what she would have to do to find the information she wanted. She also showed her the central dome, as imposing as it sounded in the leaflet, not at all as dusty and musty as she had imagined, but light and airy with windows and people moving around. She had imagined it would be redolent of death and decay, but found it vibrant with life and movement.

When left alone, Mhairi stood and gazed, transfixed by a sense of expectation. Somewhere, in all these thousands and thousands of records, was the truth. Her heritage. Almost overwhelmed by the enormity of what she was about to do, her knees buckled under her and she had to look around for a seat, where she sat for a while watching people come and go, searching through files and writing down notes.

So many lives and deaths, marriages and divorces captured for ever by writing on paper. How much laughter and joy were contained in the birth and marriage entries, the hope of a happy future recorded for ever with the flourish of the registrar's pen. Mhairi closed her eyes and listened to the choir of thousands, maybe millions of voices raised in a hymn of praise that a child was born, a marriage made.

How much was silenced by the stroke put through those lives and marriages with the same registrar's pen.

Awesome was the word that came to Mhairi's mind as she sat in the Dome, the sounds of the people around her silenced by the ability she had perfected over many years to cut out the horror she needed not to hear. This seemed a hallowed space to Mhairi. She had never entered a Church but she imagined it could feel no more sacred than this repository of life and death.

After a while, she went back to the seat she'd been given and, reading through the instructions left on the desk, she started her search.

She had held the words in her heart all the years of her exile, her father's parting words, as she was taken from her home at eight years old. 'You are your mother's bastard child and you are no longer welcome in my house.' She didn't know what they meant at the time, but she knew from the way they were spoken they were important words to remember.

Then, at the age of thirteen, she found a dictionary and looked up the word 'bastard' and understood again why she had not been wanted. Somehow, seeing the definition of the word 'bastard' set a seal on Nanny's explanation, 'He's not yer daddy.' It was official. She was illegitimate. Another man's child, not William's.

Looking out of the window beside where she sat, she paused a moment. Understanding why her father had not wanted her was only half the picture. What about her mother? What kind of unnatural mother could so neglect and fail to love her child? Audrey had been that mother.

Yes, Audrey had been not much more than a child herself when she gave birth to Mhairi, but Mhairi knew other young mothers: Carol's sister, for one. She had her first baby when she was still at school. She sat her Highers just three months after her wee girl was born. But she adored her baby. She didn't marry the father: he was too young and immature, she realised. With her parents' help, she was raising the child to be a delightful wee girl, who knew she was loved and even wanted.

No, she would not excuse Audrey due to her youthfulness. Greed and ambition were Audrey's flaws and she did not allow an unwanted pregnancy, an unwanted child, to get in the way of achieving what she wanted.

Mhairi closed her eyes and breathed deeply. She would not allow sentimentality to cloud the judgement she passed on her mother. If ever a woman deserved an adverse judgement from her daughter, it was Audrey Anderson.

A gust of the strong Easterly wind rattled the window pane beside her, reminding her she had paid for her time here and, unlike Audrey, she could not snap her fingers to get what she wanted. Work was required.

Mhairi didn't know what she hoped to find here in Register House. Her birth certificate, certainly, but, beyond that, she had no idea.

Entering Mhairi Anderson, the name by which she had been known for twenty-one years, and her date of birth, yielded no results, confirming William Anderson was not her father, if she had needed confirmation, which she didn't. Huh! She ticked any doubt of that fact off her mental list.

She sought and found records of his two marriages, the second to her mother. Using her mother's maiden name, she tried again. The only result that brought up was the record of her mother's birth, again, not really a surprise, since Audrey was a bit young to have been married and widowed or divorced before she met William. Another 'maybe' ticked off.

Entering Glasgow as her place of birth, her own date of birth, her first name and her mother's married name brought the entry she had been looking for. Also in the entry, her father's name, Charles Bellingham.

Her father.

Charles Bellingham.

She stared at the name for many minutes. So she was Mhairi Bellingham. If only she had known. She had changed her name from Anderson to Adams less than a year ago.

i have to tell you

It seemed so small a change: Anderson to Adams. Enough to make her difficult to find, enough to distance her from her past, but not so much that she would not still be her. It was a stipulation that came with the bank draft from her step-father when she was twenty-one, that she change her name and move away from Glasgow. He didn't want his name 'dragged in the mud' yet again. She was happy to lose his name since it seemed it did not belong to her. Although she never much liked the name 'Mhairi', she held on to it because it was all she had that was hers.

'Why 'Adams'?' Donald had asked.

She shrugged. 'It just seemed appropriate, somehow. I felt like it was the beginning. I had to choose something and that's what came to mind. Probably should have chosen 'Eve' to go with it.' She laughed. 'Eve Adams. That would have been fun. Wish I had thought of it.'

There hadn't been time to think about it. When she was handed the letter, she was asked the name she wished to be known by almost before she had taken in that she needed to choose one. 'Mhairi Adams,' she said, shrugging her indifference. Faced with the prospect of finding a place to live, a job and an identity, finding a new name seemed such a minor detail.

When she and Donald had been together for several months, and he was talking of marriage, she had stalled, tried to buy time. 'There's no rush, is there?' she said.

'Only that I want you to be mine forever and I want forever to start right now,' he replied, kissing her nose, her chin, her lips, making her blush because they were in a restaurant, a public place. They had finished their meal.

Donald had been sitting across the table while they ate, but afterwards, he had left his chair to join her on the soft curved sofa of the alcove in which they dined. He slid along close to her and, taking her hand in his, he asked her to marry him.

She had to tell him. If she was to marry this man she had grown to love so dearly, it had to be in honesty. So much of her life had been a lie. So much of her life lived in shadow. Like a flower pushing up through dark, suffocating soil, she sought the light. So she tried to tell him what she remembered and what she feared.

When she cried, he hugged her. 'It's all right. It all happened such a long time ago. You can forget it now.' Forget it. How could she forget it? Since she was eight years old, the past had been her constant companion. It grew with her like her skin, her fingerprint, her figure, her form. It defined her. There was no 'her' without it because it was who she was. The only chance she might forget and cast that skin was if he knew and was willing to take her past along with her. Then she could become more thoroughly the persona she had chosen with Holly Golightly's help: the persona she had been trying to be. But, in truth, they were surely one and the same, she and her past. So she tried to lay it out for him to examine.

When she couldn't remember or couldn't get the words out, he hushed her. 'It's okay, my little Mhairi Adams, it's okay.'

But it wasn't okay. He had to listen, to know the truth, to understand. What if it came out later and she hadn't told him? Even in this public place, with Donald looking round to check no-one was in hearing distance, she knew she had to tell him. Albeit in a hushed whisper, she had to tell him now, while she had the courage.

After she began and he seemed to realise the delicacy of her disclosures, he paid the bill and led her out of the restaurant. 'We'll talk as we walk,' he said.

She nodded, afraid to speak again until they stood outside, away from prying ears.

When she'd laid her past at his feet for his scrutiny, she expected rejection. Instead, he held her closer and told her, 'That's it. You need never speak of it again. No-one else needs to know.'

'No-one else needs to know.'
But, he had told his mother.
When had he told his mother? Had he gone straight home that evening, 'You'll never guess what Mhairi did,' and told her? Like it was a piece of gossip from the office. 'How was your day, dear?' 'Oh, you'll never guess what Mhairi told me.'

Had he waited till her story had time to seep into his consciousness and trouble him, so that he needed to talk it over with his mother? 'I'm not sure if I should go ahead with the wedding. Mhairi told me something that puts a whole new slant on things. What do you think I should do?'

No, it couldn't have been that. Ruth Carlyle would certainly have persuaded him to call the wedding off. Perhaps he waited till just after the wedding, until it was too late for Ruth to interfere. 'By the way, there's something you should know about Mhairi.'

Mhairi couldn't bring herself to ask him.

'You need never speak of it again,' he'd said, and she found she couldn't now. She couldn't bear to share a room with him, couldn't bear to talk about anything with him. 'With him' felt different now. He had told his mother. That he hadn't told Mhairi about his indiscretion, not in all these years, the forty and more years of their marriage, that cut her deeply. He had kept his secret but not hers.

It amazed her that he could get up every morning, shower and shave, have his breakfast, read his paper as though nothing was different, the earth hadn't shifted, the sky hadn't fallen.

It didn't help that he kept trying to talk about it, kept trying to wipe it away. "You're being overdramatic, melodramatic, even."

That particular argument failed to win her over for some reason, and she would rise from the table and scrape her uneaten food into the bucket.

"Come on, Mhairi. You need to get over this," didn't work either, and she continued to sleep in the spare room.

But, then, she hadn't told him the whole story all those years ago. She hadn't even managed to blurt out all that she could remember of it, before he had soothed her and told her not to worry about it, that it was okay, that she 'need never speak of it again.'

Perhaps if he knew, he wouldn't find it so easy to toss her life aside in a sentence.

who i am

'So, you changed your name,' he'd said. 'Lots of people change their names. What was it before?' he stepped back and looked at her, as though over a pair of half-spectacles. 'Hmm, Mhairi Adams? Who are you really?'

It irked her that he liked to call her 'Mhairi Adams,' not just because that wasn't her name, but it felt distancing, somehow, and more than a little patronising. Their relationship of boss and employee gave him the right to do it. Their romance suggested to her that he should move on from the habit. It made confidential talk harder for her. Oh, she knew it was meant as an endearment of sorts, but it acted as a restraint.

She recalled a quote by Milton about someone where he spoke of 'His peculiar art of distancing an object to aggrandise his space' and that was how she felt when he called her 'Mhairi Adams' when they were alone together: like an object, something he didn't want to get too close to, something that could make him less than he was.

But, Mhairi was nothing if not patient. She had waited fourteen years to speak. She could wait to see if this was a habit he could lose through time and familiarity. It was a small thing, after all. He had been cautious about asking her out, cautious about asking anyone out. Perhaps he needed time to fully give of himself. Besides, she was probably reading things into the gesture he didn't feel, didn't intend.

'Why 'Adams'?' he had asked.

'Why not? Like I said, a new beginning. I was coming to live in Edinburgh. Make a new start. New start, new name.' Not that that was the full story, Even before she was handed her father's terse letter, she had suspected she'd have to find herself somewhere to live. She read a book about Edinburgh, an architectural book, and decided to choose the capital as her new home, liking what she read about its history, its architecture, its famous sons. William Adams, the architect of his day, seemed a fitting personage to adopt as ancestor. A whimsical thing to do, she knew, but real life seemed whimsical at the time.

Had she only gone to Register House first, she would have known she was Mhairi Bellingham.

What would Mhairi Bellingham's life have been? She doubted it could have been worse than the one she had lived for twenty-one years as Mhairi Anderson; her childhood loveless and lonely, her teens loveless and even lonelier. For many years she had assumed she was worthless, not fit to be loved, but something inside her rebelled at the notion, and, as she grew up and looked around her at the other outcasts she was thrown among, she came to realise the life she had been consigned to was not about worthiness but about convenience. Along with the others, she was conveniently out of the way. No longer an embarrassment.

What would it have been like to be Mhairi Bellingham?

That day in Register House, she had found Charles Bellingham, her father, was a married man when she was born. Once again, Audrey seemed to have been singled out for attention by an older man, and Mhairi wondered of she had been duped by him. Duped into believing that he would marry her when he was not, in reality, free to do so. Had she told him about her pregnancy? Did he know he had a daughter? Would he have acknowledged her when William Anderson did not? She doubted it. The census records showed he had three sons and a daughter already. What need would he have of another child, and an illegitimate child, at that?

Having checked the record of her birth, housed on the first tier in the large domed area — the volumes bound in red — and Charles Bellingham's marriage recorded in one of the large green volumes on the third tier, she checked the middle tier, where the funereal black volumes of death records are held, and found that Charles had died in 1967, only two years before.

She stood and stared at the entry, written there in careful script. Some stranger's hand declaring the death of any hope of connecting to the man who had fathered her. She hadn't considered tracing him, contacting him, trying to meet with him, but, as she looked at that beautiful cursive hand pronouncing him dead, she felt bereft. The choice was no longer hers. In one afternoon, she had found and lost her father.

Having never been taught about God, she didn't know him and had never prayed, and yet, as she took in the fact that her father was dead, she wished that she could. She wanted to grieve, to mourn, to attend a funeral, stand by a coffin, see it lowered into the earth, 'Dust to dust. Ashes to ashes.' Her whole being craved to put flowers on his grave, to kneel beside it and talk to his memory, tell him he had a daughter who might surely have loved him had she known him. Might he have loved her?

Register House was no place to cry out in, yet that is what she silently did. With her face lifted to the great dome, she howled without sound to the gods, the fates, the fortune that had not allowed her to know her father. Covering her face with her hands, she hid her pain from the world and begged the gods to let her find someone to love.

Further investigation among the black volumes did not reveal any record of her mother or William Anderson having died, so she assumed they still lived. In the same large, pretentious house of her childhood memories? Might they have moved after the notoriety she would have brought upon them? To a similarly showy dwelling, somewhere else?

What if they had? Did it matter? There was to be no welcome for her wherever they lived. It would not be in any house they inhabited she would find love or affection.

Mhairi left Register House feeling adrift and rootless, having found her roots but seen them rot.

and what i've done

The day Donald proposed to her in the restaurant, Mhairi wanted to tell him everything she remembered.

She told him about her incarceration. How, at eight years old, she was sedated, strapped to a stretcher, and driven away from her home in a dark van. Not an ambulance, though kitted out as one, not that she knew that at the time. Like many of the details of her story, that understanding came at some point through the years of her enforced residence in a Home for the Mentally Deficient.

'But you're clearly not mentally deficient,' he said.

'Thank you.' She gave him a rueful smile. 'I could have done with you as my lawyer when I was locked up as a lunatic.'

'Did you have a lawyer?'

Mhairi laughed, not her usual hesitant, suppressed chuckle, but a mirthless, hollow facsimile. 'Oh, yes. My father engaged a 'gentleman' to negotiate my care.' Her voice supplied the quotation marks. 'But he was never on my side, only my father's, and my father had no interest in my 'care,' only that I be locked away out of his sight. The one good thing the lawyer won for me was that my father would make some kind of provision for my on-going care once I turned twenty-one, if I should still be alive and if I was deemed suitable for release.'

'Wow! So much has changed since the Mental Health Act of 1960.'

'It needed to.'

'Of course it did. Up till then, a child could be incarcerated without any right of appeal. In fact, you would have lost all your rights.'

'Tell me about it.' She nodded. 'I did.'

'Back then, the psychiatric care system had the awesome power to incarcerate indefinitely.'

'Mmm-hmm!'

'Strip a patient of their fundamental rights, leaving them no voice, no status, even in matters of intimate personal concern.'

Mhairi nodded.

'It was inhumane in the extreme.'

'Then you understand the conditions in which I grew up.'

'Oh, Mhairi, my poor Mhairi Adams.' He held her close to him for a while. 'So, tell me,' he said. 'How could they do that to my Mhairi? On what grounds?'

Mhairi shuddered and looked down, watching her hands twist and crush the linen napkin on her lap. 'Perhaps I was a little insane back then,' she said in a very small voice.

'Do you think so?'

She nodded.

'Who decided that?'

'My father. He convinced everyone I was a danger to myself and to the new baby.'

'Ah! I see. And were you?'

'Perhaps. I did crazy things. I was lonely, unsupervised a lot of the time. I did crazy things.'

'How old did you say you were when you were hauled away so barbarically?'

'I was eight.'

She had been locked in her room for three days. The only time the door was opened was when Nanny brought her a little food and water and the maid, who accompanied Nanny, removed the potty from under Mhairi's bed to be emptied and replaced. It was a two woman job. The maid would catch and restrain her while Nanny placed the tray on the dressing table and removed the previous one, putting it on the small hall table outside her door. Then Nanny would take over the task of holding her down while the maid removed the stinking potty, carried it to the bathroom and brought it back clean and ready for further use. Nanny had perfected her method of restraint, tying her loosely to a chair, the cloth strips she used being knotted just enough to buy them time to retreat and lock the door before Mhairi was able to rip herself free.

Her misdemeanour deserving of such punishment? She had disappeared for a whole afternoon without completing her schoolwork and she had missed dinnertime. When asked what they should do with 'the child,' Father had decreed she should be locked in her room without supper. That might have been the end of it, but Mhairi had fought the punishment, kicking and screaming, sending a vase smashing from the hall table to the floor and punching Nanny in the mouth, splitting her lip. The punishment was extended indefinitely until Nanny's lip healed to Father's satisfaction.

Mhairi was convinced Nanny picked at the wound to keep it open, because three days later, it was still bleeding and Mhairi was still confined to her room.

She had tried to escape through the window, but had been caught when lying winded in the flowerbed below, her involuntary scream as she fell from the windowsill alerting the gardener who watched her struggle for breath while he sent 'the lad' for help. Her father summoned a joiner to make the window secure. It could be opened an inch or two for air, but, try as she might, it could be opened no further. Nor could she find anything with which to break the lead-latticed panes.

She had repeatedly refused to eat and thrown the food they brought her back at them, smashing the dishes against the back of the locked door.

She had thrown the contents of the potty about the room, expecting them to have to let her out while they cleaned up the mess. Instead, they had given her the means to clean it herself and stood over her while she did it.

She was getting desperate. No amount of pleading, begging, crying, screaming, shouting or struggling secured her release.

She tried to tell them about Bobby, that he needed her, that he was waiting for her to play, that she had to go to him.

'You'll have to talk to that child,' William said to Audrey as he marched away after Nanny had requested he come to deal with Mhairi's latest tantrum. 'The damn dogs only answer to the damnable baby names she gives them! They're not supposed to be played with. They're hunting dogs, dammit!'

But Audrey didn't find the time to come into the nursery.

On the third day, Mhairi cracked. All books, toys or anything else that might soften her confinement had been removed from the room. Time hung heavily. Bobby was waiting. She hatched a scheme, an eight-year-old's scheme.

Using a chair to stand on and the heavy dinner tray, she waited for Nanny and the maid. As the door opened and Nanny looked round it to locate her in the room, Mhairi brought the tray crashing down on her head. The maid, prevented from rushing into the room by Nanny's prostrate body lying across the doorway, started to scream. Mhairi leapt from the chair and, wielding the tray as a weapon, hurled herself at the maid, raining blows on her, inflicting considerable pain.

'But, I was eight years old, a thin, scrawny wee kid,' Mhairi told Donald that day. 'The tray was huge and heavy. I'd had trouble lifting it at all. Goodness knows how I held it above my head behind that door, never mind swinging it at the maid's legs. Added to that, the maid was a strong, robust young woman. She soon overpowered me and put an end to my escape bid.'

'You were a feisty wee thing.'

'I was beside myself. Three days. It had been three days.'

'Still.'

'Bobby was waiting for me. I needed to take him some food so he would play with me. I had to escape. Desperate measures were called for.'

'But, I don't suppose they were without consequence?'

'No. The commotion had brought most of the household running. I was locked in my room again, the Doctor was called and after he had attended to Nanny and the maid, I was sedated. The next thing I knew, I was strapped to a stretcher and taken away.'

'Did you ever find out what damage you had inflicted on Nanny?'

'There was some sort of inquiry to commit me to an Institution, would that be right?'

'Quite possibly.'

'Nanny gave evidence at it. Apparently, I had knocked her unconscious, cracked her skull and she had to be hospitalised. They reckoned she would have a legacy of 'debilitating headaches."

'Ouch!'

'She gave me a damning character reference, as you can imagine, as did the maid and several of the tutors who had 'tried and failed to discipline and educate me,' according to my father. He put the case that I was an imbecile, incapable of being taught to manage myself or my affairs, that I was feeble-minded and required care, supervision and control for my own protection and the protection of others. He claimed I was incapable of receiving benefit from school instruction. He won his case and I was committed under the Mental Deficiency Act of 1913.'

'So that would be, what? 1952?'

'Fifty-three.'

'And the Act wasn't repealed until 1959. Phew! You poor old thing!' Donald leant back and put his hand to his forehead.

'By which time, I was in the system, sedated, forgotten, with no-one to fight for my release.'

He closed his eyes and shook his head. 'Of course. You'd be medicated.'

'Uh-huh! With a variety of drugs they were testing.'

'This is awful.'

'Awful' hardly described it.

Until she saw Babs Wilcox spit out her medication, the years, the lack of love and the loneliness were only hazily happening, and her memory of those times blurred into one sad, gloomy brown fug.

They were in the laundry and she looked up just as the tablets left Babs' mouth en route to join the hot suds in the tub she leant over. A light went on in Mhairi's head. This was something she could do, but it took quite a bit of practice before she got it right. The tablets had to be ejected before they dissolved in her mouth. It was essential to keep them under her tongue and as dry as possible, so she would keep her mouth slightly open, breathing in deeply through it, taking the cold air in and under the curve she made of her tongue.

Mhairi started living her miserable life at the age of seventeen, exchanging the dismal, brown fug for dismal, brown clarity.

After pouring her story out to Donald, Mhairi was exhausted and Donald walked her home in relative silence, with only an occasional sighed expletive or exclamations such as, 'I can hardly believe it.' or 'It beggers belief!'

She expected him to retract his proposal when he'd had time to digest the information.

After all, who in their right mind would want to be married to an imbecile?

let us wage war

'How long were you in the Home?' Donald asked. He hadn't spoken for a while as they walked, then, just as they reached her flat, he turned her to face him. 'How long were you locked up?'

'Thirteen years. Until I was twenty-one. Until last year.'

He shook his head. 'This changes everything,' he said.

'Yes, I thought it might.' She looked down at her hands, the long slender fingers, the freckles on the back of her hand. Twenty-eight. There used to be twenty-eight freckles between the two hands. She remembered counting them. It was something to do until lights out. She'd read her book three times over and wouldn't get another one for three more days. One, two, three … she started counting them again, shutting out the hurt, the disappointment. Hadn't she seen this coming? As they'd been walking, Donald was not the only one doing a lot of thinking.

He had a lot to take in. It was new to him, would need digesting. And when he had, what then? Why would he want to marry her now? Now he knew she had spent most of her life locked in a lunatic asylum. What guarantee did he have that she wasn't all her father had claimed she was? A feeble-minded imbecile. Her word, her story was all he had. Hanging her head, counting her freckles, she waited for him to walk away.

'It changes everything.'

'Yes.'

'I want us to marry soon, really soon.'

Fifteen. Fifteen freckles. That's as far as she'd counted when his words closed her eyes. Frozen — no, not frozen, she decided — petrified, as in, turned to stone — she felt herself turn to stone where she stood, not daring to breathe, afraid to look up, her mind whizzing inside the rocklike shell, counting freckles, sifting through dictionary definitions, anything but dare to hope, waiting for his next words.

He took her chin in his hand and tilted her face to look at him, but she couldn't. 'Open your eyes,' he said. 'Look at me.'

Tears were brimming under her lids.

'Look at me, my dear, sweet, Mhairi Adams. I know you. I know you have told me the truth and it only makes me love you more.'

A tidal wave of relief surged over her, crashing through doubts and fears, sweeping them aside as of no account, eroding the rock she thought she'd become so that she no longer had strength to stand. Her knees buckled, she was crumbling when Donald caught her in his arms.

'You are not mad. You are not an imbecile. Whatever happened back then, you were a victim. You were cruelly imprisoned and stripped of your rights, your freedom and your dignity. These are my wedding gifts to you.'

From somewhere far away, hope was shining on her with the warmth of a summer day. 'Wedding gifts?'

'Will you marry me, Mhairi Adams?'

He wanted to marry Mhairi Adams, but Mhairi Adams didn't exist. She never had. There had been a sad and lonely Mhairi Anderson, a child locked up for things she did and didn't do, a child who feared what she couldn't remember, but there was no Mhairi Adams. Mhairi Adams had been a sham, someone she made up, a pretence at being someone she was not.

He held her away a little and made her look up at him. 'Did you hear what I asked?"

She nodded.

'So? Will you marry me, Mhairi Adams?'

'Anderson,' she said through her tears.

'Anderson,' he agreed. 'Will you marry me, Mhairi Anderson?'

'Yes, please,' she said as she clung to him. 'Oh, yes, please.'

It didn't matter how or why. He loved her. Someone loved her, she was loved. It seemed incredible that the man she loved could still love her, that he could accept her past and, in accepting it, accept that it was part of her, accept her just as she was. The thoughts tumbled over one another in the undertow of the tidal wave. Clinging to him as though she might otherwise drown, Mhairi allowed herself to be buffeted with wave after wave of feelings as he whispered words of tenderness and love, kissing her tears, wiping them away with his words.

They had been standing in the street outside the tenement property where her flat was, but now, she desperately needed to sit down. Her legs were shaking and, if Donald hadn't been holding her she would surely have fallen. She pulled him into the mouth of the close and towards the stairs.

'We'll take them to court,' he said as he walked. 'Your father, the Home, all of them. We'll take them to court. We'll throw the book at them, sue them for everything.'

'No!' She stopped so suddenly that he bumped into her and they both almost fell.

'Whoops!' he said, steadying her.

Leaning against the wall for support, she shook her head. 'No. No court.'

'I'm a lawyer, trust me, I know about these things. We have a really strong case. You should not have been incarcerated all that time. They had no legal grounds to commit you to that.'

'No.'

He grimaced and held her by the shoulders. 'But, why not, Mhairi? Don't you want your day in court? To be heard? To put the record straight? Don't you want to get revenge?'

She shook her head.

'Really?'

'I don't want revenge and I don't want it all raked up again.'

'But the advocates in the firm could have a field day with this.'

She shook her head again, holding on to his arms, looking into his face with all the earnest pleading she could muster. 'There are other things, accusations...'

'It'll just be more of the same. You were eight years old, dammit! There's nothing you could have done that would merit what they did to you.'

'But, you don't know everything.'

'I know enough.'

'There were accusations...'

But he couldn't hear her any more, impassioned as he was with righteous anger at her past treatment so he continued explaining how it could be done, who he'd speak to, how it would be set in motion.

She pulled at him, shaking him, making him stop, making him look at her. 'No, Donald!' And told him with all the feeling she could muster, all the fear, all the pain that she held within her. 'I just want it to be over.'

Silenced, he looked into her eyes and, after a moment or two, 'Okay,' he said. 'It's over. If that's what you want.'

She nodded.

'Then it's over.'

With a sigh of gratitude and relief, Mhairi lowered herself to sit on the stairs before her legs gave out on her.

Donald sat beside her and put his arms round her shoulders. 'It's okay. Everything is okay. You've told me and I thank you for that, but now, you need never speak of it again. No-one else needs to know. It really is over.'

Remembering that day, his tenderness, his kindness, his unconditional love, Mhairi felt ashamed that she was angry with him now, but she couldn't seem to get past it. He had betrayed her trust. No matter how wonderful and generous he had been to marry her, he had tainted it because he had betrayed her. 'No-one else needs to know,' he said, yet he had sneaked behind her back to whisper with his mother.

There was something else rankling too: it hadn't been over. She did have to speak of it again. In the next few months before the wedding, he had asked her repeatedly if she wouldn't let him pursue it in court for her. At the time, she thought it was kindness, concern. He wanted to win the day for her, be her knight in shining armour, vanquishing the foe. But, now, she wondered if his mother put him up to it, wanting, not Mhairi's day in court, but his. He kept telling her she had an 'open and shut' case. Couldn't fail. With the advocate's help, he could win it for her. She realised it would not have been his own ambition driving him to persist with the persuasion but his mother's.

Once they were married, he never mentioned it again. Perhaps his mother had hoped for one of two outcomes: either he would have a big, public win in court, great for furtherance of his career, or Mhairi would be exposed for the feeble-minded fool Ruth clearly thought she was, and her son would be freed of his promise to marry.

Mhairi shuddered at the thought of that day in court. To have dredged it all up again, leave herself exposed once more to the accusation and malignancy of her father, would have been too much to bear. There were things she hadn't managed to tell Donald, things she wasn't sure about, that she couldn't remember. They would all come out in court to shock and horrify him. Yes, it would be great to have her name cleared, to erase the file that must be held somewhere about her. But the cost would be too high.

the wedding

Their wedding was a small affair. There was no family on Mhairi's side and little on Donald's. His father had died during the war and Ruth had worn her widowhood as a badge of honour ever since. He had an uncle and aunt on his father's side and they and their offspring were invited for the sake of politeness. Another aunt and uncle on Ruth's side, but they declined to attend since Ruth had fallen out with her sister some years before. A few of Donald's friends and colleagues, plus Carol and her husband and Letty and her boyfriend, and the party was complete.

Mhairi dusted the wedding photograph every day and it always made her smile. Carol and Letty were her bridesmaids and the three of them wore long, summery, flowing dresses and flowers in their hair: the Marianne Faithful look of the late sixties and early seventies. The bridesmaid's dresses were pastel colours, multi-hued and softly gathered at the waist, where they wore a sash of palest pink satin ribbon. Mhairi's was the same style in the softest ivory with deeper ivory sash, pin-tucks and lace edged pleating on the bodice and in panels on the skirt. She felt herself float as she walked towards Donald, her matching satin pumps hardly touching the carpet.

Her bouquet was made up of flowers from Ruth's garden tied together in a natural bunch with the same deep ivory ribbon, in a large floppy bow with long trailing ends. Mhairi loved it. She thought it was the most gorgeous thing she had ever owned. Ruth gave it a withering look and declared, 'Well, I suppose if you're only wearing a summer frock.'

'Peace' was the cry of the late sixties, early seventies, so Mhairi smiled sweetly at Ruth, 'It's lovely you dressed up, though, Ruth. Thank you.'

They looked as though they were going to different weddings. Where Mhairi had opted for innocent simplicity, Ruth wore a dramatic, formal dress and jacket in black shantung with beaded collar and cuffs on the jacket and round the neckline of the dress. It was topped off with an ostentatiously large matching black hat. Perhaps she viewed their wedding as a rather special funeral.

family

"Okay," Rhona said as she came through the back door. "I've hardly slept a wink since you told me about Charles Bellingham and I keep thinking how sad it is that he's dead."

Mhairi sighed. There was to be no let-up, then. Rhona was in bloodhound mode. There would be no peace till she'd sniffed the whole mystery out. She had really hoped, against all she knew of her daughter's character, that Rhona would content herself with the facts. Deep down she knew she wouldn't, but, stupidly, she'd allowed herself to hope.

"He'd be quite an old man if he wasn't," she said quietly.

"True, but, I was thinking, you said he had other children?"

"Yes."

"Don't you see? They're your half brothers and sisters."

Mhairi took the mugs from the cupboard. "Coffee or tea?"

"Tea please. I've already had too much coffee."

She watched her daughter rummage in her bag, grab her iPad out of it and pull out a chair, all in a series of fast, action-packed, movements. "I did wonder."

"Did you hear what I said, Mum? You've got a family."

"Yes. I've got you and Dad and Ewan, and I've got Katie and Michael."

"But you've got extended family too."

"No, I haven't."

"Yes, you have, Mum." Rhona smiled at her. "Don't you think that's rather great?"

"No, I don't." Mhairi leant her hands on the table and looked straight into Rhona's eyes. "These are names on paper. Nothing more."

"But they are your half brothers and sisters."

Mhairi shook her head, still keeping eye contact with her daughter. "They are names on paper. That's all they are to me. That's all I want them to be." Rhona started to say something but Mhairi held her hand up between their faces. "You are to do nothing — nothing — to trace them, to find out more about them, to look up who they are, where they live — nothing. Do you understand?"

"But..."

Mhairi's voice was steady and strong. "Do you understand?" she said with slow, deliberate emphasis.

Rhona stared back at her, defiance in every line of her face. "No, actually, I don't understand. Why would you not want to find out about people that are your own flesh and blood?"

Mhairi straightened up. "Because I have no room in my life for these people." She walked over to the fridge for the milk. "And I doubt they'd have room in their lives for me."

Rhona shrugged. "If it was me, I'd want to know if I had a half-sister."

"But it's not you. And they don't know. And they don't need to know. I want you to leave this be, Rhona. Do you understand?" she repeated a third time.

"No. I'm sorry, Mum, but I really can't see what harm it would do just to look up whether they're alive or dead." She turned on her iPad and logged into the site she had been using.

Mhairi slapped the cover across the iPad. "I said no!"

Rhona jumped back in the chair, clearly startled by her mother's vehemence.

"You are not to pursue this, Rhona. Do I make myself clear?"

Rhona turned away, her face tightening as her teeth clenched.

Mhairi leant across the table, her face close to Rhona's and just as tight. "**Do I make make myself clear?**"

Rhona looked straight back at her. "Yes!"

"Okay." Mhairi backed off, started to move towards the kettle. "Remember," she said. "You've to do nothing, about this, nothing at all. Right?"

Rhona nodded.

"Right?"

"Yes!"

"So you can shut that contraption down. " She pointed to the iPad. "Put it away." She took a deep breath. "And you and I will have a nice cup of tea and talk about other things. Right?"

"Right," Rhona said, with very ill grace, as she did as she was asked and put the iPad in her bag.

"Okay." Mhairi poured hot water into the mugs. "Now, tell me what I should make for desert on Sunday."

Rhona folded her arms across her chest. "I don't know. Whatever you fancy making."

"I thought maybe a crumble, because Ewan likes a crumble, but I know you and Katie like a trifle."

Rhona shrugged as she reached across and took her tea from Mhairi.

"Crumble might be a bit much after a roast dinner, anyway, I thought, so maybe the trifle? What d'you think? Strawberry or mixed fruit? What d'you think?"

A sigh and another shrug from across the table.

Mhairi sat down opposite and reached across to offer her hand. "Aw, come on, love, don't be upset. I'm sorry. I know you only want to help, but, honestly, I don't need family. Not that kind of family anyway."

Rhona kept her arms tightly folded. "You don't even know what kind of family they are."

"No, but I do know the kind of family I am, and they can do without me. I would bring nothing to them that they need, and I need nothing from them. Honestly, sweetheart. I know you mean well, but let's leave things as they are." She looked steadily at Rhona until Rhona looked up. "Please?"

Rhona nodded.

"Think about it. Would you like it if someone turned up here and told you your dad had had an affair when you were a kid and he had an illegitimate child?"

"No," Rhona said after a moment or two's reflection. "Put like that, I don't suppose I would. But I wasn't suggesting you got in touch with them. Just that you find out a bit about them."

"Then what? Just forget about them again? Don't you think the further you go with this, the more you'd want to see it through?"

"I suppose."

"So you'll leave it?"

Rhona closed her eyes and leant her head back on the wall behind. "Okay, you win. I'll leave it."

"Thank you." Mhairi reached across and offered her hand once more.

This time, Rhona put her hand out and allowed her mother to take it.

"Thank you."

They sat in silence for a moment, holding hands across the table, letting the air settle around them.

"Now," Mhairi said, releasing her daughter's hand and sitting back in her chair. "What should I make for Pudding? Crumble or trifle?"

Mhairi had, of course, thought about the fact she had three brothers and a sister. When she saw their names on the census record, she had gazed at them in awe. Three brothers and a sister, all older than her, but the youngest, Harriet, not much older. Only a year and a half. Perhaps they could have been friends, played together as children, shared clothes and confidences as teenagers.

Harriet. She would have called her 'Harry' and they would have laughed at people's confusion when she was introduced.

'Oh, you know Harry Bellingham. One of the Bellinghams of Lanark Road.'

'No, I don't believe I do. Is he the oldest of the sons?'

Then Harriet would step forward. 'No, actually. I'm the daughter!'

And they would both laugh so much they'd have to excuse themselves and go somewhere they could cling together, helpless for a while. Till they found the next victim of the joke.

Three older brothers. How wonderful would that be. Three brothers to adore her and protect her and take her fishing and swimming and look out for her that she stayed safe.

'Not too far out, Mhairi. Stay in your depth. Look, here's a good bit. No reeds or water lilies to tangle round your feet.'

'Better come out now, Mhairi. Can't have you catching cold.'

In the summer, they'd all picnic together in the park. She didn't know Glasgow at all, but there must be a park. They'd play ball and feed the ducks in the pond. There'd be a pond. They'd sit on a rug and eat dainty sandwiches and drink endless cups of tea. Or would it be fizzy juice, Irn Bru, maybe. She had never had fizzy juice, though she'd sold it in the shop often enough. Mister Foster didn't approve of it, but it sold well so he put his principles aside in order to stock it.

She laughed at her dreams and looked at the census record for the last time. She knew she could never contact these people. There would be no friendship, no fishing, no picnics. All they could ever be to her were entries in a census record. All they would ever share was the name, Bellingham, and a common father.

She felt the richer for having been in their company for an hour or two as she browsed through the volumes that contained their names.

sunday dinner

Sunday was to be perfect. Nothing must be permitted to spoil it. Not even her own anger and frustration. She would set them aside for the day and be nice to Donald. The Rover had passed its MOT after having a heap of work done on it and Ewan and Sally were definitely coming. Michael and Zara had already arrived at Rhona's and Katie was on her way. The table was set, the roast was in the oven, the trifle was made and sat proudly on the sideboard, the cream perfectly whipped and chocolate flakes crumbled over the top. Candlelight sparkled on the cutlery and serviettes sat neatly folded beside each plate.

"Goodness!" Donald said as he came into the dining room. "You've gone to town this time. What's the occasion?"

Mhairi caught herself just as she was about to snap, 'Nothing! Don't I always make the table nice?' reminding herself she was going to set aside her anger for today. Instead, she smiled and answered mildly, "Oh, nothing. Just thought I'd make a bit of an effort. Nice to have the family all together, isn't it?"

"Always," Donald agreed, stealing a flake of chocolate from the top of the trifle.

Mhairi drew her breath in to scold him, but didn't. Not today. Not today. She was determined to be sweeter than the trifle today.

She'd looked out Ewan's old Polaroid camera.

"Good grief, Mum! Where did you dig that up?" Rhona said with distaste. "It's ancient."

"My camera! You found my Polaroid camera." Ewan took it from her almost reverently.

"I came across it when I was turning out the hall cupboard. It was in a box of bits and pieces you and Rhona hadn't bothered to take when you left home. I thought it would be fun."

"There'll be no film in it, probably," said Rhona. "Or it'll have perished."

"I managed to buy a new one."

"Where on earth did you find someone who stocked Polaroid film?" Donald asked.

"I went on eBay."

They all looked at her.

"Wow! I'm impressed, Mum," said Ewan. "Thank you." He gave her a hug and a kiss on the cheek. "Right! Everyone come over beside Dad. Over there. Yes, just there, Zara. You'll have to squeeze in a bit, Mum. And you'll have to duck down, Michael. You're too tall. I can't get your head in unless you bend your knees a bit. Good, that's better. Now, say 'cheese.'" He took the photo. "Yes!"

They all clustered round as they waited for the photograph to develop.

"Oh, look! Look, it's working." Katie clapped her hands. "Oh, please can I take the next one? Please?"

Ewan handed over the camera. "Hey! Not bad! I'd forgotten what fun this camera was."

Zara burst out laughing. "Look at your hair," she said to Michael. "It's not there."

"Haha, neither it is," Rhona joined in.

"You still managed to cut the top of my head off," he complained to Ewan.

"Well, you're too bloomin' tall, mate. I told you to bend your knees."

"I did bend my knees."

"Not enough, then."

"Clearly."

"You should sit down for this one," Zara suggested. "Here, if you sit on the armchair and I sit on your knee, that'll let your mum sit here on the arm." She nodded to Rhona and patted the arm of the chair. "And your dad could go round behind the chair." She pulled Steve in the direction of the back of the chair. "There, that keeps us nice and compact. Now if you go over there." She pointed Ewan and Sally to the side of the chair. "And Gran and Gramps stand just behind and between. How's that looking, Katie? Is everyone in?"

"Quite the little organiser, aren't you?" Michael said, giving her a squeeze and pulling her in against him.

"Say 'cheese,'" Katie said...

"Cheese!" they chorused.

...and she clicked the shutter.

Another cluster round for them all to watch as the photograph slowly appeared before their eyes.

"That really is cool," Michael said.

Ewan beamed with pride. "Isn't it just?"

Without making a fuss, Mhairi took the camera from Katie's hand and made sure she took the next photograph, then Michael had a turn and Steve. Dave then reclaimed the camera and decreed that they should wait for a bit and use the rest of the film when they played charades.

There was a great whoop of delight at the suggestion and they organised the room and chose the teams.

While the photographs were laid out on the sideboard to dry, Mhairi, again without fuss, slipped the one she had taken into her cardigan pocket and took it upstairs to her room on her way to the bathroom. Once in her room with the door closed behind her, she took the photo from her pocket and studied it carefully. Yes, they were all there and all smiling. Her family. All gathered in her home, having eaten the special meal she had cooked for them and looking happy to be there. She held the memory close against her chest and closed her eyes. Enough. It would be enough. She let waves of tenderness and love wash through her. She had so much. It suffused her soul, reaching deep into her heart, her kidneys, every cell in her body.

"Mum? Where are you?" Ewan was calling up the stairs. "We need you. You're on our team. Hurry up! We need you."

She looked at the photo one last time, kissed it and popped it into the drawer of her bedside table. "Coming," she called back. "Coming."

It was way after midnight by the time everyone had gone and Mhairi and Donald were left with the last of the clearing up. To their credit, the kids had cleared the table, washed and dried the dishes and had even put them away, so there was not a lot to do.

"I'll vacuum in the morning, if that's alright, love?" Donald said as he kissed her cheek. "Don't know about you, but I'm done. Can just about drag myself up the stairs." He held his hand out to her. "You coming? I'll give you a shove up the stairs if you are."

Mhairi picked up a cushion and plumped it up. "No, you go. I just need a moment." Standing in the doorway, she looked round the cosy living room. The fire had died right down, only the faintest wisp of smoke rising from the crumbling logs. A sprinkling of ash lay on the stone hearth and she walked over and bent to sweep it up with the brush that lay at the side.

"Think it went particularly well," Donald said, pausing on the bottom step to turn and speak to her. "Don't you? Everyone seemed to have fun."

"Yes." Mhairi smiled as she turned the light out and started towards the kitchen again.

"Dave and Rhona managed to go the whole day without an argument."

She laughed. "So they did."

"And the meal was superb. Thank you. You did really well."

"Thank you."

"That was some size of roast you bought!"

"It just looked a rather good one."

"It was," he said, with some enthusiasm. "Delicious. Really tender. I'm not complaining. There's enough there for me to have a great sandwich or two."

"Yes. Good."

"Lunch tomorrow sorted."

"Mmm."

Donald paused on the second step and turned again. "You okay, love."

"Yes, of course." She smiled. "Just tired."

He yawned. "Yeah! Me too." He took another step and stopped again.

"Only you seemed a bit quiet."

"Yeah, as I said, I'm a bit tired."

"No, I mean all day. You've seemed a bit quiet all day."

"Did I?" Mhairi shrugged and pulled a face. "Didn't particularly mean to be. Perhaps everyone else just made too much noise."

Donald laughed. "You can say that again."

"Perhaps everyone else..."

They laughed together.

"Okay. If you're sure you're okay. I'll go on up,' Donald said. "I'm absolutely cream crackered!" He continued the climb.

"I do love you, you know," she said.

He stopped and turned yet again. "I know, love. I know. Love you too." He blew her a kiss. "Proper one waiting for you upstairs if you're not too long. Don't know how long I can keep my eyes open."

Mhairi nodded and smiled.

Enough. It would be enough.

She watched him pull his weary body the rest of the flight and listened to his sigh as he reached the top, his shuffling footsteps as he moved along the hall and into the bathroom. She listened as he cleaned his teeth, rinsed his mouth and gargled. All the familiar sounds of his bedtime routine. She listened and smiled, then her breath was caught in her chest and she clutched her body in anguish.

The next morning, True to his word, Donald vacuumed the house before making himself a beef sandwich for lunch and heading off to Glasgow to visit his mother.

Meanwhile, Mhairi dusted and tidied the last few bits and bobs that lay around after the family day. She polished and scrubbed till the whole house gleamed.

Donald looked round as he opened the front door. "Lovely!" he said as he bent to kiss her cheek. "You and the house." He stroked her cheek. "See you later."

She nodded, then, at the last moment, just as he stepped outside, she moved forward and put her arms round him.

He hugged her back. "Thanks, love." He smiled. "Needed that."

"Me too," she said, pushing him away and stepping back.

She watched from the door as he opened the car, got inside and drove away, giving her a last wave from the open driver's window. The car was long gone and still she stood, her eyes closed and her heart racing. Determined not to cry, she took long breaths of the cool, fresh air before going back into the house and closing the door.

Straightening her back and lifting her head, she went up to her room and changed into her jeans and a warm jumper and pulled on some hiking socks. She gathered a few precious things along with a few pairs of socks and underwear into a rucksack, took the photograph she had taken last night from the bedside drawer and put it in her pocket and walked out of her bedroom.

It was one of her favourite rooms in the house. Decorated in sunshine, with a rainbow of soft, pastel colours in the curtains and bedspread, family pictures on the walls and light natural wood furnishings. She didn't dare look round as she walked through the door.

Downstairs, she took her walking boots out of the cupboard and pulled them on, her fleece lined hiking coat from the back of the cloakroom, her hat and gloves from the drawer, put everything on, including the rucksack, stuffing her wallet and sunglasses into the front section of it, and, leaving her key on the hall table, walked out of the front door, pulling it to behind her.

Enough. It was enough.

part two

"It is enough for me by day
To walk the same bright earth with him;
Enough that over us by night
The same great roof of stars is dim.

I do not hope to bind the wind
Or set a fetter on the sea --
It is enough to feel his love
Blow by like music over me."
— Sara Teasdale

monday
donald

"Hi, Rho, Mum there?"

"No. It's Monday. I don't usually see her on a Monday. Why? Is she not home?"

"No."

Rhona clearly didn't like the sound of her father's voice. "Everything okay?" she asked, concern in her own.

"Y-e-s, at least I think so. I don't know. Mum's key is on the hall table, her handbag and coat are in the hall cupboard. Everything's supremely tidy, there's no dinner made and no sign of your mother."

"Did she say she was going somewhere?"

"Not that I recall."

"Is her car there?"

Donald looked out the window, though he knew he had parked behind it in the drive when he came home. "Yes."

"Then she can't have gone far, can she?"

"I suppose not."

"Why don't you get on with the dinner preparations, and give her a nice surprise when she gets in. She really can't have gone far without her coat and stuff. She's maybe in with one of the neighbours?"

"Can't imagine who. She keeps herself to herself, your mum. Always has. Bit of a loner apart from Carol and Letty."

"Carol and Letty! Have you phoned them? She's probably off on the razzle-dazzle with one of them. Or both of them. You know what they're like, the merry widows."

"Without her handbag or her coat? Or her house-key?" He picked the key up, turning it over and over in his hand, examining it for any clues it might provide.

"Or the car." There was a long pause. "Good grief, I hope she's not lost it."

"Lost it? Lost what?"

"It! Her mind, her marbles."

"Don't be silly." Donald put the key down on the hall table.

"You have to admit she's been acting weird lately."

"A bit stressed maybe, but weird? Do you think so?"

"She was a bit weird last night. She hugged me when we were going like I was emigrating to Australia and she wasn't going to see me for years."

"Funny, Ewan said the same thing when I walked him out to the car."

"What's going on, Dad?"

"I don't know, love. I really don't know."

"Want me to pop over?"

"Nah! Nah, your mum'll be back in a minute probably. You're right. She must've gone in to one of the neighbours." He picked up the key again and held it in his fist. There seemed something ominous about the key being there. Donald opened his fist and looked at it again. Something about it was bothering him. "It's not on her keyring. That's what's wrong," he said.

"What?"

"Her house-key. It's just lying here. It's not on her keyring."

"Why would it not be on her keyring?"

"Well, that's what I'm wondering. It's very odd."

"I'm coming over!"

After he put the phone down, Donald stood holding the key, thinking. Something was still nagging away at the back of his mind. There was a significance in the key being there like that. If he could just get a hold of it. He shook his head and put it back on the table. "It'll come to me," he muttered. "It'll come to me." He wandered through to the kitchen, shaking his head.

There didn't seem much point in starting to prepare something for dinner. Either Mhairi had told him she'd be out and he'd forgotten, in which case she might have said she wouldn't be in for dinner, or, she was going to appear any moment and be annoyed if he'd started making something and she'd planned something different. But it had been a long, tiring day and he was wearied by worry about his mother and he was hungry.

His shoulders sagged as he went to the fridge to rummage through for something to keep him going meantime.

"Great!" He'd forgotten there were leftovers. The roast beef sandwich he'd had at lunchtime was delicious. "Humph! I could fair go that again," he said to no-one in particular, as he lifted out the rest of the meat, the butter and some tomatoes. "Roast beef and tomatoes. Lovely grub!" He searched a little more and came up with the horseradish sauce.

"Perfect!" Cutting himself a couple of slices of bread, buttering it and assembling his sandwich became absorbing and he whistled as he worked, weariness and worry withering with the expectation of pleasing sustenance. Clicking the kettle on to boil and getting out his favourite extra-large mug, a feeling of well-being began to creep over him. His taste buds were tingling in anticipation as he carried his plate and mug through to the sitting room, where he placed them on the coffee table beside his chair and turned the television on.

He'd forgotten there was a mystery around why Mhairi wasn't here and was pleasantly surprised when Rhona came in the back door. "Hello, love. To what do we owe the pleasure?" he said as he took another bite of the sandwich he'd been thoroughly enjoying. "Lovely bit of beef your mum got for yesterday. Lovely!"

"Oh, is Mum back then?"
"What?"

"Mum? Did she turn up?" Rhona went to the foot of the stairs and called up for Mhairi. When there was no reply, she came back into the sitting room.

"Your Mum's not in, pet."

"Yes, I thought we'd established that. That's why I came over."

"Why are you calling up the stairs for her if you know she's not home?"

"Because I thought she'd come in or something when I saw you happily munching, without a care in the world."

"I was."

"I know. That's what I'm saying."

"Should I not be?"

"Dad! Are you not just a little bit worried that Mum's disappeared?"

Donald finished the last of his drink and put the cup down. "She hasn't disappeared," he said with a laugh.

"No?" Rhona stared at him, looking down at him sitting in his favourite armchair, while she stood, hands on hips facing him. "So where is she?"

"I don't know, love. She is allowed out of the house, you know."

"Dad! It's turned November. It's turned really cold. She doesn't have her coat on, she doesn't have her handbag with her, her car or her keys."

"So? You said yourself she's probably at a neighbour's house."

"If she'd been at a neighbour's house, why did she not come back when she heard your car? Once she knew you were home and she had a dinner to make?"

"I just had the rest of that beef. Lovely bit of beef, that."

"Dad! I don't give a toss about your beef! What you had for tea is immaterial. The whole point is, Mum would not go out like that, without taking anything with her. She just wouldn't. And she wouldn't leave her keys."

"Now, you're right about that." Worry returned to furrow Donald's brow. "She wouldn't leave her keys. She doesn't like being locked in anywhere or locked out."

"Exactly! She's positively paranoid about locked doors."

"Ah, well, that's because..." Donald stopped himself.

Rhona waited for him to say what he was going to say. When he didn't, she narrowed her eyes and moved towards him. "Because what, Dad? What's Mum scared of?"

He laughed again. 'Your Mum, scared? I doubt your mum's scared of anything. One of the strongest people I know."

Rhona looked skeptical.

"She had to be." He coughed and got out of his chair. "Right! Right, let's find your mother."

"What do you mean, she had to be? What's going on, Dad? What's Mum scared of just now?"

"I told you, your mum..."

"Is one of the strongest people you know. Yeah! Piffle!" She closed in on him. "You just sit yourself down again, and tell me what's going on."

"I thought you wanted us to look for your mother?"

Rhona looked at her watch. "We'll give her another half hour, then we start worrying in earnest, right? Meantime, I want to know what's going on."

Donald lifted his plate and mug and started to the kitchen. "Well, I can't tell you."

Rhona followed him. "Can't or won't?"

"Can't. Now, let's have a think about where your mother's gone. I'll phone Carol and you phone Letty."

Both of Mhairi's friends were delighted to hear from them, but no help at all in finding Mhairi. Neither of them had heard from her since they met up last week and were not expecting to see her again until their next monthly afternoon tea date.

"She hasn't phoned or anything?" Donald asked.

"Nope! Due to give her a bell tonight, actually."

"Well, she's not here."

"She gone awol, then?" Carol said. "You lost her?"

"Nah! Just misplaced her. She'll turn up."

"Yeah! Down the side of the cushion on that old armchair of yours. You looked there yet?"

"Haha! Never liked that chair of mine did you?"

"Not since it ate my mobile phone."

"It was hungry, what can I say?"

"Yeah, well, didn't regurgitate it for long enough."

"What you moaning about? Mhairi says you got a smart new phone out of it."

"True, true. Anyway, Duckie, I must love you and leave you. Time to walk the dog before she pees all over my carpet."

"Duckie, indeed," Donald muttered as he put the phone down. "Wouldn't have dared call me that before I retired."

"Not to your face anyway," Rhona said with a laugh. "Mum says she always did behind your back."

"Hurumph!"

"Right, when you've finished being mortally offended, let's get on with the task in hand. I'll phone Katie and Michael and you phone Dave."

"Do you really think that's necessary, pet? Will it not alarm them?"

Rhona looked at her watch. "Eight-thirty. Better now than midnight if she doesn't turn up by then."

"Midnight!" Donald shook his head. "There's no way she'd stay out till midnight."

"And there's no way she'd stay out till eight-thirty without her coat and keys, so let's just do it. They'll survive."

With a sigh and a grumble, Donald dialled Ewan on the house phone in the sitting room while Rhona went through to the kitchen to use her mobile.

Once again, when all the phone calls were accomplished, they were no further forward.

"All that achieved," Donald grumbled, "was to spread alarm and despondency and make me look a right old fool who doesn't remember where he left his glasses or his wife."

Rhona closed her eyes, sighed and took out her notebook. "Right! We're going to do this properly. Mum-style." She started a list. "Facts we have established. Mum is not at these places." She listed the names of family and friends as phoned. "She has not taken the car." She looked up at Donald. "That means she is on foot."

"Or got a taxi."

"Or got a taxi." She started a new heading. "Possibilities to explore. Walking. Taxi."

"Or a lift."

"Oh, yes, I suppose she could be in someone else's car. Hadn't thought of that." Rhona added 'Lift' to the list. "But that leaves us the question of who she would get a lift from, and where was she going. Any guesses?"

"Or an ambulance."

"Grief, Dad. Aren't you the cheery one?" But she added it to her list. "So how can we find out which of these it is?"

Donald was sitting, feeling forlorn and fragile. As they made each phone call, the realisation began to force itself upon him that there was actually a problem about Mhairi not being here when he came home. "It's the key," he said. "I'm sure there's a message in the key."

"What do you mean a message?"

Donald searched through the rusty old filing cabinet of his head, frustrated his retrieval system was so slow, sometimes didn't work at all these days. There was a time his memory was sharp and certain. Since he retired, he'd allowed it to fall into disuse. Enough getting through each day worrying about his mother's present predicament.

The key. The lone key sitting on the hall table. He was sure it was significant.

"Dad?"

"Uh?"

"What do you mean? You said you thought the key was a message. What sort of message?"

"Uh-huh."

"I mean, I know how much Mum hates locked doors, no matter which side of them she's on. I both love and hate that I can just walk in the front or the back door anytime I want. It's lovely and welcoming, but it's really not safe. Not nowadays."

"That's it, she has a whole thing about keys and locks and..." His voice trailed off as he tried again to remember what it was he should remember. Weariness was creeping into his bones again — weariness and worry, those two travelling companions.

"You said something about 'That's because...' Earlier. You started to tell me why Mum has this paranoia about locked doors."

"Yes. She does, doesn't she?"

"And that's because..." Rhona prompted.

"Well, it's because of her childhood, of course."

"What about her childhood?"

Donald looked at her. "Ah!" He realised he might have said more than he ought. "Right! What's next on your list?"

She threw the notebook across the room. "Dad! I'm getting so fed up with all this."

"All what?"

"This! All this 'can't say' nonsense." She started pacing the room. "First it was Mum with her futile attempts to stop me finding out her real name. I mean, really, who cares that she was illegitimate? Who isn't these days?" She flumped down on the sofa. "Now it's you with your nearly-letting-something-slip, then remembering you're not supposed to say anything." She folded her arms across her chest. "It's ludicrous."

Donald thought for a moment."Let's just wait a bit and see if Mum comes home soon, eh? Before we start taking her life apart."

mhairi

Mhairi felt her life fall apart. It was crumbling, collapsing round her. Everything she had built was going to become a ruin.

As she tramped the streets of Edinburgh, heading for the proverbial hills, she didn't look back for fear she'd see the dust cloud of her life's demolition as the wrecking ball of Rhona's curiosity hit its foundations.

Not that she blamed her daughter. It was a fairly normal, seemingly innocuous thing to do. So many people were doing it these days. Tracing their family tree. Seeking out the skeletons in the family closet. As she walked past flats and houses, she glanced in the windows and wondered how many daughters were sitting in front of computer screens right now, locked in to one or other of the ancestry sites, clicking on their mothers' shame.

Intellectually, she knew that the details Rhona would find there would not directly reveal her story, but her fear told her those details would lead to questions and those questions might lead to answers. She didn't walk away from her life because it was bad. She walked away because it was good. Too good. Too good to last.

With the click of a mouse, it could all be taken from her. She couldn't, she wouldn't wait around in suspended animation, her breath held, her heart stopped whenever Rhona came to tell her what she had found out now.

Head down, arms at her sides, she trudged on. Halfway through the afternoon, she sat on the wall outside someone else's house and ate the apple she'd put in the rucksack before she left home. By dinnertime, she'd reached Ratho and found a chip shop near the canal, where she bought herself a fish supper and a bottle of water to replace the one she'd finished during the day. Public toilets had been scarce and she'd made use of the facilities in hotels and restaurants she'd passed along her route, not permitting herself to feel guilty that she was not giving them her custom in exchange.

Sitting on a bench down at the canal side, the November chill began to creep through her. She'd been warm enough as she'd walked, but she felt it now and she shivered. It had been dark for some time and good sense dictated that she rest, so she got back on her feet and went in search of a room for the night. There was a hotel right there, beside the canal, but it's prices were more than she wanted to pay, so she walked a little further until she saw a Bed & Breakfast sign along the street and headed for that.

The price was better, the room was adequate and, best of all, it had a delightfully large, deep bath in which she was able to soak her aching muscles in fragrant hot water, courtesy of the bottle of bubble bath set on the shelf for her convenience. She lay back and wondered what would become of her.

Breaking her life down into three segments, she felt the second part had more than compensated for the first, but what would she do with the third? Solitude again? Was that all she had to look forward to? Anonymity and solitude?

Breaking life into four segments: childhood and adolescence; childbearing years; maturity, and the phase she felt herself entering now, old age. Childhood and adolescence had been abysmal; childbearing years hard work but mostly rewarding; maturity, when the children had grown up and left home leaving her and Donald to follow their own interests, she had been enjoying up until now. It was probably the phase she had enjoyed most, all things considered: the time she had felt most in control, most comfortable, a surety coming with maturity.

When the children were born, doubt and uncertainty were held in their wee fists, a gift to their new mother. Throughout the years of caring for them in every way a mother should, there never seemed to be a moment when she felt certain she was 'getting it right.' There were many when she knew she was getting it wrong. Donald wanted a second child after Rhona was a few years old, 'Pity to waste all that hard-earned experience we've gained through having one,' he said. But it didn't work that way. She felt just as inadequate when Ewan was born. Children have the annoying habit of all being different and what works with one doesn't necessarily work with another. That segment of life was dashed hard work, she reflected as she sponged water over her shoulders; she should have muscles like iron, in her brain as well as her arms.

It had been with a huge sigh of relief she had watched her children marry and become someone else's responsibility. She had done her best, they were both decent human beings, flawed human beings like everyone else, but decent, honest and loving. Adults to be proud of, despite all her misgivings as to whether she'd be up to the task demanded of her to produce that result.

Luxury to sit back and watch Rhona go through the same doubts and uncertainties bringing up her children, on hand to help when needed, equipped with the years of her own experience to offer advice if asked, but a relief not to carry the responsibility any more. Sweet maturity, she had enjoyed it.

Sinking down into the bath water, 'What now?' she asked.

What would this last quarter bring for her?

Had the first quarter been different, perhaps she could have looked forward to growing old, she and Donald together, dying in her bed in the house she had delighted to build into a home, children and grandchildren gathered at her bedside to wish her a fond farewell. Instead, all she saw was the lonely road she walked today.

She had signed into the B&B as 'Eve Last' and she would pay in cash. This wasn't the impulsive flight Donald would probably think it was. She had gone to the bank at the end of last week and closed her bank account. After all these years, it had seemed a liberating thing to do, to close the account her father had opened in her assumed name when she was twenty-one. The money he had placed in it was long gone, but she had continued to save in it, 'for a rainy day.' She lifted her hand and watched the water drip from her fingers into the bath. Well, this was that rainy day.

After her long soak, she dried herself and climbed into bed, where she lay studying the Polaroid photograph she had taken of her family: Donald standing behind the armchair, leaning down to say something to Michael, looking up at the last moment and smiling as she took the photograph. Dear Donald, if only he had told her, given her time to come to terms with his treachery before she had to leave him. He was a good man. He didn't deserve to be left like this, but she had to go. He would come to see that in the end. She had to go. She kissed her fingertip and placed the kiss on his dear, sweet face.

Michael, deemed too tall to stand for the photo, sitting with Zara, dear sweet, bossy Zara, on his knee. He was a lovely lad, a real gentle giant of a boy, six-foot-three and built like a rugby player. Mhairi was proud of her grandson. He was doing well at University and looked like coming out with an honours degree. Mhairi realised with a gulp that she would never see him graduate.

Enough. It was enough for tonight. She held the photograph close to her chest and closed her eyes, knowing she would look at it many times before it faded and crumpled. Tonight, that was enough or she would be unable to go any further and she knew that she must. She needed to be far away when the fabric of her life was torn apart.

monday evening
donald

By ten o'clock, Donald and Rhona had phoned all the Edinburgh hospitals. When they found that Mhairi had not been admitted to any of them, Rhona crossed 'ambulance' off under the transport heading of her list. "I don't know whether to be happy or not that she hasn't been carted off in an ambulance," she said.

"Oh, happy, surely?" Donald said, putting a cup of tea in front of her.

"Well, at least we'd know where she was."

"True. Taxi ranks now?"

Rhona sighed, looking at the long list of Edinburgh taxi companies. "Let's get started then." She gave Donald the Classified Directory and she brought up the directory on her phone. "Right, Dad. Let's scan through for the more local ones first of all. If you start working down the list, I'll start at the bottom and work up till we meet. Remember to cross them off as you go."

After they'd been working their way through the list fruitlessly for another half-hour, Rhona paused and looked up at her dad. "You don't think we should call the police, do you, to report her missing."

"Been wondering that myself."

"I don't suppose they'll do anything yet. It's twenty-four hours missing before they help, I think, but we could at least let them know she's disappeared."

"Yes."

"You or me, then, Dad?"

"You. You're much better at these things than I am."

Rhona was right, the police don't get involved until someone's been missing for twenty-four hours. "Unless it's a child or a vulnerable adult," she was informed.

"She doesn't seem to be wearing a warm coat," Rhona told the officer.

"Sorry, unless your mother is sick or very old, there's nothing we can do at this point, but I'll make a note and you can call back in the morning."

Rhona thanked him and ended the call, sitting for a while, phone in hand, digesting the information and lack of it they had. "I don't like this, Dad. I'm beginning to feel really uneasy. It's so not like Mum to do anything like this."

Donald nodded. "I know, pet." He walked over to her and offered a hug, which she accepted without hesitation. "Let's finish ringing round the taxi companies." He gave her a squeeze and kissed the top of her head.

"Oh!" she said, starting to cry. "Mum does that all the time."

Donald held her away from him a little to see her face. "Come on, pet. Let's not give up now. Your Mum's going to be fine. Whatever has happened, she'll be fine. Now, shall we make another cup of tea before we start on the taxis again?"

Rhona nodded and dried her eyes. "And I'd better give Steve a ring and let him know how we're doing. Do you mind if I stay here tonight, Dad. I don't think I could bear to go home till Mum comes back or we know what's happened."

"Of course, love. I'll go switch on the electric blanket in the spare room. Been a wee while since that bed's been used. Oh!" A bolt of pain hit him in the stomach as he remembered that was not true.

"You okay, Dad?"

He nodded and forced himself to walk away without explanation.

"I'll put the kettle on." Rhona called after him.

Between them, they finished calling all the taxi companies listed for Edinburgh, not just those local to home. Nothing.

"Looks like you can cross 'taxi' off your list, then."

Rhona did, then sat back, looking at the list. "This might sound a bit silly, Dad, and a bit obvious, but Mum does have more than one coat, you know. Do you think, if we were to go through what's hanging in the cloakroom, you'd know if there was one missing?"

"Worth a try I suppose, though I suspect you're as likely to see what's missing as I am." He got up from his chair to go to the hall cupboard they fondly called 'the cloakroom.' There were two cupboards side by side tucked in under the rise of the stairs. The taller of the two, they used as a cloakroom, the other as a 'glory hole,' where they stored all sorts of things they didn't use but were reluctant to throw away.

Switching the cupboard light on, Donald stepped inside and looked along the row of coats. "Well, the coat she's been wearing lately is here, and her good coat," he moved further in. "Her mac's still here and her old gardening coat," he shouted back to Rhona. "Hang on a minute." He stepped back a bit and checked through the coats again, pushing past his own coats and jackets, checking under them and under Mhairi's. "I don't see her walking jacket. You know, the waterproof anoraky-kind-of-thing she wears when we go hill-walking."

"Let me have a look."

Rhona double-checked. "You're right. That's what's missing." She stepped out of the cloakroom. "Quick! Check the other cupboard. Are her walking boots gone?"

"Oh, heck, how am I going to know?" Donald said as he opened the cupboard door. "This cupboard's a... all been cleared out!"

"Yes, Mum was doing it last week when I came round. You only just noticed?"

"I don't use that cupboard much. Tend to think of it as your mum's glory hole."

"Well, can you see the boots? Are they gone?"

Donald looked at the shelves at the back, where all their shoes were lined up neatly, the most used ones nearest the door. He checked the shelf where his own boots sat next to his wellingtons, with Mhairi's wellingtons beside them. "Well, mine are here," he said as he stepped back. "But I don't see your mum's."

Rhona stepped forward to look too. "No, they're gone. There's a space for them, but they're definitely gone."

"Well, at least we now know her mode of transport."

Rhona ticked 'walking' on her list as they sat down to think about the import of their find. Before either of them spoke, she jumped up again and ran back to the cupboard. "Her rucksack's gone too," she said as she sat down on her return. "It's not hanging with her other bags." She had brought Mhairi's handbag through with her and started rummaging through it.

"Her phone's gone."

"Well, that has to be a good sign."

"Do you think so?"

"Absolutely. For one thing, it means she can make contact if she needs to."

Rhona dialled Mhairi's number on her own phone and was listening. "Turned off," she said, ending the call. "Oh! I could leave a message."

"There's a good idea."

She dialled again. "Hi, Mum," she said when asked to leave a voicemail. "Where the heck are you? Dad and I are worried sick about you."

Donald snatched the phone out of her hand. "We are worried." He took up the message in a much gentler tone. "We'd just like to know you're safe, love. Maybe you could give us a call? Please?" He paused for a moment, waiting for a reply.

"Her phone's off, Dad. She's not going to answer."

"Okay. Okay, pet," Donald said. He handed back the phone. "Don't get so worked up. She might have."

Rhona snorted. "Did you check if she took her wallet?"

"I wouldn't dream of going through a lady's handbag," Donald said.

"Yeah, well, these are extreme circumstances and I have no such compunction." She continued looking through the contents of the bag. "Looks like she's got her wallet with her."

"Well, that's good too, I suppose. She can at least buy herself some food."

Rhona looked at the clock. Ten minutes after midnight. "And a bed for the night, I hope."

Donald nodded as he pushed his hands through his hair and rubbed them across his face. "Gone walkabout, then."

"Why? Why on earth would Mum suddenly decide to take off like that, without a word to anyone, at the beginning of November?"

"Yes."

"She's taken her wallet and her phone." She held up Mhairi's keyring. "But not her keys." She jingled them in her hand. "That's strange," she said, frowning. She got up and walked through to the hall, where she took the front door key from the hall table and brought it back through to the sitting room with her. "You're right, Dad, there has to be some sort of significance to her going to the bother of removing this key." She held it up. "From this keyring." She held that up too. "When she wasn't taking any of the keys with her."

Donald sat bowed forward with his head in his hands searching through his memory. That had been bothering him all night.

"What was she trying to tell us, Dad? Think. What does this mean?" She held them up and shook them.

He shook his head.

Rhona sat back and closed her eyes.

Silence flooded into the room as they both sat thinking. As the mantlepiece clock ticked off the seconds, Donald allowed himself to relax and let his mind wander methodically through the archives of his memory. But he was getting tired and the ticking was lulling him to sleep.

With a sudden rush, it came to him, clear and certain. "Safe! She doesn't feel safe any more." Donald jumped up and took the single key from Rhona's hand. "When we bought this house, just before we got married, your mother stood here, in the middle of this room and cried like a baby. 'I feel safe here,' she said. 'For the first time in my entire life, I feel safe. Safe here with you.' I gave her the keys and she took this one off the ring. 'As long as I have possession of this key, no-one can lock me in or lock me out. I'll be safe.' And she held the key so hard it left an imprint on her palm."

At last, the memory had been retrieved. He could see her standing here in the middle of the empty, undecorated, unfurnished room. They had wandered through the empty house, Mhairi marvelling at the spacious rooms again.

It had been weeks since they first looked at it as a prospective home in which to start their married life, raise their children, grow old together. He had watched with tender feelings surging through him as she waltzed and spun her way from room to room, asking him if they could put the bed here, hang some pictures there. 'Lots of pictures. Lots and lots of them,' she begged. 'Of beautiful places we've never been to, of kittens and puppies we never owned, of flowers and poppy fields.'

He laughed, his laugh echoing in the empty rooms.

'Oh, I love your laugh,' she said, coming to him, hugging him, kissing his face, his mouth. Just as he thought they might have to find somewhere to lie down, she spun away from him again. 'I've always loved your laugh. It was the first real, genuine proper laugh I ever heard in my life.'

A hammer hit his heart for her because he knew it was true. That she could have reached the age of twenty-one without hearing laughter tore him apart.

She had sat on the kitchen worktop, her legs entwined round his waist where she'd trapped him as he came to lift her down. 'I never want to leave this house,' she said, the earnest tone in her voice cutting into his soul. 'Ever, ever, ever. This is the only home I want.'

He held her to him and told her she would never have to leave this house. 'Except perhaps to do a bit of shopping now and then or to go a wee holiday or two, or...' he said, spinning away with her, carrying her through to the sitting room, spinning her round and around until they were both dizzy and he had to put her down. 'Or, to marry me in three weeks time.'

He could still remember holding her so close, folding her into himself, wanting more than anything in the world to keep her safe, to make her happy, to give her a home and freedom.

And she stood here, in the middle of this room and cried like a baby. 'I feel safe here,' she said. 'For the first time in my entire life, I feel safe. Safe here with you.' He gave her the keys and she took the one for the front door off the ring. 'As long as I have possession of this key, no-one can lock me in or lock me out. I'll be safe.' And she held the key so hard it left an imprint on her palm. He remembered kissing it.

"You okay, Dad?"

He had never cried in front of Rhona before and he felt foolish now. A foolish old man who took too many hours to bring back to mind one of the most tender, precious moments of his life. He nodded, wiping his face with his hand. "I was right. She left the key there to tell me she didn't feel safe any more."

"Why on earth would she not feel safe any more?"

"Now, that's a long story."

Rhona shrugged. "We seem to have all night, since I doubt Mum will be back tonight and I also doubt either of us will sleep."

early hours of tuesday morning
mhairi

Mhairi didn't expect to sleep, but her day's walking had exhausted her and she slept more soundly than she had in a long time. It took her a moment to work out where she was when she woke in the early hours. She had left the curtains and the window open as she always did and the light and the noises were different. Opening her eyes in a strange room, in a strange bed, confused her until she remembered that she had run away. For a moment, the thought made her feel like a silly, naughty schoolgirl and she giggled like one, enhancing the feeling. She had run away from home. Then her breath caught and the pain returned. She almost cried out, her hand flying to cover her mouth and hold back the howl. Had they missed her yet?

Of course they had, in the sense of noticing she wasn't there, but had they missed her? Did they miss her as she already missed them? It was a deep ache in her belly, a pain for which there was no painkiller. It pinned her to the bed, her limbs heavy with grief, her back weakened by its force. She turned her head into the pillow that her anguish should not be heard.

Yet, the urge to run overwhelmed every other feeling. It was primal: the same primal determination to live that had been her companion for all the years of her incarceration.

early hours of tuesday morning
donald

Donald didn't think he would sleep. He had dragged himself upstairs to lie down when he could stay up no longer. His body ached, his head throbbed, he felt light-headed and sick. He didn't bother to undress but crashed onto the bed in exhaustion and slept as he landed, sprawled across the bed, his feet dangling over the side.

It took him a moment to get his bearings when he woke. The bedroom looked strange from this angle, he was cold and stiff, and Mhairi wasn't beside him.

They had hardly spent a night apart in all their marriage. Just the few nights each time she went into hospital to have their children. She had wanted a home birth the first time, when she had Rhona. It was all planned, the spare room set up as the midwife instructed, everything in place. But there had been complications at the end and Mhairi's fear of being in hospital was outweighed by her fear of losing her precious baby and she allowed herself to be taken there.

Donald had a sudden memory of the absolute terror on her face when she was wheeled away from him to the operating theatre for a caesarian section. Nowadays, they would have let him stay with her and it would be accomplished with the aid of an epidural, he knew, but back then, husbands had no say and no place in the delivery of children and he could only watch in anguish as she was traumatised by the forced parting, her hands clawing the air for him. Remembered pain clutched at his belly and he longed to run after her now as he wanted to then.

Poor Mhairi, she seemed no more than a child herself, though she was twenty-four when she had Rhona. It was fear that made her seem so young, such a childlike terror of being alone in a strange place, of being carted off never to return, restrained from leaving by the necessity to stay.

Even with better preparation, when Ewan was to be delivered by a planned caesarian, Ewan was aware of Mhairi's fear growing as the date of the operation loomed. She became nervous and jumpy, snapping at him if he tried to soothe her, then crying, holding onto him, her tearful apologies flowing with desperate sincerity. She didn't want him to go to work, to leave the house, to leave the room. In the end, he took the last few days off work to be with her. They went for short walks and had long talks. By the time Ewan was delivered, they were exhausted and Donald had to take more time off work to look after Rhona while Mhairi and the baby were in hospital. During visiting time, he watched the fear of his leaving at the end of the hour grow over her face like a virulent, feverish illness.

Donald understood her fear but felt helpless to relieve it for her. Nothing he did or said seemed to help, though she tried to allow it to. Such a primal thing, fear.

He wondered how she had fared with sleeping in a strange bed last night, assuring himself that she had the sense to choose a warm bed over a cold bench, knowing she had her wallet with her, praying the years of security had managed to assuage some of the fear.

He sat for a while on the side of the bed, thinking about her, about her fear. She didn't feel safe any more. What a damning indictment of his husbandly care of her. Donald wept for her, regretting that he hadn't seen this coming and taken steps to stop it. With hindsight, he knew he should have been more reassuring, less offhand when she expressed her sense of foreboding.

Easy to make the excuse that he was all caught up in the anxiety of his mother's deteriorating health, both mentally and physically. Yesterday, she thought he was the Doctor and started reeling off her discomforts and complaints. After he'd come to terms with his disappointment, he stored the scene away to share with Mhairi when he got home. He thought it would give her a chuckle, not unkindly, Mhairi was rarely unkind, but a chuckle at his expense when he described himself trying to hold up his side of the conversation.

But Mhairi wasn't here when he got home.

Giving himself a shake, he scratched his head with both hands in wild, almost frenzied frustration, causing his still-thick, grey hair to stand on end alarmingly. He wouldn't use his worry about his mother to excuse himself. He should have been 'on the ball' with Mhairi's concerns. Whether he could have done anything about them, he rather doubted. Rhona was a tenacious wee creature when she got her teeth into things and he might only have spurred her on if he had asked her to drop her project, at least as far as Mhairi's family tree was concerned. "She's like a blooming barnacle," he muttered as he got off the bed to pull on an old pair of jogging trousers and a jumper.

Before he took his rumpled self downstairs to get a cup of tea, he popped his head round the door of the spare room, expecting to find Rhona still fast asleep in the bed. The room and the bed were empty and the bed was made.

"Didn't think you'd be up so early, pet," he said as he entered the kitchen. "It's not even six yet."

She turned her ash-white face towards him, her eyes unnaturally bright and red-rimmed. "Never went to bed."

"Oh dear, was that wise?"

She pushed her iPad towards him. "I was looking some more things up online. How much of this did you know?"

early tuesday morning
mhairi

Lying in a bed that was not her own, in a room that was not her own, in a house filled with unfamiliar sound and movement, unable to get back to sleep though it was too early to get up, Mhairi thought she might not be able to move. Ever. Time would wash over her in its inexorable march forward, but she would lie still.

She used to be able to do that. To lie still, very still, hardly breathing, feeling the seconds tick by, marking off another minute, another hour, praying they would stop. Time would stop. The world would stop. She would stop.

Eyes closed, shutting out all sound, letting the air flow over her, lifting her breath as it passed, wafting it away on a sigh, emptying her. Trying not to allow thought or memory any place to live.

It was easier when she was being medicated. Depending which medication they were experimenting with, she would move like an automaton, a machine, with no will or wishes, or she would tremble, her hands shaking so that she couldn't perform the simplest of tasks. For years, her body had lived when she did not. She existed, but she didn't live. Her memories of those years were overlaid with charcoal clouds that obscured reality, stealing reason and purpose.

There were days of clarity, when the medication was less powerful, or she had vomited it up as she sometimes did when the food was rancid. It was during one of those spells she had seen another inmate, Babs, spit out her pills. Mhairi had looked at her with a puzzled frown.

'You keep your mouth shut, or you're for it!' Babs hissed when she caught Mhairi looking at her.

Mhairi knew 'it' to be unpleasant, since Babs had been responsible for one or two of her trips to the infirmary already, each time assured by Babs that she had had 'it' coming to her, usually for not managing Babs share of the work as well as her own.

It might have been better for everyone if Mhairi had opened her mouth ensuring the administration of Babs' medication would be more assiduously scrutinised, but she didn't. She recognised, as Babs had, that here was a way of knowing who she was and how she felt, without the numbing effects the pills had on her brain and her being.

Whenever reality overwhelmed her, she would stop spitting them out, but for spells, she enjoyed getting to know how to think.

But now, lying in someone else's house in the early hours of the morning, before the milkman had been or the sun was up, she almost wished she had a few of those pills in her pocket.

Pulling the duvet up round her ears, she willed herself to let sleep overcome the pain of thinking for another few hours.

early tuesday morning
donald

"How much do you know already," he asked, sitting opposite Rhona at the kitchen table.

"I know she was illegitimate, her mother was already pregnant when she married the guy Mum grew up thinking was her father. I know her real father died years ago and probably never knew about her. He had other kids but Mum never tried to contact them or anything." Rhona shrugged. "Which I think is a pity, because they might have been okay with the whole thing and been family for her, since her mother doesn't seem to have been much good, as far as I can see."

Donald sighed and leant back in the chair. "Well, I think your mum was probably right to leave well enough alone. I think it's far more likely they would have been shocked to discover their father was an adulterer and I doubt they would have welcomed the illegitimate offspring of such an adulterous relationship."

Rhona thought about that for a moment or two. "Yeah, well, you're probably right."

"How do you think you'd feel in that position?"

"Yeah, that's more or less what Mum said." Rhona slumped down a bit. "It's just, well, they'd sort of be my relations too. Here's me, trying to trace my family tree, trying to find out about my family, and there's a whole branch of it, fallen off, just sitting there waiting to be found."

"More like, sitting there not knowing they're lost."

"But what puzzles me more than all that, is the fact that Mum had already changed her name before she found out about her real father. The name on her birth certificate was not the name she'd been known by nor the name she changed to."

"No," Donald said, scratching his head, his brow folding along the frown lines. "That was a puzzle to me at first too."

"Did you ever ask her?"

He nodded. "Oh, I don't remember now." He began to get up to make the breakfast. "I think she said something about wanting a fresh start."

"A fresh start? Why would she need a fresh start?"

"Well, she'd moved to Edinburgh, got her first job, her first wee flat, everything was new. She maybe just wanted a new name too."

"But, don't you find that a bit of a weird thing to do? I mean, people don't usually go to all the bother of changing their names when they move house or get a new job."

"No."

"It got me thinking and that's when I came up with this." She pointed to her iPad. "I researched into electoral rolls and trades' registers and stuff for Mum's dad, or, at least, who she thought was her dad. She told me he owned a string of shops."

"That's right." Donald sat down again. He shook his head. "You just don't give up, do you?"

"Well, he seems to have been doing great with his shops and they lived in a big house just outside Glasgow, then, as far as I can gather, the business seemed to flounder a bit and they moved out of the city to Kirkintilloch when Mhairi was about ten years old."

She looked to Donald for confirmation, but his shrug indicated this was news to him. "Did Mum never say about living in Kirkintilloch before she moved to Edinburgh?"

"No, but she wouldn't, because…"

"Because?"

"She didn't. I just mean, she didn't."

Rhona looked at him and pursed her lips. "Okay. Well, I then searched for William Anderson's name in newspaper archives from that sort of time, thinking I might find something about what happened to his business." She paused for dramatic effect.

Donald leant forward.

"And that was when I found this." She turned the iPad screen to him.

"What am I supposed to be looking at?"

"You're supposed to be looking at that article right there." She pointed it out. "And I can zoom in a bit to make it easier to read. I know it's a bit blurry, but there, see, where it says, 'Anderson Empire Struggling Following Family Scandal.' Can you read it okay?"

Donald took the iPad and read the article.

"So," Rhona said. "What do you know about the family scandal? And do you know where Mum comes into it?"

The article was in the financial section of the newspaper, so it concentrated on the effects the scandal had on William Anderson's business empire, which was so much more than the chain of shops he owned. Apparently, he also owned property in and around the city and an investment company. It was the investment company that had failed in the first instance, creating a domino effect which resulted in the fall of his clothing empire too. 'Loss of trust' was cited as part of the cause. After Anderson's family scandal, the public took their investment elsewhere, withdrawing their funds and demanding their profits. His shops were avoided, the article claimed. His name was tarnished, associated with gossip and reproach.

"I don't know as much about it as I thought," Donald said. "But, by the date of this newspaper, your mum was no longer affected by what was happening."

"She might not have realised what was happening," Rhona said. "But it must have affected her. It says the family moved house to try to disassociate themselves from the scandal."

"Yes." Donald sighed. "But your mum wasn't still living at home by then."

Rhona frowned. "What do you mean? Mum would only have been about ten when this newspaper came out.'

"Yes. She was in a Home, an Institution, by then."

"What? What d'you mean she was in a Home?"

"I mean, she was brought up in an Institution after that."

"But I don't understand. She said she lived in a big house outside Glasgow." Rhona put her hands to her mouth. "Oh, is that what she meant? Did she mean an orphanage? But that's awful! How could they put her in an orphanage? She wasn't an orphan."

"Not an orphanage. An Institution. A Home for the Mentally Unstable."

"What!" Rhona stared at her father, open-mouthed. "Mum is one of the most mentally stable people I know. She's what people call 'grounded.'" She shook her head. "I don't understand. She was only ten."

"She was eight when they put her away." Donald got up from the table and put the kettle on.

"How could they do that? Was it a breakdown or something?"

He walked through to the living room and sat in his armchair.

Rhona started to follow him through. "Was she ill? Was it like a hospital."

Donald closed his eyes. Too late to turn back. "An asylum," he said, rubbing his forehead, the word a betrayal.

"An asylum?"

"Yes." There was no way to soften it. No way to make it sound better than it was. "An asylum." Donald closed his eyes, reluctant to look at his daughter's face. "Your mother was locked away. Out of sight, out of mind."

"What d'you mean 'locked away?'"

"Just that." He sighed. "She did seem to have some kind of breakdown, as far as I can gather. Punched her nurse in the face, knocked her unconscious, injured a maid, broke up her room, went berserk, by the sound of it."

"Why?"

Donald shrugged. "I suppose they didn't know what to do with her, so they locked her up."

"Are you saying it was okay to cart an eight-year-old child off to a lunatic asylum?"

"No, I'm telling you what I remember of your mother's story. She 'lost the place' and was sedated and stretchered off to a loony-bin."

"But why? Mum's not a lunatic. I can't imagine she ever was."

"I told you, she 'lost the plot', 'went berserk', whatever you want to call it."

"This is unbelievable." Rhona had followed him to the living room but was standing in the doorway, poised to make the tea when the kettle had boiled, but now she sat in the chair opposite, a frown creasing her brow. "I just don't understand. Was it just a tantrum, do you think? Did they overreact?"

Donald shrugged. "More than a tantrum, I think. It went on for days."

"For days?"

"Yeah, I can't remember now what your mum said, but I think she said three days. They'd locked her in her room, you see, for some minor misdemeanour, and she got desperate. Went crazy."

"This is awful. I can't believe they would lock a child in her bedroom for three days."

"I think that's what she said."

"And I can't believe any parents would allow their wee girl to be taken away and locked up in a place like that. I've been in a mental hospital when I visited my friend's mum with her. It was horrible. Everyone was just sitting staring at the television. It was so depressing. We took her out for a walk in the grounds."

Donald laughed, a dry mirthless laugh. "Yeah! That might not have been so bad. But back when your mum was a kid, they weren't hospitals, they were more like prisons. There was no recreation room, no televisions. I doubt there'd be a radio." He swallowed, remembering some of the things Mhairi had told him. "Your Mum says she was mostly locked into a tiny room, with only a bed and a window high up the wall. She couldn't see out, it was so high." He shook his head, the words sounding unreal to his own ears. "She was never outside in the fresh air the whole time she was there."

"Oh, poor Mum." Rhona reached for the box of tissues. "It sounds barbaric," she said, blowing her nose. "I'm finding this too much to take in. I can't equate it with Mum. It's like a bad film."

"But it wasn't." He looked up at her. "It was what happened to your mum."

"But it's horrendous."

"Yes."

"No wonder she hates locked doors."

"Yes."

"How long was she in that place? You said she wouldn't have been with the family when they moved. That was two years later. You're not telling me they locked a child away for two years!" Rhona's eyes burned like lasers.

They were caught in a lava flow of horror upon horror. With each sentence he uttered, Donald felt scorched, seared with the enormity of what he was saying.

After all these years, the reality of Mhairi's past was punching Donald in the gut. Watching the effect of the facts on his daughter, her disbelief, her shock, was affecting his perception of them in a way that Mhairi's tearful, matter-of-fact recounting had not. When Mhairi had told him her story, he had listened, but as a man listens, with an eye on the part where he could be the hero. He had offered to take her father to court, to demand compensation for the years of her unjust incarceration. He hadn't felt her pain. Had heard her story the way he heard anybody's else's statement. As a lawyer, not a friend. Not a lover.

Swallowing, shocked at what he was saying, "She never saw her family again," he said. "She was locked away for thirteen years." The enormity of it. The injustice. The cruelty.

"Thirteen years!" Rhona's eyes were wide, shock burning in them. "Thirteen years? You can't be serious. Tell me you're not serious?"

"She didn't cross the threshold of that place till she was twenty-one." Donald had a sudden image of the famous painting, 'The Scream,' by Edvard Munch. Munch described how one evening, as the sun was setting, and the clouds were turning blood red, 'I sensed a scream passing through nature,' he said. 'It seemed to me that I heard the scream.'

It seemed to Donald he heard that same scream. *'Der Schrei der Natur,* The Scream of Nature.' Looking at the disbelief, the horror in Rhona's eyes, the affront of it came home to him. It was an affront to nature. Unnatural. Mhairi had tried to tell him how it felt, and he realised now, all he had heard were cold facts. Until now, he hadn't heard the scream.

He collapsed in on himself, clutching his heart and his stomach. How could he not have felt her pain. All these years, she must have lived with a scream in her belly and he didn't notice.

There was a break in the time-continuum and he was holding Mhairi in his arms. He had proposed to her and she wanted him to know her story before she agreed to marry him. He only wanted her to be his. His body had ached for her. His whole being had ached for her. She had tried to let him hear the scream and he had been so busy wanting her he hadn't listened.

When she cried, he held her close. 'It's all right. It all happened such a long time ago. You can forget it now.' Forget it. How could she forget it? How could she ever forget it? She must have lived every day of her life with a scream in her belly.

"Dad? Are you all right?" Rhona was kneeling by his chair. "Is it your heart?" She started dialling on her mobile phone.

"No," he croaked. He cleared his throat and tried again. "It's okay. I'm okay." He pushed the mobile away. "I just need a minute." It was the pain. Searing blinding pain piercing through his belly as it must have pierced his beloved Mhairi's. The scream.

He tried to straighten up.

"No, just sit there, Dad. Here." She placed a cushion under his head and tried to make him more comfortable. "We'll have a hot drink, then I think you should go back to bed."

Rhona made them a cup of tea and they sat in silence as they drank it.

"We'll find her, love," Donald said as he stood to take his cup to the kitchen. "We'll find her. And we'll cherish her. Make her feel safe again."

Rhona's face contorted and she began to cry. "Oh, Dad, what she must have gone through."

He tried to comfort her. Heard his voice utter the same platitudes, "There, there, it's all right. It all happened such a long time ago." Stopped himself. "No, you're right. It must have been a living hell."

early tuesday morning
mhairi

It had been a living hell. Like being buried alive.

Mhairi woke with her life replaying in her mind as though she had left the tele on last night.

The years of emptiness, unhappiness and pain.

She could see herself, a child, lost and abandoned, standing by a window. Not her bedroom window — the one she had tried to climb out of — a new window, high up the wall. She couldn't look out of it, it was so high. It gave little light. She could see a slither of blue sky if she stood back from it: a slither of blue at the top. There were bars outside the window: strong metal bars, rounded, black paint peeling off. They didn't help the light get through. The room was small, dark. She had tried to put the light on, but nothing happened when she flicked the switch. She needed the toilet but, when she tried the door, it was locked. Looking round and under the narrow bed, she found the potty. Not her potty, the dark green china one with the chip in the rim that scratched if you moved too quickly. This one was metal. White enamelled, with a dark blue rim. Her pee made a different noise. It tinkled. Nice.

She went back to bed. There was nothing else to do. The room had no other furnishings. A bed and a potty. That was all. She didn't know it then, but that was 'home' for a long time, until she was considered docile enough to move into one of the twenty-bedded wards. Home: a locked door, a barred window, a bed and a potty. The lights automatically cut out some time in the evening and came on with sudden, blinding brightness in the morning. She grew to prefer the darkness.

At first, the door was seldom opened: at mealtimes; for the Doctor to enter, syringe in hand to give her medication, and once a week for the orderly to take her for a bath.

As she lay in the comfort of a warm room in a B&B in Ratho, she shivered.

It had always been cold. The clean clothes they lay out beside the bath for her to put on were not her clothes. They were thin and worn and rarely fitted. Laundered and starched, they were scratchy and uncomfortable. It took most of the week for them to begin to soften, then they were replaced and the whole business of breaking in fresh clothes began again.

Pulling the soft sheets and duvet round her, she remembered with a shudder the fresh, cold, starched sheets that awaited her when she returned to the room after bathing. 'Cleanliness is next to Godliness,' she was told when she asked to hold on to the softer, week-worn clothes she was to take off for her bath one evening. There was a semblance of Cleanliness in her surroundings but no Godliness that she ever found. Thirteen years in God-forsaken incarceration.

When she was moved into the ward, she thought she'd found hell. Solitary confinement turned out to have been heaven by comparison. Instead of being left with her own thoughts, her private space, albeit lonely, she was thrown into noise and chaos.

Some of the women in the ward were well on their way to insanity, some of them had reached it. They were not permitted to converse, and Mhairi doubted some of them would be capable of conversation, yet they were far from silent. Nights were punctuated by snores and screams, whimpering and wild laughter. Some of her fellow inmates didn't sleep at all, wandering the ward muttering, crying or shouting, unnerving her as they loomed in the darkness by her bed, picking at her thin blanket or stealing her shoes. Days, spent mostly working in the laundry or the kitchen, accompanied again with grunts and screams, hissed threats and manic laughter.

Often, fights would break out over some imagined insult or other, and Mhairi usually managed to stay clear of them, but, one day, she found herself in the thick of it just by being there, in the dormitory.

'Whit you lookin' at?' Babs spat at her. 'Want some o' this, do ye?' She showed Mhairi her fist.

Mhairi shook her head and turned away from the feuding women.

Too late.

Babs decided Mhairi wanted the fist after all and swung it at the side of her head, knocking her to the floor, whereupon Babs jumped astride her and set about pummelling her face.

Turning her body to evade the blows, Mhairi struggled and bucked, eventually managing to squirm from under Babs, pushing her off balance, and Babs' head hit the floor with a thump, giving Mhairi her opportunity.

By the time she scrabbled to her feet, the orderly had arrived to sort out the trouble, found Babs in a dazed state, Mhairi covered in blood, and decided on the spot that Mhairi was the instigator.

Joy of joys, after three years of the ward, Mhairi found herself back in solitary confinement in her little cell, and there she stayed for the rest of her incarceration.

Babs spent a brief interlude in the 'room' next door and Mhairi could hear her at regular intervals, shouting for her release, which request was eventually granted and Babs was returned to the ward.

Mhairi was not.

Perhaps there was a God after all, and he had heard her daily plea when she was in the ward, 'Please God, get me out of here.'

Perhaps Babs had not been convicted of murder.

mhairi
tuesday
the circle of life

As a child, she had been taught to fear God. He was all-powerful and she thought perhaps he was the keeper of the keys.

She had little on which to base any other opinion of him, since she had never been to Church or Sunday School, though the Institution claimed affiliation to the Church of Scotland.

When she and Donald were getting married, Ruth insisted the ceremony take place in the Church she attended. 'God knows,' she had said with a sniff of disapproval. 'You're going to need His blessing.'

Mhairi had gone along for a few weeks beforehand to familiarise herself with the place and the practice. The building, she found intimidating and joyless, the services dull and ritualistic, and, after the wedding, she had no desire to visit it, or any other Church, again.

But she did try to read the Bible.

She didn't understand much of what she read and wished someone would sit with her, study it with her, explain it to her. The language being old and out of date didn't help. Jesus seemed a good man and she warmed to him, reading the gospel accounts often over the years, wishing she had know about them when she was in her teens. Back then, she could have done with the comfort they always brought her.

With a sigh for things that might have been, for things that could have been, and for things that were, Mhairi pulled her thoughts back to the present, and, finding a Gideon's

Bible in the bedside drawer in the bedroom of the B&B in Ratho, she sat up in bed and read a few chapters of the Book of Matthew before her thoughts made themselves heard above the calming words.

Perhaps it had been unwise to run. Perhaps she could have deflected Rhona from further research. Helped her see that having names and dates was enough. There was no need to delve further, look for more. Even as she thought it, she knew the argument was flawed. Rhona smelled a story. It would take more than Mhairi's powers of persuasion to convince her to leave it untold. Already, Mhairi knew she had made things worse. The more she showed fear and reluctance, the more Rhona had pushed these past weeks. Had Mhairi been better able to hide her fear, things might have been different, but it had risen in her gullet like bile, bitter and unbidden. From the first moment Rhona had mentioned what she planned to do, Mhairi had lost control of any semblance of equanimity.

No, she had done the right thing to run. It would be better. Having endured so much indignity in her life, she saw no reason to volunteer for more now as her daughter uncovered her past.

Washed, dressed and breakfasted, Mhairi reached the road again shortly after ten o'clock. She headed West, as she had yesterday, following the canal path today, with no set destination in mind. It just seemed the way to go. 'The Circle of Life,' the song called it. She originated in the West, and despite the horror of her life there, it was claiming her back.

The song was in her head now and she hummed it as she walked, remembering the day she and Rhona took the children to see the film it was from. What was it called again? Not 'The Circle of Life.' That was the song. It was an animated film. About animals. She snapped her fingers, pleased with herself. 'The Lion King.' That was it. They had gone for a burger meal first, a real treat for the children, a real sacrifice for Rhona and Mhairi. Then they had popcorn and pick-a-mix sweets in the Cinema. Mhairi laughed to herself. How those children weren't sick, she didn't know.

It was young Michael's treat. He had passed his cycling proficiency test and had been promised he could choose the reward.

Such memories are always accompanied by poignant yearnings for the childhood of your children and grandchildren, Mhairi knew that. The days when you were an important person in their lives. The days when they would throw their arms around you and declare how much they loved you, that they would never leave you, that they couldn't live without you. But they did leave you, they did manage without you. They grew up. It was 'The Circle of Life.'

Shaking her head to clear it of sentimentality, she strode out with greater purpose in her legs than in her mind. Glad of the sharp, crisp November chill, she turned her thoughts to other things. Her route, her toilet stops, her food stops and her overnight stops. Focus on the mundane. Focus on the mundane.

Walking alongside the canal was easy, the path was flat and the scenery was amazing. The information at the Canal Centre in Ratho had told her, 'the Union Canal simply contours its way across the countryside at a constant height of 73 metres above sea level which makes for many bizarre direction changes.'

Another sunny November day, the sky blue and mostly cloudless, the trees showing off the last of their russets and browns, greens and yellows in a continuous mannequin parade either side of the canal. At the start of her walk, she was accompanied by a family of swans. She passed ducks and drakes, geese and waterfowl, noting they hadn't all migrated South yet, though some of them surely had. There had been great, ragged v-shaped gaggles of geese in the sky yesterday, squabbling and noisy. She kept up a good pace, not allowing herself to linger to birdwatch as she would when walking purely for pleasure.

Yesterday, she had the Pentland Hills in the distance to keep her company. They had looked gorgeous, with a white frosting of snow on top, and blue sky complimenting their greens and browns. Today, she had outwalked them and the M8 motorway ran parallel for part of the way. She could hear its noise in the distance, like a comforting rumble of continuity: life continuing on without a hiccup though she was stepping out for a moment. It reminded her of when the children were young and she was making the dinner in the kitchen, accompanied by the steady flow of presenters' voices on Blue Peter while they watched television in the sitting room.

Gradually, the tranquility of her immediate surroundings blocked out the distant sounds of traffic until she was no longer conscious of it. Taking the canal path had been a stroke of genius. It was flat, level walking, virtually noiseless and free of decisions. Once she was on it, there were no choices to make other than which bench to rest on, which view to admire, and occasionally, whether to stop and share any visitor attractions she passed.

One she detoured to, quite soon after leaving Ratho, was the Edinburgh International Climbing Centre. She'd spotted a 'Climbing Arena' signpost yesterday, and, on discovering it was above the canal, she couldn't resist clambering up a steep, muddy flight of steps to have a look. She'd heard Katie talking about it and she knew Katie and Michael both went there from time to time, which increased her curiosity to see it.

What she found was a quarry which had been completely roofed-over & encased in a glass building five-storeys high to create an amazing climbing arena, 'the largest facility of its kind in the world,' Katie had told her, pride in her voice. It was impressive and surprisingly busy for a weekday morning.

Her curiosity satisfied, she didn't linger but descended the steps and rejoined her route, wondering as she walked, if 'indoor' climbing might it be like 'indoor walking' on a treadmill, though it did look rather more interesting and a lot of fun. She must ask Michael and Katie when she told them she had visited it, albeit only from outside peeping in.

A feeling of peace and calm was relaxing her, freeing her of anxiety and fear and she chose to ignore the distant nag that, unless she returned home, she might never see her grandchildren again to ask them anything. There was no room in her head to linger with that thought if she was to retain her sanity.

The wind was against her. She could see by the bend of the trees that she was walking into the prevailing wind. Her face tingled and stung, reminding her to use her heavier night cream tomorrow to protect her skin. Then she remembered she hadn't brought things like that. Hadn't thought in terms of looking after herself. All she'd been thinking of was traveling light and moving fast. Since she was heading for Linlithgow, she might buy a few things there tomorrow. After all, there can be no hurry when you're going nowhere in particular, and no reason not to look after your skin.

The canal snaked back on itself as it flowed through Broxburn and then headed over the River Almond on the Almond Aqueduct. From there she had a great view downvalley to the 36-arch Almond Valley Railway Viaduct, and she paused there for a while to enjoy it and reflect on the fact that this was fast becoming so much more than the flight she had planned. She had expected to be struggling, not with the walk, but with her feelings and her thoughts, but walking was a healer, and she found to her surprise, she could turn her thoughts to her surroundings and just enjoy being out and about.

Her route took her past the huge red-green mounds of slag-heaps, 'bings', of discarded material, the residue of the world's original oil industry, shale oil from the local shale mines. It had been a very lucrative Victorian enterprise and she remembered reading about it in a book about the explorer David Livingston, of all people. It was one of his friends, James Young, another Scotsman, who pioneered it. These geometrically shaped heaps of the industry's refuse dominated the landscape for miles and she couldn't help smiling, noting that they had begun to look quite attractive as Mother Nature dressed them in green lace, their red showing through like an underskirt.

She stopped only to take an occasional mouthful of water or eat a few of her stash of dried fruit and nuts, resting on a bench for a few minutes every hour or so.

It had been a few years since she and Donald had last done any serious walking, mostly due to the fact that his mother's health had deteriorated and she had become quite a demanding patient; demanding that her son dance attendance on her. The journey back and forth between Edinburgh and Glasgow several times a week for more than a year, and every day for the past three months, meant that Donald had no desire to be anywhere but by his own hearth and television once he got home.

Mhairi missed the weekend excursions they used to take, when they would choose a hill walk, throw everything into the car and head out with minimum fuss and maximum pleasure. They must have walked to the top of almost every accessible hill within a considerable radius of Edinburgh.

Today her feet and legs were reminding her it had been too long since their last outing. Strange, Mhairi reflected, how easy it is to assume you're keeping fit just by being active in your daily life, only to find you are far from fit when called upon to do a bit more than usual.

Before setting off again after one of her breaks, she had to massage her calf muscles. They had stiffened up in the few minutes she had been stationary and were threatening to cramp. She was aiming to get as far as Linlithgow today, hopefully before it got dark, but she knew her pace was slowing as her muscles complained about the extra work being asked of them.

A few years break from hillwalking may not have had such a devastating effect on her fitness when she was younger, but she supposed it was inevitable it should take a greater toll at her age. They weren't getting any younger, she and Donald. Mhairi laughed out loud at the banal cliche. 'I mean, really,' she said out loud. 'Who is getting younger? Point them out to me. I'd like to meet them.'

They had expected to grow old together.

Without warning, the poignancy of the thought caught at Mhairi's throat, choking her. Pain shot across her chest and she clutched at it, doubled over, coughing, spluttering, crying. Oh, it hurt so much.

They had expected to grow old together.

When she tried to straighten up she felt a knife driven into her solar plexus.

It was nobody's fault but her own that they wouldn't get that opportunity now. When she ran away from the past, she ran from the future too.

Lowering herself onto the grass verge beside the path, she bowed over the pain until it subsided and she was able to uncoil and try to stretch the last of it out. But it hurt, oh, how it hurt.

Having rummaged in her pocket till she found a tissue, she dried her face, blew her nose, and composed herself. Getting to her feet and straightening up, she took a few deep breaths and resumed walking, but she had been dealt a body blow and her legs felt weaker and shaky.

One thing for sure: she could not afford to allow thoughts like that to sneak up on her. She would have to be on guard. She drew herself up and forced her legs to stop trembling.

But, now she had allowed the thought in, she couldn't seem to push it out.

They expected to grow old together.

Neither of them had looked at anyone else. In all the years of their marriage, they had been faithful to each other. She wondered how many couples could claim that. They had been faithful and loyal.

Well, she had anyway. Where was Donald's loyalty when he betrayed her, when he shared her private business with his mother? He may not have been unfaithful to his marriage vows, but he had been unfaithful to her nonetheless.

Ah! That was better. These are the thoughts that made walking away easier. It wasn't her usual style, to focus on negative things, but she decided to indulge in it until the pain in her chest subsided and she could think of her husband without fear of breaking down again.

rhona
tuesday

Rhona hadn't gone to bed. She had dozed a couple of hours on the couch where she sat with a blanket over her, but, mostly, she had searched the internet to find her mother.

When Donald came downstairs before six o'clock and she told him she hadn't been to bed, he asked if that was wise. Health-wise, she doubted it, since she now felt sick and disoriented as well as stiff and sore, but she had been unable to stop searching. Oh, she knew she wasn't any closer to finding her mother in the geographic sense, but, it seemed imperative to find her in the sense of getting to know and understand her better. Funny, if anyone had asked her a few weeks ago if she was close to her mum, she would have answered, 'Yes, we're very close. She's my best friend.' But now she knew it wasn't true. Mhairi was a stranger: she knew nothing about her.

When Donald went to lie down for another hour or two, Rhona pulled the rug over her on the couch and tried to rest too, but her mind whirred with mental images of her mother as a young child in a lunatic asylum.

There had to be something else. Rhona couldn't see how Mhairi's parents could possibly get away with leaving their child to rot in such a place with such a flimsy excuse as a tantrum or two. There had to be more. It wasn't long before Rhona gave up on the attempt to rest and opened her iPad again to resume where she'd left off.

When Donald reappeared, she realised she was ravenously hungry. Folding the blanket and putting it away again in the old wooden storage chest that also served as a coffee table, she stretched out her back and rubbed her legs before following Donald through to the kitchen to get some breakfast. "I was looking some more things up online." She sat at the kitchen table and pushed her iPad towards him. "There's more," she said.

Donald put some bread in the toaster, filled the kettle and set it to boil, then lifted the iPad. Another old newspaper account, much like the one they'd read earlier. "Where, or how, did you find this?" he asked.

"On Google News. You can access archives of old newspapers there. Did you know the Herald Scotland newspaper used to be called The Glasgow Herald?"

He nodded as he read. "Mmm-hmm!"

"I thought that might be the best place to look for the Anderson family scandal. I've not uncovered it all yet. It's not particularly easy trawling through the archives when you don't know what you're looking for, or when it happened."

"But you found this." Donald held up the iPad.

"Yes. It seems to be the same information about the business being in difficulty, but, as you can see, the references to the scandal are stronger."

"It's talking about a death and an enquiry."

"Yes."

"But nobody died. When your mum told me the story, she said the nanny and the maid both gave evidence at the enquiry. She had knocked the nanny out, hit her over the head with a great heavy wooden tray, if I remember rightly, but the stupid woman had recovered enough to give damning evidence against your mum and get her locked up."

"Well, according to this newspaper report, someone died."

"And your mum got the blame?"

"It's looking like it."

Donald read the article again. It wasn't very long and looked like an addendum to an earlier article. "Mister William Anderson accepted culpability on his daughter's behalf. You bet he damn well did. The sod wanted rid of her." He tossed the iPad back to Rhona.

She caught it as it skidded across the table. "Careful, Dad! This is not the actual newspaper, you know."

"Sorry, love, but really, what a cad! The man should have been locked up himself."

"I wonder who died?"

"Right. I'll make you some tea and toast and you keep searching. That is, unless you want to lie down and get some kip now? You didn't even rest, did you?"

"Too fired up," she said, stretching her arms and yawning.

"You sure about that?"

"Yup! But think it'll need to be coffee instead of tea. I'm about cross-eyed looking at these old newspapers online. Don't know if you've noticed but the print was small enough to begin with, never mind trying to read it on-line on an iPad. And my arms are in agony from holding it up all night. In fact, at one point, my hands went numb and I couldn't hold the blessed thing any longer." She examined her hands, turning them over and back. "At least the colour's returned to them now. They were pure white. Didn't half hurt when the blood came back into them."

"Would it not be easier if you did it on the computer upstairs?"

"Much. I did think of it at one point, but I didn't want to disturb you."

"You wouldn't have disturbed me, pet. Once my head hits the pillow, that's me. Sleep like a baby, I do."

"Yeah! A baby revving up a motorbike!" It had been Donald's snoring that had helped her stay awake. Every time she felt herself doze off on the couch, the rhythm would change with a particularly loud snore and she would jump to attention again. "I don't remember your snoring being as bad as that when we were kids."

"Probably because I don't snore."

"Oh, my mistake!" Rhona said, tossing him the most sceptical look her weary face could muster. "It must've been a baby revving up a motorbike right enough."

"Sleep like a baby, I do," he repeated.

"Yeah, right!" She got up from the table with a sigh. "Okay if I use the computer now then?"

"Be my guest."

"I'll go and get it fired up." She turned in the doorway. "Okay if I have my breakfast upstairs?"

"I'll bring your coffee and toast up soon as."

"Thanks, Dad. You're a treasure."

donald

While Donald was buttering toast, there was a knock on the back door. "It's open," he called.

"Morning! Thought I'd look in on my way to do a job. Any news?"

"Oh, morning, Steve. No, no news. Rho's upstairs on your old computer if you want to go up. Fancy a bit of toast and a cuppa?"

"Thanks, don't mind if I do. Smelled it as I came in the door. Irresistible — toast — eh?"

With a smile and a nod, Donald put more bread in the toaster, took another mug out of the cupboard and finished buttering the toast that was ready. No sooner had he assembled and carried the laden tray up for Rhona and Steve, than he heard the back door again as he re-entered the kitchen.

It was Dave and Sally this time.

"Not at work?" Donald asked as he and Dave had a brief man-hug.

"Took compassionate leave," Dave said. "Told them my mother's ill, which, technically speaking, isn't really a lie. She has to be slightly sick in the head to go walking in this weather. It's freezing cold out there."

"Don't talk about your mother like that. She's not sick in the head, she's distressed, but that doesn't make her sick, any more than you're sick in the head, coming all this way when there's nothing to tell you."

"Okay, okay, Dad. Didn't mean to upset anyone. Just a joke."

Donald accepted the apology with a nod and a grunt and refilled the kettle. "I suppose you'll be looking for a cuppa too?"

"Mmm, yes please," Ewan said rubbing warmth back into his hands. "And is that toast I smell? Irresistible!" He went through to the living room, leaving Donald buttering the next lot of toast and putting yet more bread in the toaster.

"Rhona's upstairs," Donald shouted after him. "And Steve."

"Yeah, saw the van."

Sally came back from hanging their coats in the hall cupboard. "Thanks, Donald." She gave him a peck on the cheek. "You okay?"

"Yes, love, I'm fine. Rhona stayed last night. It was late after we'd done all the phone calls and everything."

"You must be worried sick."

"Well, yes and no. Course I'm worried. I'd like to find her, make sure she's all right, but I think I know she is all right, physically anyway. Dave told you she's kitted out with her hillwalking gear?"

"Yes. Rhona phoned last night."

"So, she obviously planned her walkabout. It's unlikely that anything happened to her, so I'm sure she'll be safe enough. I just wish she'd let us know. I just wish she'd phone. Or, even better, come home."

Sally took the cup of tea he'd made her and took a sip. "So what's next?"

He shrugged. "Not sure, really. Could do with a plan of action but not really got one."

"Maybe we could help. You know, 'in the multitude of counsellors' and all that."

"Good idea, pet. Tell you what, you go and fetch them down for a strategy meeting."

mhairi

She didn't really have a strategy. There hadn't been time to do much planning. One day she was writing her shopping list and cooking and cleaning for the special family day on Sunday, the next thing she knew, she'd made the decision to walk out of her life on the Monday. All the planning had consisted of, was emptying her bank account, then grabbing a few provisions and heading out the door after Donald left for Glasgow. Not her usual style.

Usually, Mhairi was a meticulous planner. Not much was left to chance. A list maker extraordinaire, the family called her, and she was: holiday packing lists were taped to the inside lids of the suitcases; weekend walking lists were in the pockets of the rucksacks; her cleaning schedule was taped to the inside of the cleaning cupboard door, and her shopping list and a pen lay in the top of the kitchen drawer beside her food diary where she kept a note of what they ate each day and what she planned to cook during the next week. To-do lists, appointment lists, remember-to-tell lists, if there was something that had to be done, something that had to be remembered, Mhairi would have it on one of her lists. Donald used to tease her that she even had a list of all her lists. He thought it was a joke.

It felt strange to be adrift, without plan or purpose, so, one foot in front of the other was orderly and oddly comforting, as were the long, straight stretches of the canal path. Straightforward. She had no decisions to make, just keep walking straight forward.

Decisions were always difficult. How did you know when you were making the right one? She had grown up in an environment where all decisions were made for her: what she ate; when she ate; the clothes she wore; when her hair should be cut; when her toenails should be cut; when she should take her medication; when she should go to sleep; when she should wake up, and even, when she should empty her bowels. All dictated, all decided with no input from her.

When she walked out of the Mental Deficiency Facility, she stood outside in the old coat that had been chosen for her, wearing old, badly fitting shoes that had been chosen for her with no idea where she was going to go or how she was going to get there. The warden had handed her a list, the first list she had ever seen. It was a list of bus times. That and the envelope her father had sent her, made up her possessions. The envelope contained a letter, a bank book and some money. The letter informed her she must not return to Glasgow, so even the choice of which direction to take had been decided for her.

There was a bus stop nearby and she boarded the bus for Edinburgh, paying for her ticket with the money that had been provided by her father, taken from the envelope and placed in her pocket by the warden. The first money she had ever handled.

Looking back, it seemed incredible that anyone could reach the age of twenty-one without ever having handled money. Ever.

Everything she knew of the world she was entering, she had learned from books. Once a week, one of the trustees came round with a book trolley. Once a week, her door was unlocked and she was handed a book. One book each week. Often the same book she had read a few weeks before. Some of them she had read so often, she was word perfect if anyone had cared to test her on it.

There had been no radio, no television, no music, no conversation. She used to read out loud just to hear someone's voice.

Having the peace to read was a luxury that she had appreciated when in solitary confinement. It more than compensated for the lack of human contact. Her room was cold, bare and unwelcoming, but it was quiet, and while there was enough light, she could read.

The engine of the bus was an assault to her ears. At first, she thought she would be unable to bear it, but gradually, her ears became accustomed to its constant hum and to the occasional chatter of the bus driver and the conductor as passengers entered or exited the vehicle. It was different with the bell. There was no becoming accustomed to the bell. Every time the conductor pressed it, Mhairi jumped, expecting the next part of the day's routine to start. She hated bells.

When she was twelve years old, she had been taken to work in the laundry every day, working alongside seven other girls, but they were not permitted to talk. A bell rang for them to be taken from their rooms and a bell rang for them to start work. Another signalled the start of their short lunch-break, another its end. The bell at the end of the day was the only one she welcomed.

It had been a shock to her to see people come and go as they pleased when she found her little flat-that-wasn't-a-flat-but-a-bedsit that her landlady called a flat so that she could charge for a flat. Agnes, the girl from the flat-that-wasn't-a-flat upstairs used to come thundering down the stairs every morning in a crazy, mad rush, 'Hi,' she'd say as she passed on the landing. 'Sorry, have to dash. Late for work.' The concept of being late was unbelievably alien to Mhairi.

Finding work became her priority. Not having dealt with money before had been a drawback for the first few days, but she quickly worked out that the small amount of money she had at her disposal was not going to last very long. Sitting on her bed one evening, she studied the coins and notes in her purse and worked out what each was worth in relation to the other. Such a basic thing, but essential that she learn it.

Her whole education had been basic, the formal part of it ceasing when she was eight years old. Since her father, in his testimony to the enquiry, had claimed she was incapable of receiving benefit from school instruction, the authorities gave her none. Her education consisted of only what she could glean from the books that were handed to her. There wasn't much she didn't know about Nicholas Nickleby or Oliver Twist, and she had a great working knowledge of Dickensian London from their stories, but she knew that would not stand her in great stead in 1960's Edinburgh.

The library became her favourite place to visit. After walking the streets, in and out of Employment Agencies, shops and offices most of the day, she would seek refuge in the Public Lending Library down Leith Walk and set about her education. History, Geography, Science unfolded before her with all the wonder of a long withheld gift. Carrying home an armful of books, she'd continue her studies in the sparse, cold little flat-that-wasn't-really-a-flat when the library closed for the night.

Concentration was difficult, unaccustomed as she was to having to do any brain work. Years of enforced, unnecessary medication had not helped: she felt as though thinking ability had been systematically drugged out of her. Perseverance was rewarded with increased ability, and through time and practice, she found she began to make sense of the words she was reading, the things she was learning, and she grew hungry to know more.

By the time she found the job in Mister Foster's shop, she felt a little less ignorant of the world around her than she might have had she found employment earlier than the many months it took. Working in the shop, she learned how to speak to customers, how to work with figures as well as stock and her confidence began to grow a little.

Yet, she still had such a lot to learn and, when she started working with them, she felt great gratitude to Carol and Letty for teaching her so many things she could not have learned from books.

Carol and Letty.

Closing her eyes for a moment as her steps faltered, Mhairi wondered if they knew she had gone 'a wall,' as Letty called it. 'Though, what taking unauthorised leave has to do with a wall, I've never worked out,' Letty had said, shaking her head.

'AWL,' Carol said, spelling it out. 'It's AWL. Absent Without Leave. Or AWOL in the United States. Absent Without Official Leave.' Carol knew about these things because her sister had been walking out with a GI at the end of the war.

'Aaaah! I get it! Absent Without Leave.' Letty wrote the capitals in the air. 'That's clever, that is.'

Carol laughed, and Mhairi smiled. 'I hadn't known that, either,' she owned up, happy to have learned another incidental fact, something else to squirrel away in the hollow her lack of education had left.

Carol and Letty: true friends. Even when they no longer all worked in the same office, their friendship endured. When the children were young, they called them Auntie Carol and Letty, Letty refusing to be aged by the label. 'Just let them think of me as a big sister,' she said with a grin. Carol, on the other hand, loved being an honorary aunt and delighted to be the only aunt of any kind they had.

Donald would probably have phoned by now, to see if she was with them. A frown creased Mhairi's brow. She guessed they'd be worried. She shrugged. But what could she do? They'd get over it. They'd have to. 'Worse things happen at sea,' Letty would say. Mhairi laughed. No. What Letty would actually say was, 'Worse things happen to see.'

Carol was convinced Letty's hearing was dull and teased her mercilessly about it.

Oh! Another sharp stab of longing for her friends brought Mhairi up short again.

The last time she'd spoken with either of them was when they had their usual meet-up, and, over lunch, Mhairi had shared her iPad story with them. Although she hadn't told them the whole story, leaving out that it happened because she panicked, the fact that they laughed like the proverbial drain did nothing to assuage her anxiety at the time.

"Oh, come on, Mhairi, you have to confess it was funny," Carol said.

"I'd love to have seen Rhona's face as her precious iPack went skidding across the floor."

"It's not an iPack, Letty. It's an iPad."

"Just as well it happened in your kitchen, not hers," Letty said. "Especially if it was spraying coffee everywhere."

"D'you think she'll ever speak to you again?"

"Of course she will, " Mhairi said, though she hadn't been so sure that was a good thing — depending on the subject of the conversation.

The girls would have had their own conversations with Rhona and Donald by now. Letty would probably have suggested they call out the National Guard to find her. Carol would have been much more pragmatic, pointing out the police would hardly want to know about a fit, healthy pensioner taking off in a huff and going walkabout.

donald

"As I see it," Rhona said. "The first thing we need to decide is whether or not we involve the police.

"I don't think that's necessary," Ewan said straight away. "Nothing untoward has happened to Mum. She hasn't been kidnapped. She's gone walkabout."

"But perhaps the police could help us find her."

"Perhaps she doesn't need found," he reasoned. "Perhaps she's not lost."

"Of course she's lost."

"No. She's not lost. We just don't know where she is."

"Semantics, Ewan. We don't know where she is, ergo, she's lost."

"No, we don't know where she is, ergo, we don't know where she is. That's all. She knows where she is, ergo, she's not lost."

Sally had her hands over her ears. "Would you two listen to yourselves. Ergo this and ergo that. We have a crisis here and all you two are doing is batting words back and forth at one another."

Donald laid a hand on her arm. 'It's okay, pet. It's just their way of dealing with the upset. They don't mean anything by it. Comes of growing up with a lawyer for a dad."

After they had breakfasted together, Steve had dropped a kiss on Rhona's head and taken himself off to work. "Some of us can't afford to take a day off," he said, nodding good-naturedly towards Ewan.

"You need to get that boss of yours sorted out." Ewan, in turn, nodded towards Rhona.

"Yeah! Yeah!" she said. "Am I the only one who sees that we have to do something about this situation?"

They were sitting round the dining room table because Rhona reckoned the dining room would make a good incident room. "So, what do we think? Police or not?"

"Not," said Ewan.

"Not," Donald agreed. "I doubt they'd be interested anyway since she left of her own volition and is in no imminent danger,"

"That we know of," Rhona added.

Donald shook his head. "She's in no danger, love. She'll be fine. Got a good head on her shoulders has your mum."

"Okay." Rhona crossed 'Police' off her list. "Last seen?"

"Just after lunch, yesterday."

"Time?"

Donald thought about it. "Mmmm, about one-thirty, I'd say."

"Okay. One-thirty. It gets dark about what? Five, half-five?"

"More like half-four," Sally supplied.

Rhona shrugged. "Okay, let's say she could still carry on walking a bit after dark, assuming she was somewhere not too far from street lights. You don't think she'd go up the hills at this time of year, do you, Dad?"

"Naw!" He shook his head. "Naw! Can't see it. Too cold."

"So, that means she could have walked for what? Three? Four hours? How far could she get in three or four hours?"

"Assuming she took half an hour or so to get ready and leave the house, allowing for toilet breaks and a lunch break, she may only have had about three hours at most, walking at around... What d'you think, Dad? Three, four miles an hour?"

"Yeah, four, maybe. Your Mum likes to crack on."

"So that means she could have walked a good twelve miles or more." Rhona calculated. "Now, if we take a circle with home as the centre and a twelve-mile radius." She drew a circle on the map she'd smoothed out on the table in front of her. "Any thoughts which direction she might have taken, anyone?"

"Och, this is hopeless," Ewan said. "We don't even know that she walked at all."

"She's wearing her anorak and her walking boots."

"So? She could've got on a bus to go walking in the Borders, or Perthshire. She could've got a train to the Lake District. She could be in the Pentland Hills, the Ochils or the blooming Grampians for all we know. This is a pointless exercise."

Mhairi was on her feet, leaning across the table. "So what do you suggest? That we do nothing? That we just carry on with our lives as normal? Pretend nothing has happened? Mum's just popped out for a bit?"

Ewan leant forward in his chair, his face close to hers. "I don't know, but I know this," he indicated the map, the lists, Rhona's notes. "This is all a big waste of time. You're just playing at being a detective. It's stupid."

"And you're just being a big sulky kid. Just because you don't know what to do, you think we should do nothing."

"Darn right I think we should do nothing, if this is the best we can do."

"Would you two stop it!" Sally had to shout to be heard above their bickering. "You're both behaving like kids. Rhona, sit down and take a deep breath. Ewan, sit back and shut up."

They glared across the table at one another.

"Better," Sally said when they did what they were told and sat back in their chairs. "Now." She turned to Donald. "What do you think we should do?"

He got up rather wearily from his chair. "Well, you lot can do what you want, but I have to get ready to visit Gran."

"Oh, Gran!" Rhona said, putting her hand over her mouth. "Are you going to tell her?"

"Not if I can help it."

"But what about Mum?"

"What about her?"

"Do you not need to stay here and…and…"

"And what?" Donald said, not unkindly. "Rhona, love, there really isn't much we can do. Your Mum has taken herself off somewhere for a day or two, that's all. If she doesn't want us to know where she is, then we'll not find her. Meanwhile, if I don't go through to see your gran, she'll get herself in a state, have a heart attack or something and we'll have a funeral to go to."

mhairi

Ruth was not only a demanding patient, she had always been a demanding mother. Long before she became ill, she had demanded much of her son, playing the 'you're-all-I've-got' card to great effect, making him feel duty bound to visit regularly and uncomfortably guilty when he couldn't. Mhairi hated the hold she had over Donald, though also aware that her perception was clouded by the fact her own mother had disowned her as a child. They had polar opposite upbringings. Where Mhairi's mother had been distant and uncaring, she felt that Donald's must have been almost suffocating in her fierce possessiveness.

She had opted for something in between as mother to Rhona and Ewan. Her love for them was fierce and absolute, but she had reined it in, she had tried for a balanced display of love and affection rather than the cloying, clinging gush of sentimentality that Ruth favoured. Mhairi hoped her children knew they were loved, but she hoped they knew they were also free to be themselves and live their own lives. Donald had never been totally free. When he declared that he belonged to her and only to her, she had always known that a little bit of him could never leave his mother.

The words were read out of the Bible at their marriage ceremony, 'A man will leave his father and his mother and he will stick to his wife, and they will become one flesh'. Did Donald manage to do that? Did he really leave his mother? Or did he stick to her more than he ought to have? These were questions she had never asked before and she knew she was only asking them now because she had uncovered his treachery. On one level, she knew she was being unfair to him, especially when he couldn't make a defence. On another, she didn't care, feeling jaded and aggrieved. This was the direction her thinking needed to take to enable her feet to take the geographical direction she had chosen.

During the miles from Ratho to Linlithgow, she managed to stamp out her own sentimentality by focusing on Donald's faults. Fair, she knew it wasn't, but she hoped it would get her there before the light went.

donald

Donald didn't say anything about Mhairi's disappearance to his mother. In fact, he didn't say much of anything to her because she slept most of his visit and didn't recognise him when she woke. Instead, he spent some time tracking down the Consultant and talking with him.

"We think she's having a series of small strokes now. The medication we've had her on up till now doesn't seem to be doing the job any more and we've taken some more blood tests and ordered a scan. Until we get the results of those, I'm afraid there's not much else we can do other than what we're doing already."

He left the hospital feeling frustrated and confused. He really needed to talk to Mhairi. She was great at these times: great at helping him see what he should do, what he should ask, what he should say.

Sitting in the car, he slumped over the steering wheel, his shoulders shaking with huge sobs. Not for his mother. He had always done his best for her, she was in the care of people better qualified to care for her, but for the wife he had neglected to protect.

"Where are you, Mhairi? Where are you?" He wanted another chance. After forty-odd years of marriage, he was only learning now how to care for a wife.

As he pushed back from the steering wheel and turned on the ignition, he made a silent promise he'd do it better if he got a second chance.

It was as he drove along the M8, heading East, he had the thought that Mhairi might be heading West. Full circle: she might have in mind to come full circle. He left the motorway at Harthill Services and pulled the road map out of the glove compartment. What road would she take? She's dressed for walking, so, would she choose to go cross country literally, avoiding the main roads? Certainly couldn't be on the motorway, he could dismiss that one. What about the older roads? He stared at the map, trying to see her walking this road or that. Not this one, it goes too far into the hills, therefore too arduous at this time of the year, too dangerous too, and she'd lose the light too quickly before she could reach safe lodging for the night. Not that road, it would take her through too many built up areas: no joy walking through towns on busy roads. No, she would surely choose somewhere quieter and somewhere flatter. Then he saw it. The canal towpath. She'd be on the canal towpath. He knew as surely as if he saw her there on the map, walking along the brown line that traced the route of the canal on his map. Two days walking, she'd be somewhere like… his fingers traced the line from Edinburgh, pausing at Ratho, moving on to Linlithgow. She'd reach Linlithgow tonight.

With the feeling of a dark cloud lifted from over his head, Donald turned on the ignition, put the car in gear and drove back on to the motorway, pausing only to text Rhona that he'd be late home for tea.

When he reached Linlithgow, the sun had set and the light was fading. He parked in the station car-park, facing the entrance because, from there, he had a clear view of the road that ran from the canal, down alongside the railway line, under the tunnel and down to the town. He reckoned he had about twenty-five minutes before it would be too dark to see her from here, then he would have to leave the cover of the car and find somewhere closer to watch from.

He had only been there for twenty when he spotted her familiar old anorak. The light was almost gone, yet still he knew it was her, recognising her figure, her walk, her hair. Then she was past the car park entrance and gone from his view. Relief flooded through him and he lowered his head onto the steering wheel and wept.

When he had composed himself, he restarted the car and drove home. She was safe. That's all he needed to know. She was safe. If this is what she needed to do, he would leave her free to do it and pray that she would find her way back home when she was ready.

wednesday
donald

Next morning, he crept out of the house at seven o'clock, careful not to disturb Rhona. She had stayed again, sleeping in the spare room, but he knew she hadn't gone to bed till well into the night. The tap-tap-click-click of the computer keys from next door had been his lullaby. "You're like a barnacle," he had told her before going to bed last night.

"Yeah! Yeah!" she said. "So you said already."

"You really are not going to let this go, are you?"

"I want to know what's going on in Mum's head. Why she's acting like this. I want to understand."

He ruffled her hair. "You always did."

"What?"

"You always needed to understand. 'Because I said so,' was never enough for you. Even as a wee girl, you needed reasons for things. Real explanations, even if we couldn't give them."

Rhona shrugged.

"You're like your mum. She always wanted to understand too." He shook his head. "One of the things that was so cruel about being locked away like that, not understanding why."

"And that's why I want to find out, if I can. I want to understand so I can help Mum understand when she comes home."

Donald smiled. At last. He had worked really hard earlier in the evening — after he told her Mhairi was safe, he had seen her — to convince her Mhairi just needed time on her own to work this thing out. She would come home when she was ready. At first, Rhona had been furious with him for not grabbing hold of her in Linlithgow and dragging her home.

"It's not what she needs," he said. "This is something she needs to get out of her system. Something she needs to work through."

But he wanted to make sure she stayed safe, so he snuck out of his own house at seven o'clock in the morning and drove to Linlithgow again, took up position and watched for her, assuming she would climb the hill behind the station to rejoin the canal towpath and continue her Westward journey.

Eight o'clock would be early enough to get there, he reckoned. By the time she got up, dressed and breakfasted, he couldn't imagine she'd start out till after nine, possibly closer to ten, but he wanted to make sure he didn't miss her.

By eleven o'clock he desperately needed to use the Gents. By half-past, he *had* to use the Gents. Certain he hadn't missed her and beginning to believe she had taken another route out of Linlithgow, he gave up and went to relieve himself, totally understanding how the expression originated.

There's a really good bakery in Linlithgow he remembered from previous visits, so he walked down and bought himself a bridie for his lunch before heading through to visit his mother. Instead of the euphoria he had felt on finding Mhairi yesterday, a deep gloom settled over him as he drove. Disappointment was a sorry travelling companion.

wednesday
mhairi

    Her legs were really sore this morning so she decided she would take a rest day. She was in no hurry. She had no fixed destination and no fixed time to reach it. After breakfast she booked herself in for another night and luxuriated in an extra hour back in bed followed by a long soak in the bath, by which time she was getting hungry again and went out to seek some lunch.
    Linlithgow pleased her. She and Donald had been here several times over the years and she had fond memories of summer days walking round Linlithgow Loch, watching yachts glide across it's calm surface, joining picnickers on the grass around it. She bought herself some fruit and went there now to picnic as she walked slowly round the loch, always in view of the palace that stood beside it. Too cold to sit on the grass today.
    Linlithgow Palace had always been a favourite too. Rebuilt over a long period in the fourteenth and fifteenth centuries, burned out in the eighteenth, the ruins are exquisite. Many of the apartments are still intact and, even without their furnishings and fittings, Mhairi never found it hard to imagine living here. Mary, Queen of Scots, was born here in 1542 and was often in residence during her reign. Close her eyes, and she could see her royal figure flitting about between rooms, eating in the grand dining room, dancing in the Grand Hall.
    Bonnie Prince Charlie visited in 1745. on his march South, and tradition has it that the fountain in the palace courtyard was made to flow with wine in his honour. She

wondered how on earth that had been accomplished — assuming it was true.

There was a tremendous weight of history in these walls, Mhairi reflected, touching the ancient stone. Whenever she was here, or anywhere like it, she felt her life put into perspective, another brick in the wall of history, no more. When she no longer existed, there would be others to walk round this loch, to marvel at the views from the battlements of this palace. And when this palace no longer stood, the loch and the hills would still be here, beautiful, to be enjoyed by those who walked then. Perhaps they would come across her name in their family tree and wonder if she had walked here before them. Life has a habit of going on.

Peace enveloped her. The past surrounded her and took her past to itself, blending it into a huge cosmic history, absorbing it into millennia of sadnesses, cruelties, joys and pain.

Enough.

She would think of it no more.

She returned to the B&B and rested on the bed watching TV till dinner time, then another bath and bedtime in the soft sheets, not thinking of home, the past, the future, or anything else.

donald
wednesday evening

"Perhaps you missed her." Rhona finished her bedtime hot chocolate and put the mug on the floor beside her as she sat with her feet up along the couch. "No-one can keep their eyes glued on a ten yard entranceway for hour after hour without blinking."

"Well I did," Donald said. "Well, perhaps not without blinking, but certainly without actually closing my eyes. And it would have taken more than a blink of the eye for her to go past. I didn't miss her. She didn't go that way."

"She might have got the train."

"Not while I was there. That's the Glasgow side and I'd've seen her standing on the platform."

"With the eyes in the back of your head."

"Take it from me, I'd've seen her."

"Okay. Then maybe she took a bus, or a different route."

"That's what I'm thinking."

"Unless, of course, she stayed in Linlithgow."

Donald sat up, energised again. "Of course! She wouldn't walk three days on the trot. Her legs get too sore. She's always said two days walking at a time is her limit. Genius, Rho. You're a genius!"

Rhona smiled. "Glad to be of help," she said.

"Oh, I feel so much better now. I'll go back tomorrow morning and watch for her and I bet I'll catch her this time. The canal's the only way that makes sense. It's level and it's direct. It's peaceful. She'll be able to think. Terrific!" He leant back in his armchair, smiling, feeling better than he'd felt all day.

"Are you not going to ask how my day went?" Rhona pouted.

"Sorry, love. How did your day go?"

"Rubbish!"

"Oh!"

"Apart from being up to my eyes in invoices and orders for Steve, I spent most of the day fielding phone calls from Ewan and the kids. Oh, and Carol and Letty both phoned. Great relief all round that Mum is safe and well, mixed with concern that she isn't home."

"Oh," Donald shifted uncomfortably in his chair. "I suppose they thought I should've made her come home?"

"No, actually, the general consensus is that you did the right thing."

"Hmmm! Good. Nice to get that affirmation."

"So, I didn't get much research done today, but I got through a lot last night."

"And?"

"Have you any idea how hard it is to read sixty-year-old newspapers online?"

"No idea at all."

"Well, can I tell you? It is damn difficult, almost impossible. Even using your magnifying glass, there were some pages I just couldn't read."

Donald shook his head. "Tell me you're not really reading sixty-year-old newspapers?"

"Trying to. Well, not really read them, more scan through them. But it's a mammoth task. Assuming Mum was actually eight when whatever happened, happened, I started off going through editions of the Glasgow Herald from October nineteen-fifty-three on. Have you any idea how many editions that is?"

"No, but I get a feeling you're going to insist on telling me."

"No, I'm not. I didn't keep count, but let me tell you, it's a lot. Some of them are almost indecipherable, some of them are totally indecipherable. I've had to go on headlines only for the most part and that's not always easy."

"So why on earth do it?"

Rhona stared at him. "You know why."

"Not really," he said with a sigh. "I wish you'd let the whole thing drop. In fact, I wish you'd never started the whole sorry, damn business."

"But I have a right to know."

"No, you don't! You have no right to know anything. No right to know anything at all."

"Well it's near impossible to find anything out anyway."

"Good! Maybe you'll let the damn thing drop now."

"I've no intention of letting it drop."

Donald was getting tired. It had been a long day. Starting early, staring at a ten yard strip of roadway for hours on end, driving to Glasgow, sitting beside a sleeping parent who wakes not knowing you, getting hold of a consultant, hearing what he has to say, digesting the information, worrying about your mother, worrying about your wife, driving home, looking at every person walking on the pavement or crossing the road, now listening to a list of impossibilities. "Why the hang are you doing it, if it's so darned impossible!"

Rhona started. "I...I want..."

"You want to understand. Yes, I get it. I get it." He heaved himself out of his chair and walked across the room. Leaning down to Rhona where she sat on the couch, he spoke slowly and carefully right beside her ear. "Well, understand this. Leave your mother alone. It is her past and she is entitled to leave it where it is." He straightened up. "In the past."

"But..."

"If you hadn't been so bloody-minded about all this, maybe your mother wouldn't have felt the need to disappear."

"Oh, you're not going to put that on me!"

"No?" he said. "Watch me."

"Dad!"

Leaning down again, he wagged his finger in her face. "You stop all this damn detective work and let your mother's past alone. Right? D'you hear me?" When Rhona didn't say anything, he raised his voice. "Right? Got it?" Ignoring the stricken, injured look on his daughter's face, he turned and stomped out the room and up the stairs, muttering as he went, "Bloody barnacle."

His conscience kicked in an hour or two later after tossing and turning in bed, first of all angry, then penitent. It wasn't like him to shout at his daughter. But, then, it wasn't like Mhairi to disappear like this. It was, however, just like Rhona to persist in what she was determined to do. With a sigh and a promise to himself that he'd apologise in the morning, he rolled over and managed to get a few hours of sleep, interspersed with hours of wakeful wondering what on earth his next move should be.

thursday morning
donald

His apology choked in his throat. Rhona was up before him, had made the spare room bed, left him a note and gone home.

"I'll need to get some office work done for Steve. Want to start early because I'm going to go through to Glasgow to access the actual newspaper archives. I'm guessing they're easier to read," her note read.

Crumpling it in his fist, he cursed and threw it in the wastepaper basket by the bed and stormed out the room. "Wee besom! Hasn't listened to a word I said!" Grabbing some toast and a cup of tea before he stormed out to the car, he allowed the heat of his anger to glow, stoking it with the thought that it was Rhona and her damn 'project' that drove Mhairi away in the first place. He had refrained from pointing that out to her until last night, but she clearly hadn't heard him. He just might have to drive the point home when he saw her tonight. "That's if she has the brass neck to show her face tonight," he muttered as he swung the car out of the driveway.

His bad mood was lightened a few hours later, at half-past ten, when, from his vantage point in the station car park in Linlithgow, he watched Mhairi trudge up the hill towards the canal.

She was safe. That's all that mattered. She was still safe.

Her legs must be aching, he could see it in the way she almost dragged herself up the hill and out of his sight. How many more days could she walk ten or twelve miles a day? It had been a couple of years since they had done any serious walking together, a fact he suddenly regretted.

They used to enjoy their hillwalking so much, not just for the exercise and the scenery, but for the bonding too. Sometimes they would talk as they walked, especially if they were on a long straight stretch where they could walk side-by-side. They would hold hands at these times and he closed his eyes remembering the feel of her gloved hand in his, how she would slip her glove off and he would do the same and they would walk on, feeling one another's warmth through the contact, feeling one another's love. He almost ran after her just to hold her hand again.

"Patience. Patience," he told himself. "It's not about what I need. It's about what she needs." And he knew that what Mhairi needed right now was time, quiet time, reflective time. And who knows what else? Whatever it was that drove her onward on tired, aching legs, ever Westwards.

He started the car and was driving out of the car park, the car pointing down the hill towards the main road, when he had a sudden thought.

She might have changed her mind and be walking home.

Slamming the car into reverse, he drove back up the hill, parked again, jumped out and ran up the hill to the canal. By the time he got there and ran a little way along the path, he was panting and he had a pain in his chest.

Doubled over, clutching the pain, he peered into the distance both ways.

There she was. He recognised her just as she rounded a bend and was taken from his sight: walking West.

A mixture of disappointment and relief washed through him. Disappointment she wasn't coming home. Relief to see her walking fairly easily with a relaxed stride. He didn't want her to be in pain.

He, however, was in agony. It might have been years since they had hillwalked; it was even longer since last he ran. And uphill at that. And from a cold start. Breathing was ragged and painful and his left calf muscle was in spasm, probably pulled, and it was with considerable difficulty he limped down the hill to the car, which he found unlocked and askew in the carpark.

After getting his breath back and letting his heart rate settle, he drove out and started the drive to Glasgow and another tortuous day, he was sure, sitting at his mother's bedside.

He'd never been more grateful to have chosen an automatic, with no need for his left leg to do any pedal work.

Whenever he was anywhere near the canal, he would slow the car and crane his neck to try to catch a glimpse of her old, dark green walking coat or her glorious auburn hair. Oh, he knew her hair was shot through with grey now, but the auburn still burned holes in his heart.

His intellect told him she would still be miles back at the start of her trek, his heart would not allow him not to look anyway.

thursday
mhairi

The day started well enough. Despite all the languorous hot baths she'd taken, her legs ached and were a bit stiff, and the climb up the hill to get to the canal path had been murderous. Once there, she felt good and soon got into her stride. Thankful that she had chosen this route and not literally headed for the hills, she reckoned she could make reasonable headway and reach Falkirk tonight.

Blessed with another dry, bright day, she zipped her coat against the sharp wind and pulled the woollen hat out of her pocket and onto her head. The canal cut through beautiful countryside here and she began to feel relaxed and mellow as she walked.

Relaxed and mellow, that is, until she spotted a dog up ahead.

It was coming towards her.

A labrador, by the look of it, though it was still some distance away.

Her heart did a little skip, a jump into her throat, preparing her for flight.

She tried to swallow, to push her fear back down.

Still coming, sniffing in the reeds at the water's edge, but still coming.

Pulling her gloves on tighter, she drew her hands in close to her body, feeling her heart rate quicken.

Was it on a leash?

Cold, clammy perspiration trickled down her brow.

It should surely be on a leash?

Breath coming in short, shallow pants now.

The dog was not on a leash.

It kept coming.

There was nowhere to go. Canal on one side, thick hedge on the other.

It had her in its sights.

She stopped. Stood perfectly still.

The dog kept coming.

Her legs started to tremble.

The owner whistled.

The dog ignored the summons.

Mhairi closed her eyes and prayed,"Oh, please let him pass! Please let him pass!"

Eyes still closed, bent arms crossed across her chest, she felt the dog brush past her. Biting back the scream that rose in her throat, she heard it pant and snuffle as it ran.

It didn't stop.

She opened her eyes and turned to see it racing on down the path away from where she stood, unable yet to move.

"Nice day," the owner said, his silly grin telling her he had observed her pantomime of fear. "Nippy wind, though!" he added as he passed.

Mhairi managed a grunt of greeting and waited until she was certain the dog and its supercilious owner were well gone before she shook out her fear and uncoiled her body enough to walk on. It was half an hour or more before she could enjoy her walk again and appreciate the beauty of her surroundings. Stupid dog should have been on a leash.

She hoped there would be no more such encounters to mar the crisp beauty of this November morning. The few dogs she saw yesterday had been on the leash, which had been easier for her. She had simply stopped and stood aside for a moment to let them past. Stupid dog should have been on the leash.

Taking a break on the awesome Avon Aqueduct, 'the tallest in Scotland,' she read on the brass inscription plate on the rail, 'second tallest in Britain, 250 metres long, 26 metres tall,' numbers that would be meaningless to her if it wasn't that she could see its length ahead of her as she read the plaque, could look down from its great height and get the feel of being 26 metres high above the ground.

She marvelled at the views the aqueduct afforded down to the fast-flowing River Avon below. Breathtaking. But freezing cold to stand too long in such an exposed place and a wee bit scary to be up so high. She felt more than a little vulnerable being buffeted by the wind, so continued carefully along the well-maintained path. Times like this she could do with the warmth and security of Donald's large hand holding hers.

Her shoulders slumped a little as she walked. She missed Donald. True, she still felt a residual anger that he had broken her trust, but it did happen a long time ago and maybe it was time to let him off the hook. He had, after all, proved his love and loyalty to her over and over again so many times in the years since then.

She began to feel totally selfish in her initial outrage at his disclosure that he had told his mother she had a past to hide.

With the clarity hindsight can bring, she realised she had been selfish in many ways throughout their marriage.

Marriage is not, should not be, for you. You don't marry to make yourself happy: you marry to make someone else happy. Frowning, she tried to be honest with herself, to look into the mirror and see herself and her marriage undressed, naked, exposed. What had she hoped from it? Stability, certainly. A home, yes. More than anything, she had wanted a home. A proper home. Somewhere she could feel safe but not imprisoned. She remembered holding the front door key in her hand the day they gained entry to their house, their first and only house. That key represented everything she wanted at that moment. She would feel safe as long as she could hold that key in her hand, as long as no doors in this house were locked to her.

What else had she married for? Love? Yes, she wanted, needed, craved to be loved. Until she met Donald, there had not been a single day in her life when she had felt loved or wanted. It had been intoxicating that someone should want to hold her, kiss her, look after her, care for her. It took her breath away. When Donald looked at her that way — that special way he had of looking deep into her eyes as though he could see her soul, as though he could see everything that she was and everything she could be — her knees felt like jelly. She melted in his scrutiny.

Her knees almost buckled now as she thought of it. How long had it been since they'd taken the time to look at one another, really look at one another? Not just to see if his tie was straight, his jumper clean, his face shaved; if her hair was tidy, her petticoat showing, her trousers unmarked. How long since they'd looked inside one another through the window of their eyes?

His eyes were hazel, his lashes long and dark, lashes any girl would love to have. There were well-earned laughter lines radiating from the corners of his eyes. She loved his eyes; the way they laughed when he was amused, smiled when he smiled, clouded with her pain, but most of all, she loved how he looked at her, *that* look.

Another craving: she had married for a future, for a family. Not for in-laws and all of that nonsense, a ready-made family — which was just as well, since Ruth never warmed to her, never was the family she craved. But for children. Donald's children. The children he would help her raise. She wanted him to be her son's role model, her daughter's hero.

But should it have been about her? About what she wanted? About what she needed, what she craved? Should it not have been about Donald?

A sharp gust of insight almost blew her away.

She should have married to make Donald happy, not for him to make her happy.

To see him smile every day, to make him laugh, to give him what he needed, not just to take what she needed. A true marriage and true love should not be about you. It should be about the person you love. Selfishness demands, "What's in it for me?" while Love asks, "What can I give?"

She crouched down in a ball at the side of the path. "Oh, please, I want another chance," she prayed. "I want another chance!" She screamed it into the wind. She cried it into the flowing waters. "I want another chance."

She didn't know how long she crouched there, but she was stiff and cold when, at last, she was able to gather herself together enough to stand up and continue walking. Tears had dried on her face and it was tight and sore so she stopped at the next bench and took the cream she had bought in Linlithgow out of her rucksack and rubbed some into her face, roughly at first, then slowing, thinking about Donald and how he had dried her tears so many times, his thumbs wiping them away with gentle tenderness, all the while looking into her eyes, telling her it would be all right, telling her he loved her.

"What have I done?" she asked the wind. "What have I done?" she asked the water.

She had given up. She had stopped trusting him. Somewhere along the line, she had stopped trusting that he would dry her tears, that he would look after her. She'd taken the easy way out. She had run away. She had given up.

Getting off the bench, she started back along the way she had come. "I have to go home," she told herself. "I have to go home."

Anyone can give up. That's the easiest thing to do. But to hold it together when you have reason to give up, that's true strength. She saw it now, clear as this sharp, cloudless autumn day. She had to go back and face whatever Rhona was going to unearth. She had to tell Donald the whole story. She would make him listen, she would make him understand. She would throw herself at his feet and pray that he would still love her when he knew the heinous thing she had done.

donald
thursday

Ruth died while he held her hand.

She had given up the struggle when he arrived by her bedside. The nurse told him she had been fighting for breath, would not allow them to increase her morphine until he came, though her pain had clearly increased.

As soon as he took her hand and spoke to her, she visibly relaxed and nodded to the nurse to turn the dial that regulated the drip of morphine entering her body. "You have to listen," she said in a whisper.

Donald leant closer.

"I'm going to find out all about her."

"All about who?"

"That girlfriend of yours. Don't marry her. She's no good."

Donald sighed. "We've been through all this, Mother."

She gripped his hand tighter. "I won't allow it," she hissed.

"You're too late. We've been married a long time."

But she didn't hear him. "I've hired a private detective."

He started.

"Mmm! Didn't know that, did you?" She started to drift off to sleep.

"What private detective?" He gently shook her shoulder.

"The boy. About the boy." She was getting weaker. The fight was leaving along with every other care and thought. She opened her eyes. "Ah! There you are," she said. "I knew you'd come." Her grip tightened for a moment.

"What about the boy?"

"Only had the one. Just you, son. Just you." It was too much to keep her eyes open now and she surrendered herself to sleep, her hand holding his and tightening round it every now and then.

During that long afternoon, she woke once or twice more, but each time, she only checked he was still there and closed her eyes again.

Nurses came and went, checking her pulse, her blood pressure, her temperature, oxygen saturation and the drip. None of it disturbed her. For once, she made no complaint.

Donald asked in a whisper what were the readings and the nurse shrugged and pulled a face.

"Not good, then?" he asked.

She shook her head. "Afraid not. We can only try to keep her comfortable now, and pain-free."

So this was it. This is what it all comes down to. All the years of struggle, all the petty hates and jealousy, all the grand loves and romances. They all come to this. Nothing. What did it matter now whether Mhairi was all Ruth hoped for in a daughter-in-law, whether he had made his mother proud or disappointed her? It was all coming to this one moment when her heart was going to stutter and putter and stop.

It all felt so futile. All the striving, all the struggles, the grand gestures and the weak posturing. Futile.

Ruth had tried her best to be a good mother, he knew that. Perhaps she didn't always get it right, but who did? Perhaps she became over-possessive, but he was all she had. Perhaps he shouldn't grudge her his time and attention as he sometimes had.

Raising her hand to his lips, he kissed it and whispered, "Sorry, Mum."

He didn't know the moment she left him. He had been sitting for so long, his back was aching, his bottom numb and the hand that held his mother's also numb. The nurse came back to check things again, but saw there was no need. "She's gone," she said, resting her hand on his shoulder for a moment, before she left him alone to make of it what he would.

He was glad he'd been here. Glad his was the last face she saw, the last voice she'd heard. Huge shuddering sobs rose up in him and he bent his head to her hand and let them come. He owed her his tears and his grief. She was his mother and he loved her.

Some hours later, after he had done all that he had to do with consultants and doctors, undertakers and lawyers, registrars and tinker, tailor, soldier, sailor... he left Glasgow and drove to Falkirk, where he found somewhere to park where he could watch for his complement. He needed to be made whole again.

Everything had taken too long and, when he arrived in Falkirk, it was already getting dark. Although he waited for an hour or two more, he didn't find her. As he drove home, he thought that, for her sake, perhaps it was just as well. Had she been there, he would not have been able to stop himself. He would have run to her. He would have clung to her. He could not have let her go again.

mhairi
still thursday

She hadn't gone far along the path back towards Linlithgow when she stopped.

She couldn't go home.

Not yet.

Certainty hit her with a slap that made her flinch.

There was something she had to do first.

At last, she knew why she was on this journey, why she was going back.

There was unfinished business she had to see to.

Then she could go home.

So, she turned back around and started to hurry.

Even against the wind, she picked up the pace, almost running, panting with effort, not noticing whether it was pretty around her or plain.

While the canal began to meander along, under old stone bridges, past fields and built up areas, she began to walk with purpose, looking neither to right nor left, but straight ahead, looking for the signs that would lead her away from the canal at Falkirk where she could get a bus to Glasgow.

There was something she needed to do.

Fired with urgency, she could hardly stand still as she waited for the bus, then, once she was on it, found herself willing people to get on and off quickly at each bus-stop. "Come on! Come on! Hurry along, there!" she shouted in her head.

It took all her self-control not to get up, go forward and tell the driver there was a faster route, more direct, no need to stop and start. Why go through towns and villages, the motorway would be quicker.

An hour and a half later, she stood in Buchanan Street in Glasgow for the first time in her life, with no idea how to find where she needed to be. There was a newsagent nearby that was still open, though it was well past tea-time, and she went in and bought a map and some chocolate. The map to work out where to go and the chocolate to help her get there without fainting from hunger. She had no time to stop and have a meal, though she did eventually have to stop to study the map. Trying to do it as she walked was fruitless. For one thing, she didn't have a clue in which direction she should walk.

She found the hospital on the map, and wondered idly if Donald had visited Ruth today and how she was.

But that was not where she herself needed to be.

She continued searching the map, her eight-year-old self reciting the address in her head. At last, she found what she was looking for and realised she still had a good way to go and would need to take a bus or the underground train. Opting to stay above ground, she queued for the appropriate bus, hopping from one foot to the other while she waited.

Sixty years melted away as she stood in front of the tall, wrought-iron gates. They looked the same as she remembered them, painted black, with swirls and curls and pretty patterns wrought into them. Unable to resist the prodding of memory, she placed her index finger on the metal and allowed it to trace the pattern, feeling again the remembered dips and curves. Overcome with weariness and emotion, she leant her head against the gates and closed her eyes.

How many times had she stood on the other side of these gates, her tiny fingers following these curves, her eyes looking way beyond them, peering through, waiting for adventure to find her.

And it had.

And it had changed the course of her life for ever.

But she wasn't strong enough to follow that memory trail yet.

Opening her eyes to shut out the picture of her young self leaning on the other side of the gates, she drew back and looked through them. The long, curving, gravel driveway drew her gaze towards what she could see of the house.

Having so rarely been on this side of the gates when she lived here, she had little memory of this limited view of the house, but she didn't suppose it had changed much. Still imposing, still pretentious, the honey-coloured stonework resplendent in its elegance. It should have been blackened by time and pollution, but it had clearly been scrubbed and blasted clean in recent times. If anything, it looked better than she remembered it.

The front steps and the door were hidden from her view by the curve of the driveway and the trees and bushes that lined it, though she craned to the side in a vain attempt to see them. It somehow felt important that she did, though not important enough to draw her through the gates to crunch up the gravel to approach the door and what lay beyond.

Three floors of large elegant rooms with servants quarters in the attic, the house stood tall and proud. Two floors up, the schoolroom and the nursery windows were to the front, but she remembered her bedroom had been at the back, so she started to walk round outside the long perimeter wall, her view of the house becoming obscured by the height of the wall and the tall trees beyond it, but she remembered there had been a back gate and she kept going in the hopes of stumbling upon it.

And, at last, there it was.

The publicly maintained surface had finished even before she turned the second corner of the boundary and she was now on a rough, grassy road marked 'Private.' Halfway along this side of the wall, she stood at the back gate.

It was almost hidden by creepers: she recognised the winter leaves of Ivy, Honeysuckle and Virginia Creeper stretching over the wall and draping down to the rough road for long stretches of her walk round the boundary and they almost covered the opening. Rhododendron bushes pressed up against the single, wrought-iron gate, making it likely it had not been opened in years. Why would it be? It led only to this unmade road or the fields beside it, and the rough road led only round the outside wall and back to the front gate.

In years gone by, when she was a child, the coal man, the woodsman and the gardener used this entrance. Peering through the gate, she doubted the present owners still employed a gardener. The untamed look reigned as far as she could see.

Sniffing the air, she could detect no smokey smell from a wood burner or coal fire and saw no smoke from the chimneys of the house. Being November and cold, she assumed the present occupiers had some other form of heating.

Present occupiers.

For all she knew, that could still be her family. A shiver ran through her and she leaped back from the gate. Instinct told her to flee from here as fast as she could.

But she had come this far.

'Here I am, at the gate,' she thought, and a line or two of Tennyson drifted across her consciousness: 'Come into the garden, Maud, For the black bat, night, has flown, Come into the garden, Maud, I am here at the gate alone.'

Mhairi closed her eyes and took a long steadying breath, pulling the sharp air deep into her lungs, holding it there, letting it go in a slow, controlled stream through her pursed lips. Courage. Another quotation ran in her mind. Amelia Earhart said it: "Courage is the price that Life exacts for granting peace."

If she was ever to have peace again, she knew she must now find the courage to go through this gate.

Moving forward, she felt along the top of the wall for the loose stone, a shell of a stone, hollowed out to hide the key. A crude but effective method of ensuring access for the coal man, while discouraging it for the casual passer-by.

No, not the top of the wall. Not quite the top. Memory tapped her on the shoulder, correcting her hand.

Her little eight-year-old fingers counted up the stones from the bottom to as far as she could reach, 'Then another two,' she told him, pointing him to it. The remembered finger pointed it out again and she worked the stone loose. Gasping, she stepped back to lean against the wall.

The key, the same key, was still secreted here.

It lay in her hand, a good sized key, but smaller than she remembered. She stared at it for a moment as it burned in her hand, then threw it from her with an anguished cry.

She had told him where to find it.

Thinking she was going to faint, she slid down the wall to sit on the ground among the red and brown leaves and rhododendron flowers that had fallen before her. Oh, to turn back the clock. To erase that moment when her little fat finger had pointed. To bar him from this garden.

Turning her face to the rough stone of the wall, her stomach heaved and clenched. It might have been a relief to be sick, but she was spared that indignity and gradually her body stopped shuddering and her stomach settled.

When she had regained her balance and her composure, she stood up, and, with trembling fingers, picked up the traitorous key, inserted it in the rusty lock and tried to turn it. Relief flooded through her when it refused to turn and, at that moment, she might have walked away.

'Courage is the price that Life exacts for granting peace.' Amelia Earhart's words echoed in her head.

She tried again, with more determination and more muscle. With a squeal of pain, the key turned and she pushed the gate open.

The point of no return.

'Come into the garden, Maud, For the black bat, night, has flown, Come into the garden, Maud, I am here at the gate alone.' She muttered the words again, daring herself to accept the invitation.

If she walked through this gate, she knew she was unleashing the past and she might not be able to stand the weight of it.

donald
thursday evening

Donald let himself into the empty house. Rhona had not forgiven him his outburst of last night, then. Throwing his coat in the direction of a chair, he sat down heavily at the kitchen table, exhausted and lost without Mhairi's comforting welcome at the end of a bad day, and this had been a particularly bad day and he needed that comfort more than he ever had. When she hadn't shown up in Falkirk, he entertained the slender hope that she might have turned around and come home. The hope had held him together on the drive home from Falkirk and was now in tatters around him.

When Rhona came through the back door, she found him asleep with his head on his arms on the kitchen table. He hadn't eaten, he hadn't even taken his shoes off or made a cup of tea.

"Dad?" she said, her hand laid lightly on his shoulder. "Dad? You okay?"

"Hmm?" he tried to rouse himself.

"You look awful."

"Sorry, love. Feel pretty awful, actually."

"Should I get the Doctor?" She had her phone out already.

"No, no, not that kind of awful." He wriggled his shoulders to loosen them up. "Just stiff and tired."

"And miserable?"

"And miserable."

"Have you eaten?"

He shook his head. "Naw! No appetite. Cup of tea wouldn't go amiss though."

"You need to eat." She flicked the kettle on. "I'll make something. Mum always has something quick and easy in the freezer 'for emergencies.'" After a bit of a rummage, she drew out a fish pie. "This do? Six minutes from frozen." Before the kettle had boiled, she had the fish pie out of the packet, film lid pierced, and the pie on a plate and in the microwave.

Donald doubted he could eat it, but, after he'd had a cup of tea, he revived a bit and thought he'd give it a try, since she'd gone to the bother. To his surprise, he polished it off in less time than it had taken to cook. "Hadn't realised how hungry I was."

"Did you eat at all today?"

"D'you know, I don't think I did."

"Not even at the hospital?"

Slap, bang, wallop! That's what his grandfather used to say. Whenever Donald snuck up on him and said, 'Boo!' his grandfather would pretend he's been hit by a bolt of lightening. 'Slap, bang wallop!' he'd say, clutching his chest.

"The hospital!" Donald said, clutching his chest. "You'd better sit down, pet."

mhairi
thursday evening

Stepping inside the gate was possibly the most courageous thing Mhairi had ever done in her life. It isn't courage unless you're afraid. It isn't courage if you have no choice. It is only courage when you choose to conquer your fear and do what you're afraid to do. Mhairi was certainly afraid. She knew she had a choice. She chose to step inside the past.

The log-house was still there. Battered and bruised but still there. The door was weathered and warped. It no longer closed properly, making it easy for Mhairi to pull it open and step further into her fear.

Something awful had happened here and she'd been running from the memory all her life.

No longer used to store logs, it looked like it had become a refuse tip: old rusting bits of machinery and tools; half empty tins of paint; paint brushes that had gone rock-solid where they sat in jars that probably once held white spirit or turps; rags and tatters, and there, in the far corner, a few mouldy, mossy old logs of wood.

It smelled different too. Instead of the smell of newly-cut logs, that fabulous, living smell of resin and sap, there was the all-pervasive smell of death and decay. Light filtered in, as it always had, through the slats of timber the hut had been constructed of, only now the gaps were wider, some of the slats were broken or missing, so there was more light to showcase its disintegration.

Something awful happened here and she thought it might have been her fault.

Tears were flowing freely down her face. The doorframe creaked and gave a little under her weight as she leant against it to support herself. Her legs were buckling under the weight of her guilt and her grief. Heedless of the dirt and what may be living in it, she sank down against the wall, her body wracked with great, silent screams, as she made herself remember what she had spent her life trying to forget.

He delivered the newspaper every day. She watched him cycle up their front drive, his bag slung across his body, resting on his hip. By the time he reached their house, his bag was empty, theirs being the last on his round. Perhaps that's why he didn't hurry away when she talked to him.

It was he who started it. He grinned up at her one day, pulled a silly face to make her laugh as she watched him through the nursery window. Then he was gone, cycling back down the driveway, whistling, his thin little legs pumping too fast, making the bike wobble.

The same the next day, and the next. Then she got brave and waited in the garden, stepping round the corner of the house just as he pushed the paper through the letterbox. He pulled another silly face and jumped the steps, all four of them in one leap. She was in awe. After he disappeared out of the gate, she stood on the top step and looked down. He must have had wings on his feet.

When he came the next day, she was already there, standing a few feet away, waiting to see if he had, waiting to see if they unfolded from his ankles as he launched himself into the air. This time, his ungainly flight took him even further, another foot beyond the bottom step, but she couldn't see the wings. He called to her as he jumped on his bike. 'See ya!'

'See ya!' She said it first the next day when he was picking his bike up ready to climb aboard.

He grinned. 'What's yer name?' he asked.

She felt the colour rush to her face and she turned and ran.

'What's your name?' she asked the next day.

'Bobby,' he shouted as he cycled off. 'What's yours?'

'Mhairi,' she whispered to the space he left.

On Sundays, he came earlier in the day, close to lunchtime and she dared not wait in view because her mother liked to give him his tuppence herself when he handed her the Sunday Post.

But he must have known she was watching from somewhere because he waited till Audrey closed the door, then performed his leap, his time with a twist in it, landing the wrong way round, facing the door. He scratched his head, pretending confusion, turned around and his face lit with surprise and joy to find his bike waiting for him. She could hardly stifle her giggles and received a reprimand from Nanny for disturbing the baby's nap.

He couldn't have heard her, but he must have guessed she was in the nursery because, before he cycled off, he gave a cheery wave up at the window. She stepped back guiltily, her face suffused with colour, her heart suffused with love.

That Monday was a particularly warm day for early May, and Mhairi had carried a glass of homemade lemonade all the way from the kitchen, where she'd begged it from cook, out of the back door and round the house to the front step, setting it on the top step where he was bound to see it. When he did, but hesitated to touch it, she stepped forward and said, 'It's for you,' before running to hide part way behind a rhododendron bush to watch him drink it.

Instead of putting the glass back down, he waited, holding it out for her to take from him. 'It's okay,' he said. 'I'm no gonnae bite ye.'

She stepped forward cautiously and took the glass from his hand.

'Thank ye!'

She blushed.

'What's yer name?'

'Mhairi.'

'That's a nice name.'

'So's Bobby.' She thought it was a wonderful name. A hero's name.

'How old are ye?" he asked.

'I'm eight.'

He stood tall and proud. 'I'm ten,' he told her. 'Eleven next birthday.'

She was impressed. He must have seen the adoration in her face.

'Ye can have a go on my bike if you want.'

She shook her head. 'I don't know how.'

'I'll teach ye.' He looked around. 'But no here. It's too stoney.' He kicked at the gravel. 'Come on doon tae the road.'

'I'm not allowed.'

'Whit about yer back garden? Have ye a flat bit of grass?'

Mhairi nodded.

'I'll come early the morrow and I'll teach ye tae go ma bike. Is there a back way in?'

And she told him about the back gate and the false stone and the key.

donald
thursday evening

There were phone calls to be made. They split the list between them and called everyone who needed to know that Ruth had died.

Ewan had wanted to come right away.

"No. No need for that, son," Donald told him. "I'm all right. Rhona's here and she'll stay again. If you want to come, come tomorrow."

"If you're sure, Dad."

"I'm sure, son. I'm tired now. A long day. Too tired for company." And he was. He didn't want to talk, didn't want to reminisce or grieve. He just wanted to sleep. To hold all the feelings at bay until he could deal with them. The only person he wanted to share them with was Mhairi.

When he told her about her grandmother, Rhona had fallen apart a bit and he had comforted her as best he could, trying to let some of his sorrow wash away with hers, but he felt numb, almost as though he couldn't give himself properly to grief until he had Mhairi there to help him.

Not that Mhairi would grieve for Ruth. He knew Ruth had kept herself firmly outside Mhairi's affections, never giving Mhairi any inkling that she had a softer side, a gentler side. To Mhairi, she was only ever abrasive, deliberately scratching her daughter-in-law's feelings whenever she could, scouring her, with no expectation of burnishing her sufficiently to merit approval.

This was the harsher side of his mother, one she rarely turned on him, treating him as someone to be cherished the more for his 'unfortunate' choice of marriage mate. On the rare occasions Mhairi was with him, his mother made a point of leaving her to the side and pouring affection liberally over her son.

Once Rhona had settled for the night, having cried for her grandmother and clung to her father, Donald filled a hot water bottle and took it to bed for comfort of sorts, looking round the spare bedroom door as he passed to make sure his daughter slept peacefully. Lingering a moment to watch her sigh and sough in her sleep, he allowed a tenderness to soften his loss. Ruth had loved her grandchildren. He was glad of that.

As long as Mhairi was not with them when they visited, which she rarely was, Ruth would show her playful side, joining in their childish games, laughing or nodding seriously at their recounting of teenage escapades, and listening attentively to their grown-up news and plans.

Over the years, the children stopped wondering why Mummy chose to do the shopping while they and Dad enjoyed lavish Saturday lunches with Gran. It became the norm and they accepted it. If they continued to wonder, they kept it to themselves and had long-since stopped asking.

Shrugging off the discomfort the situation had always given him, he hugged the hot-water bottle closer and went to bed, leaving the hall light on for Mhairi, as usual. She didn't like the darkness.

He remembered the first night she asked if she 'please might leave the hall light on.'

They had been married for a few weeks and were getting ready for bed. They had had their cuddle and 'the rest', as Mhairi jokingly called it, and he was ready for sleep. 'Night, love!' he said.

'Donald,' she said, her voice whispered against his neck. 'Would you think I was being a baby if I asked for the hall light on?'

He kissed her forehead, laughing softly. 'I didn't know you were frightened of the dark.'

'I'm not. Well, not really. Not *frightened*. I just would like to know I can have the light on all night if I want.'

Giving her a sleepy squeeze, he kissed her again and told her, 'This is your home. You can have all the lights on night and day, if you want.'

'Just the hall light will do,' she said, hugging him, kissing him, arousing him again. When she returned to their bed after turning the light back on, sleep was far from his mind.

The memory tugged at him as he climbed into the empty bed, releasing tears at last. Once more, his tears were not for his mother; not even for Mhairi this time, but tears for himself and another lonely night.

Donald reckoned he had cried more tears this past few days than he had in all his adult life. Hard, choking stuttering tears that didn't flow easily, but felt as though they found their way through rough cracks and fissures in his body. The thought of losing Mhairi had dug a well in his centre from which tears were being drawn daily. Only with Mhairi's safe return would it be stopped.

friday morning
mhairi

Mhairi woke up, stiff and cold, wondering where she was again. It was still dark, with the palest hint of light falling on and around her in broken strips. She had fallen asleep, cried herself to sleep, lying on the filthy earthen floor of the log-house, her head on her rucksack and her crooked arm, which was now numb, and with her legs curled up close to her body. She could hardly move a muscle. Everything hurt. She could hear scuffling sounds as she tried to move, and they didn't come from her. Spiders crawled over her, having adopted her into their space as she slept.

With a shudder, she forced herself to sit, then stand, brushing off her clothes, riffling her hands through her hair, shaking out whatever might have crawled in to nest there. Dampness had seeped into her bones and every movement caused more pain. Dust and dirt clung to her clothes, the smells of decay and fungus seeping into them, making her long to tear them off and burn them. Stepping out into the early morning, pre-dawn twilight, she breathed in some fresher, frosty air. The rawness of it caught in her throat, making her cough, letting the cold air penetrate deeper into her lungs like long, sharp icicles.

Common sense told her she needed to move, to get out of this mausoleum, to walk warmth back into her limbs, but she was not ready to leave. Not yet. There was more she needed to remember.

After she told him about the back entrance, he cycled round the wall until he found it, found the key under her instruction, opened the gate and joined her in the garden.

She remembered feeling very shy the first time, aware she was now the hostess: he was in her territory. With sombre face, she welcomed him by walking him round the secret part of the garden, where hardly anyone else ever came, her playground. With her heart bursting with pride, she accepted his amazed appreciation for her workmanship when she revealed the tunnel she had made under the boughs of a very old, large rhododendron bush. The tunnel led through its dense branches and leaves to a clearing she had made in the middle, where she had dragged old tree stumps for table and chairs. His amazement that she had been strong enough to drag them, was expressed with a whistle through his teeth. 'Thought you said you were only eight,' he said.

She had been playing in it that day and had brought some bread, some cheese and an apple she had stolen from the pantry, intending a solitary picnic which she now gladly shared with her guest. Watching how he wolfed the food, she realised he was very thin and probably didn't eat well. Even at eight, she had a womanly way of seeing a need of nurture. 'Wait here,' she said, squirming her way back through her tunnel and running through the fruit trees, past the raspberry canes, the strawberry beds, the vegetable garden and across the wide expanse of lawn, round the flowerbeds and the kitchen garden to the back door of the house.

It was still early enough that final preparations for the evening meal were not in full swing, though she could smell the advance ones of meat and a pie in the oven. Sneaking into the pantry, she hacked off a few more hunks of bread and chunks of cheese, stole another apple and, folding them into the tea towel that hung behind the door, she raced back to the hide-away. 'For you,' she said, breathless, panting, but proud.

His eyes widened when he saw the stash and he closed the cloth back over it carefully before putting it into his empty newspaper satchel.

'Aren't you hungry any more?' She was disappointed, had anticipated further pleasure in watching a hungry child fill his belly from her largess.

He blushed a little, probably recognising his own weakness. 'It's me wee sister,' he said. 'Don't think she's had an apple before.'

'Is she hungry too?'

'Aye.'

'I'll bring another for her tomorrow,' she said, setting in motion the custom that would become a cause.

They played in the hide-away for a while, until Bobby knew he ought to be going. 'I'll come earlier tomorrow and I'll teach you to go my bike,' he promised.

She didn't need to wait for him by the front door any more. After delivering the paper, he would cycle round to the back gate, retrieve the key and let himself in the gate as though he had every right to be there.

True to his word, Bobby taught her to ride his bike. He turned out to be a good teacher, she turned out to be a quick learner and it was not many weeks before she could cycle along the path outside the gate all the way to the corner, a daring feat, since she was not supposed to leave the confines of the garden for any propose whatever.

Every day, she would steal food for him, some to appease his appetite there and then, and some for him to take home for little Molly, who was the same age as herself 'but not so grown,' Bobby told her. 'She's just up to here on me.' He showed her, indicating a spot on his chest.

'And I'm up to here,' she said, measuring herself against him.

She smiled at the memory. They had been so young, so innocent, so unaware that danger lurked in their friendship. Frowning, she forced herself to remember what happened. The memory was reluctant to come and she walked about in the garden a while, reliving the games they had played.

Hide and seek, when he climbed one of the old apple trees and she couldn't find him for such a while, until, hot and frustrated, she heard the rustle of leaves behind her and turned in time to see him jump from the tree and sprint for the den. 'Den!' he shouted, grinning with jubilation. 'Home free!'

Hunt the apple, another favourite. 'Warm, warmer, getting hot.' And she would clap her hands in delight when he found his prize, hidden deep under a bushy hydrangea, laughing as he emerged, pretty blue flowers clinging to his hair.

The garden crowded round, almost hiding the picnic table from view, but Mhairi had not forgotten where it was and she searched it out, pleased to find it still here, where it belonged. If it could speak, what stories it would tell: of summer days and summer picnics, no doubt. But these were not her memories. They belonged to some other time, some other family. The table had always been there. It was old when she was young. Neglected and forgotten, it endured where those who spread their food upon it had not.

Pulling the long grass and weeds that stood between her and it's dark, weathered wood, she cleared the old, broken bench that served it and was part of it, and sat down. Memories flooded in unbidden: her father throwing still warm carcasses upon it, skinning rabbits and hares with more pleasure than was seemly; her mother flirting across the wooden slats with her lover as though a child of six or seven would have no notion of what was in play; lonely picnics with dolls and teddies instead of playmates, marigold food on rose petal plates.

Stretching her arms flat across the table's width, Mhairi lowered her head and wept. One memory surpassed all others. One summer day when she was eight and he was eleven, their last-but-one day together, a picnic of stale bread and some thick slices of ham, 'A banquet fit for a king,' he'd said, thanking her for what she'd managed to steal from the pantry.

Her tears fell on the old, gnarled surface of the table, making tiny pools of mud in the dust. Using the sleeve of her coat, she scrubbed at them, revealing the dried-out, grey beauty of the wood. Although broken and decaying now, it had aged well, better than one could have expected in the Scottish climate, but it had been wisely placed in the shelter of a towering sycamore tree, hedged around by rhododendron bushes. Even on dreich, wet, winter days the table was dry, a great place to bide out the storm. In summer, it's situation afforded shade from the noonday sun.

When she wiped the debris of too many autumns from the end of the table that had been swallowed by the bushes, her fingers found the crude carvings of that childhood summer. M & B. No heart wreathed the initials: it was not a declaration of love, but a statement of friendship. They were but children, after all. Her fingers traced the all but flattened initials, her heart remembered the joy with which they'd been carved.

'Ah can do ma letters,' he told her proudly, taking the old, rusty penknife from his pocket. 'Your name starts with a M.' The knife dug into the wood, guided to form a crude capital M.

As young as she was, instinct told her not to crush his pride with her own, warned her not to declare she had known her letters since she was four years old.

'And mine with a B.' That too was carved into the wood, more time and concentration needed to get the curves looking anything like a capital B. 'See,' he said when it was done. 'M and B. You and me.'

'Ah,' she said, smiling her adoration, running her fingers across the rough cuts.

'Watch out for splinters,' he told her, his wise warning coming too late. 'Here! I'll pull it for ye, it's no too deep.'

Eyes closed, breathing the scent of decaying leaves, rotting wood and moss, she allowed herself the luxury of recalling that perfect day, morphing the smells to summer roses and rhododendrons. The garden had been theirs, all theirs.

Reluctant to move away, yet stiffening from the November chill, Mhairi touched her fingers to the initials one last time before rising from the bench to leave the decaying table and move on.

Looking round, she tried to remember where her tunnel, her old hideaway would have been, finding it at last, completely overgrown, the bushes almost impenetrable, but not quite. Certain she could push her way through, she put up the hood of her anorak and pulling on her gloves to protect herself from sharp branches, she fought her way in to the centre of the bushes. There was still a tiny clearing. She could make out the moss-covered shapes of tree stump table and chairs. Imagine! After all these years! Tears stung behind her eyes, emotion choked in her throat. That there could still be traces of her childhood drawing room. Crouching in the tiny space, her gloved hand smoothed the mossy tablecloth and she felt again the joy of entertaining a special visitor in her special place.

Time rushed past in a whoosh of wind and she could see him sitting opposite her, wiping his hands on the seat of his pants as though they might be any cleaner, thanking her graciously for her kind hospitality. 'I might no be rich,' he told her, 'but I know ma manners.'

The ropes she had used to tie branches aside were long gone, but somehow, the years of being held back in that position had trained the boughs and they, in turn, held back the new growth. It was almost unrecognisable as the wide space she had created and she couldn't straighten up in it, but then, she laughed to realise that an adult probably never could.

Delighted to have found the one place in the world she had felt safe and free as a wee girl, she closed her eyes and breathed in the smell of it, the essence of it. This had been her place. The only other person to know of its existence was Bobby Wallace, her first love. Here they had whispered and laughed together every day for four or five blissful weeks in the early summer of nineteen-fifty-three. They had played Ludo and Snakes and Ladders, and shared bread and cheese and eaten apples.

Drying her eyes and smiling at the warmth of the memories, Mhairi pushed back out through the undergrowth.

With a sudden cruel clarity that knocked her to her knees, she remembered what she had seen the last time she pushed through these rhododendron bushes.

friday morning
donald

When Donald pulled his weary body from bed and washed, dressed and went down to breakfast, Rhona was sitting at the kitchen table, the facsimile of an old Glasgow Herald lying open on the table in front of her. When she looked up, he could see that she had been crying and her face was gaunt and pale. "What is it, pet?" He sat beside her.

She pushed the paper across to him. "I keep reading and re-reading it. Trying to make sense of it. Trying to find the loophole that would let Mum off the hook."

"What loophole? What are you talking about?" he lifted the paper. "Nineteen-fifty-three," he read. He looked up at her. "Where did you get this?"

"The Scottish Newspaper Archives. Through in Glasgow. Yesterday."

Rhona had spent yesterday searching through the archives, reading old newspapers, fascinated by the feel of them, the smell of them, struggling to read some of the more faded of them. They had been put on microfiche and she had first of all to go through slide after slide until she had found what she hadn't known she was looking for.

It had been May 1953, just before the coronation of Queen Elizabeth II. Mhairi was eight years old.

As Rhona had scanned the microfiche slides, she came upon daily updates on a missing child. She had thought nothing of it until the news report of his being found and the enquiry that followed a couple of months later. Then she knew she had stumbled on the Anderson family scandal, because the boy was found on their property and it was estimated he had been dead for ten or twelve days at least.

It was difficult to know for sure, the body was in such bad shape. Rhona chose at first not to read the details. A sentence or two of description had sent her rushing to the Ladies to part company with her lunch.

The enquiry had involved a second child, one Mhairi Anderson, a girl of eight.

Character witnesses were called, none of them rising to her defence, and her father declared she had been incarcerated for some weeks already in a facility for the mentally deficient. She did not give evidence at the enquiry, it being felt that her mental condition was unstable and therefore any defence she made could not be relied upon. Her father acknowledged her culpability on her behalf. It was ordered that she continue to be detained and restrained for her own safety and that of other people, until she be deemed fit to reenter society, or the age of twenty-one, whichever came the sooner.

The facts were there, in black and white. Rhona had read and reread them. It was a heinous crime Mhairi was condemned of. The boy had been tortured and beaten — severely, according to the enquiry. He had bled to death from a blow to the head. There had been more than one blow: one of them had cracked his skull, another had smashed into the side of his head and that had probably been the one that killed him. Witnesses testified to the fact that Mhairi had previously delivered a blow to her nanny's head, rendering the woman unconscious. Although only eight years old, her 'manic disposition gave her the strength of a man,' according to the Doctor who had been called to the family home to treat the nanny and the maid, who had also sustained several serious blows.

Donald pushed the paper back across the table towards her. "No," he said. "This is not true." He got up and went to fill the kettle. Rhona had done her best. The kitchen was clean and tidy, but not everything was where Mhairi liked it to be, so, while he waited for the kettle to boil, he straightened things, put them back where they belonged. "No," he said again. "I don't believe it."

"They said…"

"I know what they said," he shouted. "But it's not true."

"I don't want to believe it either."

He swung round, kettle in hand. "It's not a matter of not wanting to believe it," he said. "It just plain and simple is not true."

"But the evidence showed…"

"The 'evidence' was circumstantial, at best. The child had been dead for weeks." He poured water into the two mugs he had laid out ready with teabags in them. "Nineteen-fifty-three, the forensics would have been pretty rudimentary. They would not have had much to go on other than the testimony of these…" He put the kettle down and turned to pick up the paper. "These so-called 'character witnesses' and her father." He threw the paper down. "Her hypocritical, scheming, cold-hearted, arrogant pig of a father!"

"He wasn't actually her father."

Donald swung on her. "I know that. You know that. Back then he didn't have the gumption, he didn't have the humility, or whatever else it would have taken to let the world know he had been suckered into marrying a woman who was already carrying another man's child." He swore, calling William Anderson a few more choice names. "The brute saw this as his chance."

"His chance to do what?"

"To disown her." He swept the paper off the table. "This pack of downright lies, gave him an excuse. He could disown her. Say she was no longer his daughter. No longer!" He stomped through to the sitting room, turned and came back into the kitchen to pick up his tea. "She was never his daughter. Thank God she wasn't!" he said, nodding heavenward. "Thank God she has none of his genes flowing through her body." He snatched the mug up, slopping the tea over the brim, not heeding the spill, marching back to the sitting room. Setting the mug on the wee table beside his chair, he sat down with a heavy flump.

Before Rhona reached the chair opposite, carrying her own mug of tea, he was up again. He marched through to the kitchen, picked the newspaper facsimile off the floor and brought it through in his fist, waving it at her. "I'll show you what I think of this parcel of poison," he said as he ripped it in two, then four, then threw the pieces into the wastepaper basket that sat by Rhona's chair.

"Hey! I paid good money for that!"

"Then you wasted it. It's a load of drivel."

"You don't know that."

"Oh, yes, I most certainly do! And you would too, if you stopped for a minute and thought about your mother. That woman doesn't have a cruel bone in her body. 'Torture!' I don't think so."

"But it was a long time ago."

"Damn right it was a long time ago. And it's just as well that man is dead. If he wasn't, I'd get off my backside right now and stuff his so-and-so paper down his so-and-so throat!" He glared over at Rhona. "And don't you so-and-so smirk at me like that. Your mother wouldn't have swearing in this house. Protecting your so-and-so ears!"

Rhona couldn't help it. She spluttered into laughter.

He couldn't help it. He started to laugh too.

They both rocked with great, uncontrolled gales of laughter, silly laughter, painful laughter until, as shockingly as it had started, it stopped and left them staring at one another's pain.

friday
mhairi

For the first time in her life, Mhairi had shared something. For the first time in her life she had somebody to share something with. She had shared this special place with Bobby. He was her first friend. Her only childhood friend. It was her fault he was dead.

She should not have told him about the key, she should not have invited him into her garden, taken him to see her hideaway, encouraged him to come again, day after day. She should have known there would be a price to pay for happiness.

For weeks they'd played together for an hour or two every day. He had taught her to ride his bike, she had taught him the names of the trees and the flowers.

But then their idyl was broken.

They had been in the hideaway, picnicking on the spoils of her latest pantry raid, sheltering from the threat of rain. It was time for Bobby to go home, 'Before the rain starts proper,' he said, indicating the spatters that had already penetrated the thick cover of rhododendrons, and she wrapped some food and an apple in the tea towel for his sister. He put it in his satchel as usual. It had become a routine. Each day, he brought back yesterday's tea towel empty and each day he took it home full. 'Ta, Mhairi!' he said as he took it from her. The last words she remembers him saying.

He went ahead of her into the tunnel that led back out into the garden. Sounds were always muffled from the central clearing, due to the thick bushes surrounding it, otherwise Mhairi might have warned him of the dogs.

Her mouth opened in a silent scream, her eyes closed and her hands went up to ward off the memory. This was what she had forgotten, this is what had happened that day. Monstrous waves of revulsion knocked her to her knees, shaking her head, fighting off the memory.

It was the dogs.

Her father must have been rabbiting with them. From deep in the bush, she became aware of the commotion as the dogs snarled and barked at Bobby, as he emerged from the mouth of the tunnel. She started to hurry, pushing through the bushes to reach him, to stand by his side and talk to the dogs. 'Choochie! Cuddles!' she called, knowing even as she called, the dogs wouldn't hear her above their own din.

She was almost out in the open, when she stopped, horrified by what she could see beyond her hiding place.

The dogs were jumping on and around Bobby in a confusion of snarling mouths and wagging tails. She was about to step out and try to soothe the beasts when she saw her father, a string of dead rabbits hung over his shoulder, his walking stick raised to rain down blows on the intruder.

She couldn't move, immobilised by fear and horror

Bobby ran, but, at her father's command, the dogs were faster. They had been hunting, they were trained to hunt and kill; the rabbits on her father's shoulder, the blood on their mouths, bore witness to their success.

'Get him!' her father shouted.

They had the scent of his blood now, having already scratched and bitten him, so they flew at him before he could reach the gate, tearing at his skinny, bare legs and arms.

She had seen this once before, when her father had taken her with him to hunt vermin, as he called the rats and rabbits the dogs sniffed out for him. After they had caught something and had pinned it down, injured and unable to flee, he would call them off and step up to finish the vermin off with a sharp blow of his stick to the head. At the end of the hunt, he would not call the dogs off, but would let them have the last few victims as their reward, allowing them to tear at the flesh, devouring it raw, sharpening their teeth on the stripped bones.

She had vomited on the ground at his feet, appalled by the barbarism of the scene.

Holding her head up by the hair to ensure she was watching the spectacle, he spoke roughly, close to her ear, his voice cruel and guttural. 'Where are your cuddly, baby doggies now, then?' It was one of the things that enraged him most about her, this attachment she had to the dogs, her affection softening them, blunting the killer instinct in them. That was the sole purpose of taking her with him that day, to show her the true nature of the beasts.

And the dogs were putting it on show again. Putting her little hands over her ears to shut out the uproar of the dogs snarling and barking, Bobby screaming, and her father shouting, she stepped back, shaking her head in denial.

Powerless to halt the vicious pantomime playing out before her eight-year-old eyes, her pupils wide with shock, she watched from her hiding place.

Watched as Bobby struggled to hide his face from their teeth.

Watched as her father stood back and let the dogs go in for the kill.

Watched as her father finally called the dogs off and gave them a rabbit instead of the child.

Watched as her father kicked him in the stomach. 'Vermin!' he said. 'I won't have vermin on my property.'

Watched as his walking stick came down on Bobby's head with a loud 'Thwack!'

She flinched.

Bobby's head snapped forward, his face smashing onto the sharp gravel of the path.

Again. 'Thwack!' He tried to protect his ear. Blood spurted from the side of his head. She fell to her knees, her hands covering her mouth, catching the scream.

And a third time. 'Thwack!' Bobby went still. She curled into a ball and rocked back and forth, back and forth.

Her father was done. His rage subsided.

Immobilised by fear and horror, she watched as he rolled the boy's body over with his foot. 'Aye, you'll live.' He spat on him. 'But you'll not trespass on my property again.'

He grasped the collar of Bobby's shirt and dragged him down the path to the gate and threw him outside, as though he was the trash can for the bucket men to uplift tomorrow. He turned the key in the lock and replaced it in the false stone. Then, wiping his hands on his trousers as he walked, he returned to round up the dogs, whistling at them with a long high note that pierced the air, rending what remained of the day asunder.

Silence crept in on cautious belly.

Calm fell about her in torn-up, floating pieces as the sound of the pack and their master faded into the distance. The air vibrated and shimmered around her, the only sound the pattering of rain on broad, green leaves. With a whisper, the wind lifted a scattering of dead rhododendron flowers at her feet.

young mhairi

A few spots of rain fell on her hand, where she lay in foetal position in the bushes. A branch blew softly against her face, waking her from her shocked trance with its gentle kiss.

Panic used rougher tactics as consciousness brought memory rushing in behind it, and she jumped up in a rush.

Tears blinding her, she stumbled out of the tunnel and ran to the gate.

Unable to reach the stone where the key was hidden, she looked around for something to climb on, ran to the log-house, there and back several times until she had a precarious pile of logs she could stand on.

Still it took three attempts to make them firm enough to take her weight and she scraped her hands and knees against the wall, ripped her dress, and lost her shoe, before she managed to pull the stone out and get the key.

Once through the gate, she flew to his bloody body. 'Bobby! Bobby!' she cried, trying to rouse him, shaking his shoulder, raining tears on him.

At last, he groaned, but he couldn't open his eyes. They were bloodied and already swelling. There was a deep gash down one side of his head, another across the top. It had started to rain in earnest, washing blood from him to run in rivulets down the unmade road. She looked around frantically for someone to help, but she knew in her heart there would be no-one. This was a private road, seldom used except by delivery men and her father after walking the dogs.

She had to get him to shelter. She had to get him out of the rain. And what if the dogs came back? "Bobby! Bobby! I don't know what to do.' Crying and shivering, she sat beside him, immobilised once more, this time by her own inadequacies. 'I wish I was eleven, like you,' she told him. 'But I'm only eight and I don't know what to do.'

donald
still friday

Donald shook his head. He could not, would not, did not believe the old newspaper article.

"So, did Mum tell you what *did* happen, then?" Rhona asked.

He scratched his head. "I think she tried to, or as much as she could remember, which actually wasn't much."

"Did you try to help her remember? I mean, let's face it, I expect you needed a bit of reassurance she didn't murder that poor boy."

"You just don't get it, do you, Rho?"

"What?"

"That your mother is not capable, never was capable of anything so grotesque."

"Well...she was capable of knocking out a strong, healthy adult."

"That was different. That was desperation. She was locked in a room for three days, damn it!"

"How do you know the boy hadn't done something awful to her, made her desperate again?"

Donald stopped pacing and stood in front of her. He reached down to the wastepaper basket beside her chair. "I'm telling you and I want you to hear this," he said, speaking slowly and quietly. He shook the basket at her, making the pieces of torn newspaper rustle. *"Your mother did not do this."*

Rhona shrugged.

"If you really believe that she did: that she was capable of such a cruel, horrendous, heinous crime, then you are no daughter of mine and you can get out of this house."

Donald threw the basket from him, newspaper pieces spewing from it as it arced in the air.

She shook her head. "You don't mean that."

Grasping her by the elbow, he pulled her up and marched her towards the sitting room door. "Try me!" he said.

"Okay! Okay!" She shook herself free. "If you're so convinced of her innocence, convince me." She rubbed her arm. "You hurt me."

"Not as much as you're hurting me." He shook his head. "She's your mother, for pity's sake."

"Yeah, well I daresay Myra Hindley could have been someone's mother given a chance."

"Can you hear yourself? Can you hear what you're saying?" He pulled her off the chair again and hauled her upstairs, struggling against him.

"Stop it, Dad! Stop it. Please, Dad. You're frightening me."

Throwing open his bedroom door, he sat her down on the stool in front of the dressing table mirror. "Look at yourself," he commanded her. "Look at yourself and tell yourself that your mother is a killer."

"Dad, this is silly." She turned away from her reflection.

"Look at yourself and say it. Tell yourself that your mother is a killer."

She lifted her head. "I can't," she said.

"Try!"

"I can't."

"Why not? Eh? Tell me. Why not?"

She looked at his reflection in the mirror, then at her own. "I can't." She put her hands over her face and started to cry. "Oh, Dad. I'm sorry. I'm so sorry. I don't want to believe it. I don't know what to believe."

Donald bent down so that his face was level with hers, lifting her head so that they looked at one another in the mirror. "Know this," he said. "Your mother is not a murderer."

"I want to believe you, Dad, honestly, I do, but the evidence..."

"The evidence is bullshit!" Donald swept everything off the top of the dressing table with the side of his arm as he straightened up and turned away.

Rhona cried out, cowering from his rage, but still she asked, "But how could they get away with saying that if it wasn't true?"

He shook his head and sighed. "Because there was nobody there to defend your mother. No-one to tell the truth." His shoulders dropped and he sat on the end of the bed.

"So what is the truth?"

"I don't know, but I do know that newspaper report is not it, because I know..." He stood again, his elbows bent, his fists clenched in front of his chest. "*I know*, your mother is not capable of torturing and killing another human being."

Rhona looked at him; studied the passion in his face, the flame in his eyes, the tension in his body. Closing her eyes, she leant her elbows on the dressing table and rested her forehead on her hands.

Donald sank onto the bed, his elbows on his knees, his posture a reflection of his daughter's, panting deep, exhausted breaths.

After a few minutes, Rhona got up and fetched the photograph of Mhairi from Donald's bedside table, staring at the image, searching Mhairi's face, her eyes. She shuddered. "No." Her head shaking, her face etched with pain. "You're right," she said at last. "You're right, Dad."

"Damn right I am!"

"She couldn't have done what they said. She just couldn't, could she?"

He lifted his head, looking straight at Rhona. "Absolutely not."

"Mum couldn't hurt someone like that." She shook her head, putting the photograph down. "Not in the cold-blooded way they said."

"Not in any way!"

Her hand lingered on the photograph frame. "Well she did knock her nanny unconscious."

"But she would not, could not torture and kill a child."

"No. You're right." Rhona shook her head. "It's different. It is different. You've always told us never to believe everything we read in the papers."

"Exactly."

Rhona started to cry again. "Oh, Dad. I'm sorry. I'm so sorry. I should never have doubted."

"No."

"I feel awful. I feel so disloyal to Mum." She put her hands over her face, huge gulping sobs shaking her shoulders. "Oh, Mum. I want my mum. I just want my mum." She fell onto the bed, lying across it, her knees drawn up and the duvet gathered in a clutch at her chest.

Donald sat closer and drew her in against him. "I know, pet, I know."

She turned to him, holding on round his waist. "I'm sorry Dad. I'm so sorry. I didn't mean to make you angry."

"And I'm sorry too." He leant down and stroked her hair as she lay with her head on his lap. "I didn't mean to be rough. I just wanted you to wake up to what you were saying."

She nodded, drying her eyes with a tissue she took from the box he offered from the dressing table.

"I just needed you to look at yourself, look into your heart. You know in your heart, you must know, deep inside, just like I do, that your mum was never, ever capable of doing something as wicked, as evil as that report makes out."

Rhona sniffed and nodded again. "Oh, poor, poor Mum. I do know. Really, Dad, I do know. Mum couldn't have done that. Oh, Mum, I'm sorry. I'm so, so sorry."

"It's okay. It's okay," he soothed.

"But I should never have doubted her. It would break her heart…"

"She'll never know," Donald held her away from himself and gave her a long, meaningful look. "She will never know." Then he let her cry for a while before he spoke again. "Let's go back downstairs and I'll make you a nice cup of tea. It's your Mum's answer to everything, you know, a cup of tea."

She nodded and laughed as she let him lift her into a cuddle before they went downstairs.

mhairi

Mhairi paced out the distance. Twenty yards, maybe more. She had dragged him twenty yards. True, his frame was slight, but she was only eight years old.

She had put her arms under his armpits and, bending her back to the task, she had dragged him, walking backwards, all the way to the log-house. Three or four times, she stumbled and fell, never slackening her hold on him, so she cushioned him as they fell together. Three or four times more, she had to pause to get her breath. She felt as though her arms were going to come out of their sockets, her back was going to break. But she gritted her teeth and she dragged his poor bleeding body twenty yards. Once inside the log-house, she had collapsed under him on the floor. He groaned as she let his head fall onto her lap.

And all the while it had rained, soaking through both their clothes, washing his cruel wounds clean, his blood soaking into the grass and the gravel, washing away all trace of her exertion. Afternoon passed into evening while Mhairi sat nursing his broken body. The trauma of what she had seen rendered her incapable of words or thought, so she sat with his head on her lap and crooned and keened. She heard someone call her to dinner, but the words were meaningless and she didn't respond. There was a second call, a last chance call. 'Come now or you will be in trouble.' Again, meaningless.

It was only later, when her name was being called by two or three voices and the voices were coming nearer, that she roused from her trance-like state, a flow of fight or flight adrenalin jump starting her into action. If they found her here, they would find Bobby too. They would tell her father. He would bring the dogs.

With a last gargantuan effort, she pulled him further into the hut and propped him, semi-sitting, against the pile of logs. 'I'll come back tomorrow,' she whispered to him. 'When you're awake and we can play.'

While the voices were still a little way off, she slipped out of the hut and into the bushes, reappearing some distance away and running through the fruit trees, the raspberry canes, the strawberry beds, the vegetable patch and across the grass towards the back door.

'There you are, you wicked child. You're mother has been worried sick about you!' Mhairi knew that not to be true, since she had never known her mother to care where she was or what she did, but she whelped her apologies while being whipped across the ear with the back of Nanny's hand.

Bedraggled and filthy, she was hauled upstairs to her room. While she was stripped and bathed, her father was informed of her behaviour and consulted as to suitable punishment. She was to be put to bed and locked in her room without supper.

Mhairi hated being locked in her room and she remembers that she fought the punishment, kicking and screaming, remembers the crash of a vase as it hit the floor, the feel of her fist smashing into Nanny's face and remembers the punishment being extended way beyond that evening, extended indefinitely until Nanny's lip healed — which was unlikely since she remembers Nanny picking at it.

Going back inside the log-house, Mhairi sat in the far corner, on the floor, in a huddle, remembering the last time she had seen Bobby, just before she left him in response to the final summons to bed. Bitten, battered and bleeding, blood running down his face from head-wounds inflicted by her father's walking stick mixing with rainwater. Remembered she had taken her socks off and used them to wipe his poor face, all the time chatting away to him in a whisper, then she wound the filthy socks round the bites on his wrists, tucking them in on themselves to keep them on. Same thing with her hair ribbon, using it as a bandage too. It was all she had to play nurse with.

During the three days she was locked in her room, Mhairi became frantic and tried everything she could think of to escape. The first evening, she imagined Bobby waking up and finding her gone. He would go home and perhaps his mother would not allow him to come and play with her again if he went home so dirty and bleeding all over her carpet.

The next afternoon, she tried to listen for his bicycle bell coming up the drive to deliver the paper, but her room was to the back of the house, the letterbox on the front door. She listened instead for the back gate creaking open, the wheels of his bike crunching on the stones of the back path, though the gate was too far from her window for the sound to carry. Would he give up if she wasn't out waiting for him, if she wasn't at the nursery window to pull faces, if she didn't get out to play?

She managed to climb through the window, but her involuntary scream as she fell from the windowsill alerted the gardener, who sent someone for help while he stood guard over her as she lay struggling for breath. Once more kicking and screaming, she was hauled upstairs to be locked in her room. Her father summoned a joiner to make the window secure. It could be opened an inch or two for air, but, try as she might, it could be opened no further. Nor could she find anything with which to break the lead-latticed panes.

Another day passed and the thought crossed her mind that he was hurt and might not be able to ride his bike. He might still be waiting for her in the log-house or the hide-away. He'd be getting hungry, so, in temper and frustration, she refused to eat and threw the food they brought her back at them, smashing the dishes against the back of the locked door.

She even threw the contents of the potty about the room, expecting them to have to let her out while they cleaned up the mess. Instead, they gave her the means to clean it herself and stood over her while she did it.

She was getting desperate. No amount of pleading, begging, crying, screaming, shouting or struggling secured her release, so she tried to tell them about Bobby, that he needed her, that he was waiting for her to play, that she had to go to him. They assumed Bobby was either one of the dogs or an imaginary friend.

When all these things failed to secure her release, she made one last desperate bid for freedom, and brought the heavy dinner tray crashing down on Nanny's head and thirteen years confinement on her own.

Sitting in the log-house sixty years later, she marvelled that she had done all these things. With hindsight, she realised she was probably suffering from post traumatic shock syndrome. The terrible scene she had witnessed in the garden had unhinged her, she had lost all sense of reason, 'reason' being limited for an eight-year-old child anyway. She had what she would call today 'a total meltdown.'

When frightened and disturbed, children can do strange things, often things that are counterproductive. How many times she had been in the situation with Rhona, watching Rhona have a tantrum to get what she wanted, every kick and every scream pushing that desire further from her grasp.

Shaking her head, she marvelled at her eight-year-old self: the physical strength she had. To drag someone heavier than herself all that distance, to stand on a chair behind her bedroom door with that huge, heavy wooden tray above her head, then bring it crashing down on Nanny's head with enough force to knock her unconscious. It seemed incredible to her now that she had done it. But she had, and she was locked up for her trouble.

Through the years of her incarceration, she had often thought of Bobby and as those years passed and her understanding matured, she wondered about him. No-one told her what had happened. No-one told her about his body being found, the enquiry being held, her father firmly pinning the blame on her. She had to read it in an old newspaper the warden of the Institution thrust in her face the day she was being released.

'I trust you have learned your lesson,' he said, his face stern and unforgiving. The newspaper had been with her file. He had it on his desk, along with the envelope she would be given as she left.

Mhairi stood in front of him, reading the account of the enquiry, and found out for the first time, with a punch in the gut, that Bobby had died that dreadful day. According to the newspaper, she had been found guilty of torturing and killing the boy. Her blood-soaked socks had been found beside the body, her bloodied hair ribbons wrapped round his ankles as some kind of bond from which he had partially struggled free. There was no evidence of any other person being in the woodshed where he was found: only the poor dead boy and Mhairi. Nanny testified to the effect that Mhairi's clothing the night in question had been filthy and bloodstained, and she had lost her socks and her hair ribbons: just one of the reasons she had been confined to her room.

The murder weapon had not yet been found, but police were raking in the undergrowth around the garden, certain it would be. One of the blows to his head had proved ultimately fatal, but there were so many injuries the boy had clearly been badly beaten, possibly after being rendered semi-conscious by the blows to his head. Semi-conscious rather than unconscious because the injuries to his arms suggested an attempt on his part to protect his face as his clothing was ripped from his body, his flesh ripped from his bones. The police forensics team agreed with the prosecutor; it was feasible these horrendous injuries could have been inflicted by a mad, feral child, out of control and malicious. The first bite, the first taste of blood would have been enough to send such a child into a frenzied attack.

An explosion of pain ripped through her body at the enormity of what she was accused. Her knees gave way under her and she vomited on the warden's carpet as she sank to the ground. She lay, curled into a foetal ball, her stomach retching and heaving until there was nothing more to vomit, until the dry heaving stopped and she lay spent on the floor, lying in her vomit until the attendants came and escorted her away to be cleaned up before returning to be given her envelope and released into the world outside the Institution.

Although she had no memory of such repugnant, bestial behaviour, and found it inconceivable she had been capable of it, she couldn't be sure because the whole episode was shrouded in a thick, black veil. Until she read the account, she had no memory of the momentous day: the day blocked out by trauma and subsequent medication.

Her last memory before being sedated and incarcerated, was the frantic need to escape from her bedroom to go to Bobby, the need so strong it drove her to assault her nanny. Her memories of Bobby were sweet, tinged with a slight apprehension that something had gone wrong and he needed her.

donald

"So what about you, Dad?" Ewan asked. "Do you think Mum did this?" He had come to comfort his father, unaware that something else had arisen to eclipse the death of his grandmother.

"Do you need to ask?"

"No, not really." He tossed the bits of paper down on the table. The three of them were still sitting in the kitchen. Rhona had managed to find some salmon and vegetables in the freezer and made them a meal which they'd eaten in partial silence, each mulling over the enormity of the story Donald had related to Ewan. "It might've been easier to read this drivel if it was still in one piece."

"Yes, well, I was angry."

"Yeah, I can imagine. Bit late now, though, no? Time to get angry might've been…" He looked at the date on one of the pieces of paper. "Nineteen-fifty-three."

"I'd have been thirteen, son."

'Yeah, well. Pity you hadn't been a bit older. Sounds like Mum could've done with someone in her corner. Fascists!"

It took a lot to ruffle Ewan's feathers, but he'd been visibly shaken by his mother's story, the colour draining from his face, his eyes wide with disbelief. "I don't know what shocks me more, the fact that Mum was accused of murder, or the fact that she was locked up in a loony-bin for most of her life."

"Hardly most of her life," Rhona said. "Thirteen years. She's sixty-eight now, so more like…"

"A fifth. A fifth of her life. Still a heck of a long time to be banged up in a loony-bin."

"I wish you'd stop calling it that. It was a Correctional Facility. A Home for the Mentally Deficient."

Ewan looked to his father for support. "A loony-bin."

Donald shrugged.

"Can't we just call it a Home?" Rhona suggested.

"Doesn't sound like the kind of place I'd want to call home."

"Look, kids, that's hardly the point. What we need to discuss is what we are going to do with this information.

Ewan scuffed the paper across the table. "Burn it, is my suggestion."

"He doesn't mean the actual written information, dope!"

"I was being facetious, actually." He pulled a face. "You know the kind of thing, a joke? One of those things other people laugh at and you never get?"

"What is it with you two," Donald said with a sigh. "As soon as you're in the same room, you revert to being teenagers." He rubbed his hand across his face and stood up to start clearing the table.

"I'll do that, Dad." Rhona got to her feet. "You look tired."

"I'll wash," Ewan said.

"Why should you get washing? I'll wash, you can dry."

But Ewan had rolled his sleeves up and was running the hot water into the basin as she cleared the table.

"I hate drying."

"Yeah, well, suck it up, Princess."

Ignoring him, Rhona turned to Donald. "You go through, Dad. I'll make us a cup of tea when we're finished the dishes."

"Lovely, pet. Not much a good cup of tea can't put right, according to your mother."

While he dozed on and off in the chair in the sitting room, he could hear the banter continuing in the kitchen. He was very proud of his children, both of them. They were good kids and, much as he scolded them, he loved to hear them having a go at one another because it reminded him of years gone by, when they were both still at home. When all was right with his world.

"I've been thinking about it," Rhona said when they were sitting together having the promised cup of tea. "I don't think we need to tell Katie and Michael any of this."

"No."

"How will you explain why Mum went walkabout?"

With a long sigh, Rhona closed her eyes to think about that.

"Can't you just say she needed a wee break?"

"Without telling you?" she said to Donald.

"Well, maybe you could say she had told me, but I'd forgotten."

"You are getting a bit forgetful, right enough."

"But *that* forgetful?" Ewan wondered. "Is it likely Dad would forget something as important as that? Would they swallow that? I mean, I know your kids are thick and all…"

Rhona threw a cushion at him.

"Hey, watch the tea!" He held his cup out of danger.

"Did they know she was away?" Donald asked.

"Well, yes, of course they did. Besides, it may have escaped your notice, Mum isn't actually back yet. We have no way of knowing if she's coming back."

"When." Donald said. "Not 'if.' When she's coming back."

Rhona shrugged. "Anyway. What I tell them is my problem. I'll think of something."

"But you'll not tell them everything?"

She shook her head. "No. I don't think they need to know. Do you?"

"No."

"For Mum's sake, I think the fewer people who know the better."

"Agreed!"

"Well, that's nice," Donald said with a smile. "Nice you two agree on something."

He lay back for a while, letting their discussion of who should be told what wash over him. It was a habit he had, the ability to seem not to be listening when he was or, conversely, to seem to be listening when he wasn't. Sometimes a useful habit, sometimes a bad habit.

He hadn't listened to Mhairi all those years ago, before they married, when she'd tried to remember what had really happened to the paper boy. She tried to tell him what she remembered of the poisonous report in the newspaper the warden had handed her two years before, but she got distressed.

'It's okay,' he said, putting his arms round her. 'You don't have to remember. Whatever happened, it wasn't that. That's all we need to know.'

'Maybe we should try to get a copy of the paper.'

'It was a long time ago.'

'But they hold on to copies in the newspaper office, don't they?'

'Probably.' He remembers admiring the courage in her face, the brightness of her eyes. 'But do we really want to read what was clearly a biased account? Probably a load of circumstantial evidence at best?'

'But don't you want to know I didn't do those things?'

He remembered smiling at her earnestness. 'Oh, little Mhairi Adams, you don't have to convince me.'

'But, if I could remember, you could be sure.'

'I am sure. I'm telling you, you are pushing on an open door. You have no need to try to remember in order to convince me. I am convinced.' He kissed the top of her head. 'It all happened a long time ago and I think it's just as well you don't remember.'

He wanted to protect her. Whatever horrors she had witnessed, he was glad she couldn't remember them. Wanted to protect her from more pain.

Sitting here, listening to his children talking through the whole thing, talking it through in order to make sense of it, in order to come to terms with it, he realised that is what he had protected her from. From coming to terms with it. From making sense of it.

Mhairi had needed to remember, needed to convince him of her innocence for *her* sake, not for his. She needed him to believe her story because it was the truth, not because he loved her. Not because he trusted her. Because it was the truth. And to do that, she needed to remember.

Painful or not, she needed to remember and he had helped her to forget.

saturday morning
mhairi

He had died. Her lovely, cheeky paperboy had died. It had hurt when she had learned that. She had always hoped he had been all right. But he had died in this very hut. It had never felt possible that he could have died at her hand, and now she knew he had not. Now she remembered: now she knew. She had not killed him. But nor had she been able to save him.

She looked around.

There was one thing more she needed to do here.

She had fallen asleep, exhausted and hungry, as the light had faded into evening and the birds had grown silent, making way for the sounds of the night. Once again, she wakened stiff and sore from the cold and damp of the hut, with an added headache — probably dehydration since she ran out of water yesterday afternoon. To keep the headache company, there was a gnawing pain in her stomach from lack of food.

The sensible thing would be to leave this place now, but Mhairi found she couldn't yet, not before taking her leave of Bobby.

It was early morning, the dawn chorus had broken through her troubled slumber: blackbirds, house sparrows and blue tits probably. There seemed to be a robin nesting in the eaves of the log-hut, she could hear its angry flapping that she had invaded its territory, its distinctive syrupy song. It was the male blackbird's wonderful, fluting song that dominated now as she stretched and rubbed her limbs to coax warmth and feeling back into them. There would be a blackbird's nest in the nearby bushes.

"Can you hear him, Bobby?" she whispered. "Remember, I taught you how to sing back to him. Remember? You were good at it. Better than me. We could probably find his nest. Wrong time of year for eggs, of course, but we could see the nest."

Creeping out of the hut, careful nobody was about, Mhairi peered into the hedge behind it. "Yes," she said. "There it is. See it?" She put her hand out to halt him. "Shh!" she whispered. "Look! A chaffinch." It was just under the hedge, a few feet from where she stood. "Looking for insects for breakfast."

When the chaffinch moved on, "Do you hear him? Such a funny song, eh? Do you remember what I told you. How to tell it was him? The song starts out with a few slow clear notes, 'Chip, chip, chip,' remember? Then it speeds up, finishing with a real flourish." She laughed. "D'you know what Donald says it sounds like?" She inclined her head. "Donald? Well, he's my husband. You'd like Donald. He's a kind man. Like you would have grown up to be, I know." Closing her eyes, she sighed and bit her lip to stop herself from crying. "Anyway, Donald reckons Mister Chaffinch here sounds like a medium paced bowler. A few plodding steps, picking up speed and then a crescendo as he bowls. What d'you think?" She listened to the birdsong for a while.

Straightening up and stretching, "Tell you, Bobby, I'm not as young as I was when we last were here. Sixty years ago, Bobby, sixty years. You would be seventy-one." She sighed and wiped tears from her face with the back of her hand. "I'm sorry, Bobby. You should be a granddad by rights." She shook her head. "I'm sorry, Bobby. I'm so sorry."

There were a few Nerine lilies still flowering nearby, looking tired now, but still pretty. Because it had been a good summer and a mild autumn, they must have bloomed longer. Mhairi picked the best of them and looked around for other flowers to compliment them, finding some winter jasmine and honeysuckle, which she also picked. "Lovely!" she said.

She knew she was talking to herself. Despite what it would have looked like to an onlooker, she hadn't really flipped, knew fine that Bobby wasn't there to hear her. But she felt comforted, imagining his presence. Never a believer in ghosts or any sort of afterlife, her Bible reading having established that much at least, she wasn't talking to his spirit or anything else. Just to his memory.

Arranging the bouquet as she walked, Mhairi went back to the log-hut, where she knelt beside the remnants of the log-pile at the back. "Goodbye, Bobby," she said, kissing the flowers before she lay them down on the logs.

One last lingering look round as she pulled on her rucksack, and she left the log-hut, left the garden, closing the gate behind her, but not locking it. She threw the key deep into the bushes. She hated locked doors.

saturday morning
donald

Ewan was already up when Donald came down to put the kettle on.

"Manage on the couch okay?" Donald asked him.

"Yeah, no bother. I can sleep anywhere."

There was a pot of tea already made and bread in the toaster. "Thanks, son."

"No bother."

"What time you heading home?"

"No rush. Saturday." Ewan stretched. "You decided what you're going to do about Mum? You know, about trying to find her? What with Gran dying and everything."

Donald poured himself a cup of tea and buttered some toast, bringing it over to the table. "Yes, I have, actually. I woke up knowing exactly what I'm going to do."

"Great!"

"What you are going to do about what?" Rhona asked, coming into the kitchen in her mother's old dressing gown.

"Morning, love." Donald kissed her and poured her some tea. "Here, you take that toast. I'll put some more on."

"Thanks, Dad. Lack of sleep and too much stress catching up on me, I'm afraid."

"Was a bit late, last night, before we headed up."

"And well seen you need your beauty sleep," added Ewan, pulling a face. "Digging the wild look."

Rhona put her hand to her hair. "Oh, and I suppose you were up and showered hours ago."

Before they could start another argy-bargy, Donald cut across their banter. "I've decided I'll go through to Glasgow for a few days. I need to sort things out for your Gran's funeral and things like that, so I'll stay in her house and do everything from there."

"Do you want me to come? Moral support and all that."

Donald rumpled her hair as he passed her to sit down at the table. "That's okay, love. There's one or two things I'd like you to help me with here, if that's okay?"

"Anything."

"Since you're the business with the computer, I've some things I need you to look up for me." He drew a list out from his trouser pocket.

"You have been busy." She looked at the list. "Cemeteries. You want me to find a list of cemeteries in the Glasgow area?"

"Right."

"I thought you'd already spoken to the undertaker? I thought Gran was going to be cremated?"

"That's right."

Rhona waved the list. "So you need this, because…?"

"Just something I've been thinking about. Not sure about it, whether I'll need the information or not, but, if you wouldn't mind?"

"On to it right after breakfast."

"Anything I can do?" Ewan asked.

"There might be, if you're up for it."

"Just tell me what and I'm your man."

"Well, if you really want to help…"

Ewan nodded.

"I told you I found your mum down on the canal path?"

They both nodded.

"Well, I reckon she's headed for Glasgow, or Maryhill, probably. The thing is, I doubt if she's got too many days' walking in her. It's been a while since we last did much. So, I reckon she might get the train or a bus at some point. What I thought you might do for me, son, is to check if she's still following the canal."

Ewan's face lit up. "I could do it on my bike," he said. "It's years since I cycled the canal route." He got up from the table. "I'm on to it. I'll head back home and load the bike on to the back of the car and Sally can drop me and the bike at, where? Ratho? Linlithgow?"

"Well, it was Linlithgow I saw her three days ago, so, by my reckoning, even allowing for a rest day in Linlithgow, that she'll have made Falkirk or even a bit beyond by now."

"Right. I'll start in Linlithgow, just to be sure. Don't want to miss her."

"And, son," Donald put his hand on Ewan's arm as he passed by his chair, making for the door. "Remember. You've not to let her see you. I want to be first to speak to her myself. Understand?"

"Got it."

"If you find her, you'll know her by that old anorak she wears."

"And her hair. I'd know Mum's hair anywhere."

"That's because it's the same colour as yours," Rhona said. "And almost as curly." She pulled a 'sweet' face, knowing she had touched on a tender spot.

Ewan chose to let the tease pass this once and ignored the comment. "Right, Dad." He held up his mobile phone. "I'll phone you as soon as I catch sight of her."

"Fine, son. That'll give me an idea how many more days till she hits Glasgow."

"Unless she's taken the train or the bus already?"

Donald pulled a face. "Unless she's taken the train or the bus, in which case.."

"In which case you're stuffed," Ewan supplied as he pulled on his jacket and opened the back door. "Right. See you, guys." He took his car keys out of his pocket and waved them. "A man with a mission. No time to lose." And he was gone.

"Always supposing his stupid car starts," Rhona muttered.

mhairi

Mhairi expected to feel some sort of closure as she walked away from the house. She had avoided looking at the actual house since the first look when she arrived outside it, but now she stood, scrutinising it from the front gate. Because the long driveway bent round as it swept up to the front door and past it for cars to park round the side, the view from the gate only showed half of the front. It was enough to show her that it hadn't changed much, only gotten a little older, the stonework a little cleaner than it used to be, she was sure. The curtains were different, of course, but the windows were the same. Small square panes, framed by white paintwork needing a fresh coat. If she moved as far to the left as possible without her view being totally blocked by the wall, she could see the front door and the front steps. It caught her breath.

He flew down those steps with wings on his feet. Oh, how she longed to watch him do it again. Fearless, sure-footed like a mountain goat. "Oh, God, please," she prayed. "Take care of him. Take care of my Bobby." She had her hand over her mouth to stop herself crying out. She wanted to scream. She wanted to push open the gates and run up to the door. "Killer!" she wanted to shout. "Murderer!"

But her father was long dead too, she knew he must be. Whatever guilt he'd carried in his heart for the dastardly deed, she hoped it pained him every day of his life, that he'd gone to his grave scorched by it, scarred by it.

With a last scathing look at the building that had housed such a monster, she turned and walked away.

And she expected closure.

donald

There was nothing much he could do about tidying up his mother's affairs, it being Saturday. He'd been in the house, but hadn't touched anything: didn't feel like going through any of his mothers things. The house had an old-lady smell about it: the smell of small accidents on the way to the toilet, cabbage that had been boiled too long, and talcum powder. Which of these smells was stronger depended upon which room he was in.

Wandering from room to room, Donald realised he couldn't do this. With a groan that was almost a sob, he sank onto the sofa in the front room; the parlour, his mother liked to call it, the room where she received guests and entertained family. Familiar furniture filled the room: a china cabinet whose shelves were crammed with china tea services, silver spoons, thimbles, glass ornaments, china ornaments and various other assorted nicknack; the old piano on which he had learned to play as a boy, his piano tutor tapping out the rhythms with his hand on his knee, the top of the piano covered with silver-framed photographs mostly of Donald as a boy, a man, a graduate, a lawyer; stuffed chairs and a long stuffed sofa, sagging now, the imprints of too many bottoms denting and dipping the cushions, and coffee tables and plants and so much stuff.

Donald held his head and hurried from the room. Nightmare. How would he ever deal with all this paraphernalia? What would he do with it all? He rested against the wall in the hallway, clutching his chest, trying to breath as evenly as he could till the spasms passed.   Tension. It would just be tension. Stress.

Looking round, he realised he couldn't stay here, not for another minute, never mind a night. He pulled at the open collar of his shirt. Suffocating. Drowning.

It wasn't until he was standing outside the front door that he realised he hadn't found the paperwork he would need, hadn't looked for it, hadn't opened the bureau drawer where it would likely be, couldn't go back in to do it now. Saturday. Nothing to be done till Monday.

So he sat in a cafe, far from the house, drinking coffee and studying the list of cemeteries Rhona had printed off for him. There were telephone numbers beside the name of each cemetery and he started phoning their offices, then remembered it was Saturday for them too, and they'd probably be closed for business. He'd have to hoof it.

Downing the rest of his coffee in one swallow, he paid his bill, left a tip and headed back out into the cold to put his plan into action.

mhairi

After walking for quarter of an hour or so, it occurred to Mhairi that she didn't have a plan, and, if she didn't buy food and water soon, she would become incapable of making one. Going into the first shop she came to, a small supermarket, she wandered the narrow aisles with a basket over her arm, unable to think what she was here for until, as she passed the cold meat counter, the smell of roasted meats assailed her nostrils, reminding her she was desperately hungry. With a 'huh!' she realised she had managed to forget she was hungry. Her stomach embraced the smell and shouted a loud reminder, growling its longing for food.

As soon as she left the shop, she started ripping into the bags of meat and cheese, cramming her mouth full, hardly able to chew properly, she was so ravenous. A bottle of water to wash it down and she'd exchanged hunger pains for indigestion. Clutching her stomach, she doubled over, expecting to part with her purchases in less time that she'd taken to buy them, but the spasm passed with a loud belch, followed by loud, hard hiccups.

Berating herself for her haste and stupidity, she started walking again, looking around to gauge where she was and where she should be going. Twice she stopped to relieve the pain in her stomach with another unladylike belch, and twice she stopped to take another mouthful or two of water in a vain attempt to relieve the hiccups.

There was a park nearby and, as she approached the wrought-iron gates, hoping to find somewhere quiet to sit and work out her plan, with sudden clarity, she knew where she needed to be. Unable to take the time to find a bench, she squatted on the grass just inside the park gates and snatched the map out of her rucksack.

Smoothing it out on the grass at her feet, she scanned the area where she reckoned she must be. Yes, there was the park. She looked up at the nearby sign. Yes, that was the one. Then her fingers traced back to the road where she had found the house and around its immediate vicinity. She hadn't realised she had walked so far. Closing her eyes, she tried to remember what she had passed, but, either there had been nothing of note, or she hadn't noticed.

She ran back the way she had come till she found the shop again.

Bursting through the door, she launched herself at the checkout, skipping neatly in front of a young woman toting a basketful of groceries. "Have you always been a supermarket?" she asked the girl on the till.

"What?"

"Was there a shop here before?"

"Before?"

"Yes, before it was a supermarket?"

The girl shook her head and shrugged her shoulders. "Did you want anything?"

"Oh!" Mhairi stomped out, letting the door slam behind her. "Useless!"

There was an old man walking toward her on the pavement.

She rushed at him. "Have you always lived around here?" she asked him.

He stepped back and looked out from under startled brows. "Do I know you?"

"How long have you lived in this area?"

"Man and boy," he said. "But who needs to know?"

"What was this before it was a supermarket? Please," she added, suddenly realising how rude she must seem. "I'm sorry. It's very important."

"Well, now." He settled in for a chat, leaning back on his heels, hands in pockets, eyes raised in concentration. "Before it was a supermarket?"

Mhairi nodded, smiling her encouragement.

"Well, when I was a lad, it was old Granny Morgan as used to have these here premises. Inherited it from her father, she did, oh now, let me see..." He took his cap off and scratched his head. "Nineteen-thirty-three, she must've taken over when her old dad died. I were just a wee bairn, no more'n five or six, but I remember it because she started selling newspapers that had comic strips in them. Her old man disapproved of comic strips, but once he was gone, well..."

"Nineteen-fifty-three. Who had the shop in nineteen-fifty-three? Did it still sell papers?"

"Och, aye, hen. Her boy was running it by then. It was aye a newsagent though."

"With a paperboy?"

"Och, aye, of course. A good run he had an' all. Some big houses over yonder." He swung his arm in the general direction from which she'd so recently come, from the road that led to the house. "Did the run myself in the forties, till I left the school and got a proper job. Aye, it was a good run. Good tips of a Sunday. Like I say." He nodded back up the hill. "Big, fancy houses. That's where the nobs lived."

Mhairi was hardly breathing at all now, but she had to stay focused. She tried to ask the next question but it came out as a croak. "Did you.." she coughed, cleared her throat of the debris of her pain. "Did you have a bike."

"Och, no, hen, we didn't have the money for a bike." He laughed. "We were the poor folks down here. The plebs." He looked up the hill again, his lips set in a sneer of contempt for remembered slights. "Aye, we were the plebs." He made to move away. "The shop had one, though. A bike. I got the use of that for the papers."

Mhairi put her hand to her throat, made herself swallow, made herself breathe. "In the fifties?"

"Aye, it'd still be the same. Still the Morgans' shop. They didn't sell up till well into the seventies. When John went to Australia."

"There'd be a paperboy then, in the fifties?"

"Aye, aye, hen." He started to walk on past. "There was aye a paperboy."

Closing her eyes, letting him shuffle away, she tried to picture the shop as it would have been. The paperboy collecting his bundle of papers, loading them into the satchel, climbing onto the bike, riding off up the hill on his round. Hers was always the last house, Bobby told her. After delivering her father's paper, he was finished for the day. He would cycle back here, leave the bike and run home for tea.

Hardly daring to breathe, she looked around at the tenement flats that lined this street and the ones beyond. This is where he would have lived. Somewhere not far from the shop. Somewhere here. Wrapping her arms around herself, she shivered, her knees weakening as she stood, unable to move yet knowing she must. How close must she be to Bobby's home? How she longed to turn back time, see the bike come hurtling down the street, his little legs turning the pedals at break-neck speed, his socks falling in folds to his ankles. Smiling at the vision she had conjured up, knowing he would be riding fast. Didn't he have wings on his feet, after all?

Checking the street name, she perched against the window of the shop and consulted her map again, her fingers working over the area until she found what she was looking for. There was somewhere she needed to be.

But, first, there was something she needed to buy, so she retraced her steps and went back into the shop.

donald

"There's no sign of her anywhere on the canal towpath between Linlithgow and Maryhill." Ewan told him over the phone. "I can't see that she'd even have gotten this far by now, so I don't see much point in going on," he said. "But I will, if you like."

"No, no point, son. I'm sure she wouldn't go any further and, like you say, I doubt she'd even have walked that far. No, you go home, son. Sally picking you up?"

"Yeah, light'll go soon and I've no lights on my bike."

"Fine. Thanks, son."

"So, what's next?"

"I'll take it from here," Donald said, preparing to end the call. "You get off home. I'll give you a bell, anything happens. Bye, son!"

It didn't take him long to find what he was looking for: it wash't a big place. Exhausted from the fast pace he'd imposed upon himself after parking the car, he sat on a bench at a little distance to catch his breath and wait for Mhairi.

He didn't have too long to wait, vindicating the speed he'd chosen to get himself here. The bench was discretely placed at a distance from the main path, partially hidden by some bushes and he was able to watch her unobserved. She had brought flowers and she knelt on the grass in front of the gravestone.

mhairi

Mhairi had found it with ease in the small, neatly kept cemetery. As she expected, his grave was near the back among others that looked as though they'd been here just as long as he had.

Robert Wallace
1942-1953
Beloved son and brother
R.I.P

The starkness of the inscription stung. She wanted there to be eloquence, explanation, exposition. Did someone speak up for him at his funeral? Not just some paid minister who didn't know him. Someone who loved him, who could tell of his kindness, his fun, that he had wings on his feet. Someone who could tell stories of his love for his sister and his mother, how he had cared for them, brought gifts of bread and cheese, and always an apple for Molly.

Dropping to her knees, she thanked God she had found his resting place. As she placed the flowers on his bed, she collapsed beside them with a low moan of pain.

donald

His whole being ached to run to her, but Donald held himself in check. Not yet, not yet. This time he would let her remember, let her grieve, let her feel the pain she had to feel.

Wiser today than yesterday.

At first, the only way he knew she was crying was by the heaving of her shoulders, the shaking of her frame, but it wasn't long before he heard her howl.

Still he waited.

mhairi

When the pain that ripped through her had passed, she lay on for a time, reluctant to leave him. She whispered all her sorries, all her goodbyes. She left him flowers: roses.

'I like them flowers there,' he'd said. 'Yon red ones.'

'The roses?'

'Aye. Yon ones.'

She'd picked one for him.

He'd beamed at her before placing it gently in his satchel. 'Ta,' he said. 'I'll gie it tae ma Ma.'

She brought him roses. Laid them on his grave. Red roses, beautiful, closed flowers that would open in the next day or two. She took one out from the bunch and placed it in one of the bottles of water she had bought. "This one's for your Ma," she said. "To tell her I'm sorry."

Enough.

It was enough.

She had remembered. She had relived that dreadful day and she had said her goodbyes.

As she stood and turned away, Donald walked forward with his arms open to welcome her home, and she knew it was going to be alright. The fact that he was here meant he knew. Somehow he knew. "But how?"

He led her to the bench.

"How did you find me?"

He encouraged her to sit with him. "A long story."

"Like mine," she said.

"Like yours."

"Shall I tell you?"

"When you're ready. That's why I'm here. Why I'll always be here."

They looked at one another, neither knowing quite where to start, but both knowing there was a lot to be said. Donald knowing he would help her remember, Mhairi knowing he would help her forget.

"Rhona?" She looked at him, fear in her eyes.

"Rhona's fine. She needs you to come home now."

"Does she know?"

He nodded. "Yes, she knows. She's there at the gate." He nodded towards the gates of the cemetery. "I phoned her while I was waiting for you to come. Her car's just drawn up and she'll wait out there till you're ready to forgive her."

Mhairi smiled. "She's at the gate. I keep remembering the poem. I think it's Tennyson? You know the one. 'Come into the garden, Maud, For the black bat, night, has flown, Come into the garden, Maud, I am here at the gate alone.'"

"Yes, Tennyson."

"There has always been a darkness inside me. No matter how happy I've been, it's always been there. It followed me about like a black bat, haunting my nights, hiding in a corner during my days, flapping out at me at odd moments, scaring the wits out of me. I couldn't get rid of it because I couldn't remember what happened beyond that garden gate. Whenever I thought about that time…" She looked at Donald. "The time before I was taken away."

"When you were eight years old."

"I knew something happened in the garden. But I could never get beyond looking in through the gate. It was as though I was standing outside and I could see all the bushes and trees, the rhododendrons and roses. I could even smell the roses — and the honeysuckle — and I could see myself playing in the garden, but then the gate would swing shut and I was outside and suddenly it was dark and I couldn't see what happened. The black bat, night, flapped round the memory, obscuring it."

"So you went back to the garden?"

"Yes."

"And?"

"And I remembered."

Donald took a deep breath and let it go on a long sigh. "At last."

"Yes, at last. 'The black bat, night, has flown,'" she said. "Once I got inside the gate, it all started to come back to me."

"Good."

"And I've Rhona to thank for driving me to it with her determination to delve into the past. I had to know myself what she might find." She turned to look at Donald. "I didn't kill Bobby, you know."

"I do know," he said. "And so does Rhona. And Ewan. We never doubted for a moment."

"I did."

"I know." He smiled at her. "But we didn't."

"Thank you," she whispered.

Donald held her to him and they clung together, Mhairi watching her own tears fall on her hands. "Rhona…"

Donald drew back to look at her. "Yes. You need to talk to her."

"I need to tell her what happened."

"Yes." He got up. "I'll bring her to you. She's here at the gate."

Enough

the author

Christine Campbell is a novelist, who also enjoys writing poetry and short stories.

You can follow her on her blog
http://cicampbellblog.wordpress.com

her Facebook author page
https://www.facebook.com/WriteWhereYouAre

her Goodreads page
https://www.goodreads.com/author/show/7126731.Christine_Campbell

on Twitter
https://twitter.com/Campbama/status/406092654733053952

or YouTube
http://www.youtube.com/watch?v=lcJCfT1nHHQ

the books

also by **christine campbell**

Family Matters

http://a-fwd.com/asin-com=B00BR9JUV8

Making It Home

http://a-fwd.com/asin-com=B00BR9YS0G

Flying Free

http://a-fwd.com/asin-com=B00HUHGQW2

Amazon Author Page

http://www.amazon.com/Christine-Campbell/e/B00BRGC0C2

Sarah's husband, Tom, disappeared without trace eleven years ago.

Now her son, David has died.

Tom appears at David's funeral and tries to reestablish contact, which Sarah refuses but Kate, her daughter accepts. The growing closeness between Kate and her father worries Sarah because she believes that Tom is dishonest and unreliable, at best.

Then Sarah finds David's diary and follows the steps he took in search of his father.

It becomes a journey of self-discovery: what she uncovers forces Sarah to reassess her view of herself, her origins and her certainties.

A relationship novel, but also a detection novel with a difference: this story traces a woman's drive to uncover and understand the truth about a family she thought she knew…her own.

Kate had a home, but her heart wasn't in it...or in her marriage. So she left them both.

Phillis had a home...and her heart was in it...but she wanted something more. So she shopped.

Naomi had no home and her heart was in cold storage, frozen by grief and fear. So she shopped.

They found one another in a department store. Shopping.

The problem with 'retail therapy': you can overdose.

As friendship grows between these three women, they help one another face up to their problems, realising along the way, that every heart needs a home and it takes more than a house to make one.

A contemporary novel about women who want more.

When Tom asks Jayne to marry him, he unwittingly opens her personal Pandora's Box, and now she can't seem to close the lid on all that rushes out at her, whirling her into a cycle of self-sabotage.
Unable to commit to a relationship, she pushes Tom away… along with everything else that's important in her life.
There are things she had chosen to forget. There are others she can't remember even when she tries. What she does remember is fear.
Feeling emotionally trapped by her past, her biggest challenge is to break through its bars and fly free.
Then she finds someone to help her make sense of what's happening, but, instead of slamming the lid shut on all that

has been let loose, he helps her open it wider and makes her face her fears in order to overcome them.
Remembering the past helps her make sense of the present and allows her to begin the process of healing and she finds that, as in the fable, there is one last thing left in the Box. That thing is hope.
But, when she is ready to commit to a relationship, will Tom still be waiting?

This novel traces a woman's struggle to become the woman she wants to be in order to marry the man she loves.
A contemporary novel about someone who could be your neighbour, your friend, or even you.

~~~

Lightning Source UK Ltd.
Milton Keynes UK
UKOW03f2256270514

232400UK00001B/62/P